"Eimear McBride is that old-fashioned thing, a genius. . . .
The adventurous reader will find that they have a real book on their
hands, a live one, a book that is not like any other."
—ANNE ENRIGHT, THE GUARDIAN

"Brilliant . . . bracing, unrelenting, and audacious."
—THE MILLIONS

"I loved it. . . . You'll be horrified, you'll be crying, but most of all
you'll be transported by how beautiful the writing is."
—CAITLIN MORAN

"Wild, brave, moving, and darkly cryptic."
—CHRIS CLEAVE

"Simply a brilliant book . . . I can't recommend it highly enough."
—ELIZABETH McCRACKEN

"An astonishing literary debut."
—THE INDEPENDENT

"It's hard to imagine another narrative that would justify this way of telling, but perhaps McBride can build another style from scratch for another style of story. That's a project for another day, when this little book is famous."

—*London Review of Books*

"Brilliant . . . bracing, unrelenting, and audacious . . . a literary sensation."

—*The Millions*

"Spellbinding . . . This is brave, dizzying, risk-taking fiction of the highest order."

—*Minnesota Star Tribune*

"One of the most remarkable things about [*A Girl Is a Half-formed Thing*] is hearing the thoughts of a woman from the inside out. There are very few authentic literary examples of the inner workings of a woman's mind."

—*The Independent* (Ireland)

"The language is expressionistic, confiding, and plays havoc with the normal rules of syntax and structure. For the reader, the impression is of a voice so close to your ear that you can almost hear the breathing."

—*Irish Independent*

"An astonishing literary debut."

—*The Independent*

"Eimear McBride very deliberately set out to recapture in her own writing what Joyce had done for her in his—opened up parts of life that couldn't be described in conventional language."

—*The Telegraph*

"*A Girl Is a Half-formed Thing* is to modern fiction what bare-knuckle fistfights are to the Marquess-of-Queensbury-ruled boxing—this is the savage and fucking hard-hitting end of the genre. . . . absolutely brilliant."

—*The Only Way Is Reading*

"I urge readers to step outside their literary boxes and experience this remarkable book."

—*Shelf Unbound*

"McBride has created a world that is not just accessible but positively drags you in, surrounds and infiltrates you. Her innovative approach to language is sometimes shocking, but it's the only way that we can genuinely experience the whole of the character."

—*Tales From a Bruce Eye View*

"I'm left with great admiration for the author's skill."

—*Bluestalking Journal*

"A wonderful but harrowing first-person stream of consciousness . . . It truly is one of the most extraordinary things I've read in the last year."

—*Harper's Bazaar*

"At its most fundamental level this is a heartwrenching story of love, loss, and an exceptionally strong sibling bond. The sadness of it was almost unbearable; it didn't remind me of grief, it felt like it. But in as far as grief can only spring from love, there is something beautiful about that, and about much of the writing."

—*PaperBlog*

"Eimear McBride's victory in the Bailey Prize with *A Girl Is a Half-Formed Thing* is a heartening though rare instance of a difficult book being given a reward from mainstream publishing, not just from independent readers and reviewers."

—*Quadrapheme*

"Applause and credit is well earned, for the voice is like nothing you've ever heard before."

—*Kingston Creative Writers*

A Girl Is
a Half-formed
Thing

Eimear McBride

HOGARTH
New York   London

Published in the United States by Hogarth, an imprint of the Crown Publishing Group, a division of Penguin Random House LLC, New York.

www.crownpublishing.com

HOGARTH is a trademark of the Random House Group Limited, and the H colophon is a trademark of Penguin Random House LLC.

Originally published in 2013 by Galley Beggar Press, Great Britain. First published in the United States in 2014 by Coffee House Press, Minnesota.

Library of Congress Cataloging-in-Publication Data
McBride, Eimear.
A girl is a half-formed thing / Eimear McBride. — First United States paperback edition.
pages   cm
"Originally published in 2013 by Galley Beggar Press, Great Britain. First published in the United States in 2014 by Coffee House Press."
1. Brothers and sisters—Fiction. 2. Dysfunctional families—Fiction. 3. Brain—Tumors—Patients—Fiction. 4. Domestic fiction. 5. Psychological fiction. I. Title.
PR6113.C337G57 2015
823'.92—dc23
2014041404

ISBN 978-1-101-90343-8

eBook ISBN 978-1-56689-378-7

Printed in the United States of America

Cover design by W. H. Chong

10 9 8 7 6 5 4 3 2

First Hogarth Paperback Edition

for Donagh McBride

PART I

Lambs

1

For you. You'll soon. You'll give her name. In the stitches of her skin she'll wear your say. Mammy me? Yes you. Bounce the bed, I'd say. I'd say that's what you did. Then lay you down. They cut you round. Wait and hour and day.

Walking up corridors up the stairs. Are you alright? Will you sit, he says. No. I want she says. I want to see my son. Smell from dettol through her skin. Mops diamond floor tiles all as strong. All the burn your eyes out if you had some. Her heart going pat. Going dum dum dum. Don't mind me she's going to your room. See the. Jesus. What have they done? Jesus. Bile for. Tidals burn. Ssssh. All over. Mother. She cries. Oh no. Oh no no no.

I know. The thing wrong. It's a. It is called. Nosebleeds, headaches. Where you can't hold. Fall mugs and dinner plates she says clear up. Ah young he says give the child a break. Fall off swings. Can't or. Grip well. Slipping in the muck. Bang your. Poor head wrapped up white and the blood come through. She feel the sick of that. Little boy head. Shush.

She saw it first when you couldn't open your eye. Don't wink so long wind'll change and you'll stay that way. I'm not

3

Mammy. It's got stuck. She pull it open. Hold it up. I can't it's all fall down.

And now Holy Family on a Saturday night. He is leaning you are sleeping she the chair me whirlabout. Listen in to doctor chat. We done the best we could. There really wasn't much. It's all through his brain like the roots of trees. Sorry. Don't say. That. He's running out I'm afraid. I'm afraid he's running down. You should take him home, enjoy him while you can. He's not. He is. Can't you operate again? We can't. Shush. Something? Chemo then. We'll have a go at that.

Gethsemane dear Lord hear our prayer our. Please. Intercession. Night in hospital beds. Faces on the candlewick. Lino in the knees. Please don't God take. Our. Holy Mary mother of all, humbly we beseech thee.

You white-faced feel the needle go in. Feel fat juicy poison poison young boy skin. In your arteries. Eyeballs. Spine hands legs. Puke it cells up all day long. No Mammy don't let them.

Weeks for you. Weeks it. Scared and bald and wet the bed. Dark trees outside for me when it weather rains. She praying in a coat until I am froze. Hard chapel kneelers bare-kneed real repents. She does. And our father was. Where? Somewhere there. I think.

There's good news and bad news. It's shrunk. He's saved. He's not. He'll never be.

So like it lump it a short breath's what you've got. Jesus in her blood that minute. Rejoice sacred heart of Christ. But we'll never be rid do you understand? he says. Shush now she says shush.

Your pink face make that sitting up the best thing she's ever done. Watching you going growing hair. Scabby over slices where scalpels were. Don't look. Telling what's the time and where you are. Makes her happy. Makes our father. Walk down corridors alone.

He says I can't be waiting for it all the time. I'd give my eyes to fix him but. The heart cannot be wrung and wrung. And she like calmest Virgin Mary sitting on the bed. Hands warming up her sides for. What're you saying? Breath. Going? Leaving? But he's just stopped dying. This one's to come. Please don't no I won't stop you. Could never make you do a thing. You'll support us. Aren't you great? Oh the house is mine. It's for the best. For who you me? Board my body up. I'm not for loving. Anymore. I'll live for housework. Dressing kids. And you for mortgage new shoes spuds. Can't live short hope but gas bills long and paid on time too. Oh so kind. Aren't you the fine shape of a man.

He left her with a fifty-pound note. Take care! Stroke combing full untidied hair.

Thinking I think of you and me. Our empty spaces where fathers should be. Whenabouts we might find them and what we'd do to fill them up.

But didn't time continue still. Where's Daddy? Gone. Why's that? Just is. And yelp she at the strength growing to your tips. Poke belly of baby that's kicking is me. Full in myself. Bustling hatchery. And I loved swimming to your touch. Lay on the lining for your strokes for you secret pressed hellos. Show my red foot. Look. Look there. Baby when you're born I pick your name. See you and me were busy with each other long before I came.

She was careful of you. Saying let's take it slow. Mind your head dear heart. And her guts said Thank God. For her gasp of air. For this grant of Nurse I will. Learning you Our Fathers art. And when you slept I lulled in joyful mysteries glorious until I kingdom come. Mucus stogging up my nose.

Scream to rupture day. Fatty snorting like a creature. A vinegar world I smelled. There now a girleen isn't she great. Bawling. Oh Ho. Now you're safe. But I saw less with these flesh eyes. Outside almost without sight. She, asking after and I'm all fine. Hand on my head. Her hand on my back. Dividing from the sweet of mother flesh that could not take me in again. I curled there learning limb from limb. Curdled under hot lamps. Sorrow lapped. I'm so glad your brother's lived. That he'll see you. It'll all be. But. Something's coming. Wiping off my begans. Wiping all my every time. I struggle up to. I struggle from. The smell of milk now. Going dim. Going blank. Going white.

2

Two me. Four you five or so. I falling. Reel table leg to stool. Grub face into her cushions. Squeal. Baby full of snot and tears. You squeeze on my sides just a bit. I retch up awful tickle giggs. Beyond stopping jig and flop around. I fall crack something. My head banged. Oop. Trouble for you. But. Quick the world rushed out like waters. Slap of. Slap of everywhere smells kitchen powder perfume soap of hedges in the winter dogs and sawdust on a butcher's floor. New. Not new. I remember. Patterned in my brain. I feel the carpet under that scratch me when you drag my leg. I know its gold and turquoise coils. Flowers on. Leaves for green. The couch leg I drawn red biro in the grain. Digging. Singing long long ago in the woods of Gartnamona I heard a blackbird singing in a blackthorn tree. Oh. That's come from. Come from where? I can't remember any before.

You bent over. Don't cry don't cry. Trot it out. I think I might. Don't. Whinge get beats for you or me. Wooden spoon worse than hands or clip on the ear. I'll give you something to cry about. Making a holy show with that big lip. Stop your gurning. Sorry Mammy. I won't cry so, though something's happen in my head. I woke up. And stare at your brown hair.

Soft boyish bob on your round face. Must be the washing brushing combing of it. Attentive loving mother. I remember. I have seen. Such a pride and joy in him. Those doctors nurses said it would not. Dead in follicle dead in root. But there it is she says sprigging away. Don't pull it you, giving slap hand for me.

I flee from washing brushing. Get the teeth in good and deep. Too much. That knuckling scrubbing. Like soapsuds scalp scratched in. She'll work her arms out. No lice here. No disease. No psoriasis or dandruff for many miles to see.

I'll jump the bath when she has me. Running with my headful of shampoo shouting no Mammy no no no. Cold chest where water hits windscreen belly in the rain. Down those stairs fast as I can. Shampoo on my forehead. In my eyes. Nettle them. Mammy. Yelling Lady you come back or you'll get what for. A mad goat I'll be. Rubbing bubbles. Worse and worse and hotter like mints I'll turn my nose at. Always get me. In the hall. You by wormy bit of hair. Lug me rubbing ankle skin up the stairs. She in suddy ocean. You just settle down. Quicker over the quicker's done. I am boldness incarnate, little madam little miss. Put back your head I'll wash it down and off your face. Haaaa wat. Blow spit. Thhh. Bubbles. Muckle face with a cloth. There for your bubbles. Eejit. Don't you want hair like your brother's? See that lovely shiny bright. I do. Out in handfuls but two years on—as good as you. Doctors nurses. So now so. For little limp and tunnel vision aren't bad when you are well.

Teeth is though. Worse you than me. All rotted yours. Nothing even like milk. Just keep an eye it's normal after all he's had. His news'll come in and should be fine. Not black, she said and threw them out. Spoiled not washed or washed enough. And would not keep them in a matchstick box.

Mine are safe. Don't touch. Safely in my head. When yours weren't you wouldn't like to see the look on her face. Being reminded. So you make secret seconds in Wrigley's spearmint gum. Stick in the gaps in case she said open up. She says wash your teeth God's sake every other child has theirs. But the doctor said. You could have kept a few I'm sure. Yes Mammy. Don't just yes Mammy me. Mammy yes. You said always yes when I did no. Poor teeth yours and not the fifty p's I'll sue. For no good reason either. Lucky. Blessed I was. Your second lot were hard sturdy. And you take care. Though you'd have liked them better then, I'd say, than now.

3

We're living in the country cold and wet with slugs going across the carpet every night. Now when you are seven eight. Me five. This house, green growing up the outside.

You and me having slug scum races from the doorway to the source where is it. Get that dirty thing out of this house I don't know where they get in. We wondered ever, seeking slug nests in the sofa. Under the grate and found a lizard running hell for leather in the ash. Come in with the coal black buckets but it was hot too hot. Under the fire in cinder we rake back and forth. It bolt out you were faster still than me. Scoop it up in time it might have been a newt I think. Get a jam jar get it. Stuck in that twig. I wallowed in its turning eye. Sickish in my throat, thinking it feels scum like slug roads. Never you ever touch it. A slap for every word of warn we get. Never. Ever. Touch. That. Dirty. Thing. It'll. Give. You. Warts. That. Is. Di. Sgust. Ing. Still we kept its jam jar in the shed until I broke it it died of fright you said and threw it at the cat who ran. Fat cat full of shit. Oh-e oh-e oh-e what you said. Yellow squirting if you touched him. Don't. Pick. Up. That. Dirty. Cat.

Blasted in the winter. Pelted and rain rush under the

kitchen door. She slap it with a broom away. Bunch up papers under there. Look at that. Streaming down the walls and windows full of damp. Godforsaken house it is look out it's lashing down.

You and me swimming star wars in the puddles of it. Lino reefs of other worlds. My dirty fingers picking bigger holes. And made the stairs Niagara Falls and threw men over tied with wool. Lie on our stomachs eating piece of bread with butter sugar on top. A glass window Mammy I want one. Don't get it on my floor.

Howl winter all through the night that year in the trees where we climbed on and the hedges on the road. No cars here. No one comes. Things crying in the fields for me. Say they want me and coming down the walls for. She's coming Mammy. Who? The banshee. Don't be silly. Sure isn't your brother here? Won't he mind you if anything comes along. Should I close the door or leave it open? I don't know. Shut bad out or shut it in? Worse you. And said They are coming. For you and me. Stop it. Coming for us and we're without the knife. What knife? The one that goes with the magic machine. What is it? Makes the noise for killing bad things. A big dark tunnel bangs. How do you know? That's what I had, me shouting it burns awful ahhhh. The doctor said fire came out my eyes. He didn't. He did and these aren't mine. They are so. Mine melted. These are goat's. Goat eyes and the devil wants them back. My throat's closing. Shut up. Ugh shut up. Mammy? But wakes me in the night. Goat eyes riding off into the sky.

Always in the house, drifting round the stairs or sitting by our puddles little beast in your head. Sleeping happy homed up your brain stem now and fingers only strumming on your bad left side. Don't you knock your brother's head.

You stumble. Not that bad. And walking into doors a laugh. Is blind eye at side like in eyelid? No. Lake water? No. Like glass? You said it is like nothing at all. It must be something what? And words, trace stammer of. At school why do you talk like that? Notoriety it likes maybe. It's in your sums X and red lines through a copy book for no no no. Wrong, the teachers writing, I explained this all to you. Wrong you do not understand. Wrong not listening paying attention in class. Again. No, you were not.

It's clear it's clear it's there it's there. Cosy kernelled in your head. It must have strings pulling all the time. Sly in affection. Nasty thing. Having a chew. Nails dug for claws. Her blind spot I think when you were small. No you're better. No you are, turned her good eyes blind.

4

Whose is that car? Do you see it she said, parking at the gate? Oh God let it not be the PP and the state of the place. Who's that now? Don't pull the curtain back. No it isn't. Well he's coming up the path. Oh Jesus Mary and Joseph. Go wipe your nose you.

Daddy. I didn't recognize you. You gave me the fright of my life. I didn't know who it was at all. Is the car different? I thought that. Surely you didn't do all that drive today? Sacred hour. It's a terrible long old journey. Come in God and sit down. Anyways you're looking well.

That's it. Is Mammy with you? Ah no of course. Ach she's not able. She said that alright before. And can the doctor not give her something, just to relieve her a bit? You must be worn out. Will you have a cup of tea?

Come in here and say hello to your grandfather. He's come all the way to see you, isn't that right? Just slip on that kettle as you come past. And can you get any sleep? Desperate at your time of life. Come you in and say hello like your brother. Oh god, look at the face on that. Would you not think about getting some help in? No she's not a bit shy. For a break in the mornings even? Will you have a sandwich with that? I haven't made a start on dinner. So we'll not eat til six I'd say. You know, I haven't a thing in the house. Sure I wasn't expecting you. I'll just nip out. It's only five minutes down the road. No stay where you are. You've driven enough. You sit there and talk to your granda while I go get the messages. Oh now Madam's away upstairs. Don't mind her. She'll be down soon enough exercising her ears. You tell Granda the result of your IQ test. Average. Yes. Now isn't that good? It is. You know well what I was worried about. Look, I'll talk to you when I get back. No now it is good love. Daddy I didn't mean to snap. No of course I'm glad you came. Look let me go get these few things in. You show Granda your Octons love. I really won't be long.

That man was sterner stuff than us. A right hook of a look in his eye all the time. Thin tight gelled hair. Mustache brown eyes. Clark Gable—alike when he was young, she said. But every man was I think then, when she was growing up. Under the thumb of him. Under his hand. Movie star father with his fifteen young. His poor Carole Lombard fucked into the ground. Though we don't say those words. To each other. Yet. They were true God fearing in for a penny in for a pound. Milk-soaked mackerel for every Friday night. Mass every morning for all children over three and the wrath of God for anyone saying Jesus out loud or even in your head. For what's unsaid's as bad as, if not worse. Saturday til afternoon dedicated to praying with his wife—when none of the little could enter without a big knock. Such worshipping worshipping behind the bedroom door. With their babies and babies lining up like stairs. For mother of perpetual suffering prolapsed to hysterectomied. A life spent pushing insides out for it displeased Jesus to give that up. Twenty years in bed and a few after this before she conked. Ah desperate for him in his nice tweeds with his nice cane. Seven sons to carry his coffin. Seven daughters to follow and cry and one extra to make him martyr—surely toddlers die but she would have been the best. Sons for breaking chairs on the backs of. Daughters to shoo from the bath for a wee. Rich-ish husbands or they got a crack in the jaw. Chaste-ish wives or the boys got more. Goodfornothinglumpofshitgodforgiveyou. Ours got for her wedding a glare though he paid. He, at least, knew how to behave. Though a man like our father could be nothing to him. Not to lick his boots. Not to be his dog. Of course he wasn't even surprised when he ran off. Walked she said. I knew it would happen for what could you expect? Psychiatrist indeed and what rubbish is that? Poking in vegetables' heads for a living or calling good people mad. He knew the type. Didn't even guess his son was sick. Busy thinking he was so great, no doubt. What kind of father is that you tell me? She didn't, or he wasn't a brain surgeon either.

And he came, this grandfather, like bolts from the blue. Not a bit of warning just a rap on the door. No one expects the Spanish Inquisition late Saturday afternoon. Would they drive four hundred miles without checking you'd be in? But he did because you wouldn't dare not. Not be in, indeed. Stay for a week us beck and called. Still children loved him and the lollies in his pocket. In the post office they'd say he was a real type of gent. Held doors for women. Kind to dumb animals. Gave generously to the plate on Sundays and could teach you a thing or two about a godly life. Gave up the drink for his mother on her deathbed. Bad he was and all with it. He says himself it was the hardest thing he ever did but if you're bad to your mother you'll never have luck. He doesn't know about that but he knows what's right.

Never touched a drop again after. All those children too and each one a regular communicant. A daily one himself and us when he's afoot. You'll scorch eternity in hell then you'll wish you'd gone to church. Don't turn your face from the father or he'll turn his face from you. And he's a saint with that wife of his also. They say she got very hard. Bitter-like with him and sharp. He never says a word. Offers it up as penance. Oh he has his cross to bear—but sure, hasn't everyone? Besides it's as nothing to the death of a child. He doesn't mind telling you his faith was sorely tried. There's no grief like a parent's. No there's no pain like that. Set him off with the drinking. And this grandson just brings it back. His daughter could have spared him descriptions of the little cut-open head, should not perhaps have phoned crying he'd only six months to live. But he reminded her he'd not had as much himself. So show some gratitude for what you've got. A lot my girl. A lot.

Sit down youngster and tell me what have you been at since I was here last. Have you grown? So you won't be stunted? Thanks be to God. How's school going? Are you top of your class yet? Ah you will be soon enough. And how are the tests? And arithmetic? Well, that's not up to much. You can't be trying that hard. Your mother was good at sums. You should ask her to explain. Well then ask her again. And how's the head? Have you been for any more scans? Well that's good. And how's your mother doing? No sign of that feckless father I suppose? I knew the minute I laid eyes on him. No sense of responsibility. I hope you won't turn out like that. Well, I'm very glad to hear it. And how old are you now? What class are you in? Have you been saying your prayers? Going to communion? How often? And confession? Every week? You know it's important never to receive the host in a state of sin. Your body is a temple for Christ. Did they teach you that at school? So why do you not go more often or are you just so good? Never tell a lie to your mother? Never fight with your sister? Well there's no arguing with that. But you know pride's a deadly sin we should all be humble before God. Your father was a proud man. He wouldn't come to mass and look what happened to you as a result. So you beware of pride. Well now, say a Hail Mary and we'll forget about it but the next time you go you tell the priest. Go on then. Hail Mary. Go on Hail Mary full of . . . Grace. You pick it up. The Lord is . . . How can you forget? Do you not say the rosary in this house? Then how can you not know the Hail Mary? No, this'll not do. This is a terrible carry-on.

And what about you Miss Piggy? Come in here and talk to me. You are. You do look like her. Don't you be cheeky. You're the image of her. That snout you have on you. Now see. I've got it. Say please and you can have it back. Don't you hit your grandfather. There. Have it so. Bold brat. If you were mine you'd be over my knee but then my little girls were well behaved. They'd certainly never slap their grandfather on his sore leg. Because it would make him cry. Now I'll have to tell your mother and you'll get a beat on your bot. Because I'm her daddy so if I say it she has to give you a smack.

I've just been talking to your son. And your daughter. Well . . . But first what have you done to upset your sister? That's not what's been said to me. She said you knew she was sick and you never called. It could've been asthma. She could've been admitted to hospital. Well so far no card's arrived and I've no reason to think she'd tell me a lie. Well I don't know. You might. You could be twisting it all round. You're that turned in on yourself. Isn't there a phone box in the town? As she said herself she made all those calls when that boy took sick. But since the day and hour he did you'd think you're the only one has worries. So listen here, I have more children than you and I love them all equally and I won't be made to pick and choose. You are. You are asking me to. You're trying to make me take sides. You probably want me to give out to your sister. Well get that out of your head for starters. Oh you don't fool me. You're not bothered about anyone even your family. Well you never thanked me at the hospital for that money I sent. I didn't say anything at the time but I was deeply hurt. Of course there was time. There's always time for gratitude. Truth be told you've just assumed we'd always be there for you and we always have. But not a word of thanks. None whatsoever. Oh I'm sure. I'm sure you didn't mean it. You never do. And when I went to have that eye test you never called. It could have been. I could have had glaucoma. Both your grandparents had. But sure what's the point. It's like talking to that brick wall. You were always a selfish. No. Don't please Daddy me now.

And that child only made his communion a year ago and he can't even say his Hail Mary. Have you no morals? I mean what kind of way is that to rear your son? But of course you're so clever. I forgot. Too good to marry a man who'd want his children to believe in God. Oh we look down our noses at those sorts, don't we? We wouldn't want to be like that, would we? You've always looked down your nose at me and my beliefs. You're above that sort of thing. But I couldn't care less because I'm grateful for how God has worked in my life. You do laugh. Of course you do. But I'm the one put food in your mouth. Your superior husband, where is he now? And you still think that's the way to rear a child? I was a daily communicant by nine. I was serving too and there was none of this Do we have to? If they're asking that then you're doing something wrong. That boy has a lot to be grateful for. It mightn't have left him that bright but he's not six foot under and don't tell me that's not the power of prayer. Half the parish doing novenas night and day. It was not remission. No it was not and you be careful because what he gives he can also take back.

And look at that one. What way is that to rear a girl? Look at her. Forward rolls in a skirt. It's disgusting. It's perverted. Underwear on display. What kind of carry-on is that? How is she supposed to be a child of Mary? Well, you shouldn't let her away with it. I never reared you that way.

There must be something wrong with you. You're not right in the head. Just as well I left your poor mother behind. Well it's little wonder why your husband left. If I had to live with this kind of Godlessness going on under my roof. You don't realize we're talking about their immortal souls and that doesn't get a second chance. Can you live with their damnation on your conscience? It doesn't matter what they want or not. It's for their own good. And as for you. As Christ said Better a millstone be tied around their necks. No. No it was mistake to come here. I feel the evil in this house. I'm not staying here. I cannot stay. No don't you speak to me. I don't want to hear the words of the evil one from my own daughter's mouth. You don't know what this has done to me. My own daughter. The shock. No, stay you away. Well I'm sorry they'll be upset but get out of my way. I don't want to hear any more of this. You'll only poison me with your bitterness you Godless creature. I pity you. I really do. Don't come near me. God forgive me I never knew. I never knew I'd reared a . . . No. Enough. That's it. Good-bye.

Such a quiet house after. Car blistering road beneath. She

covered face up and whooping in her throat. Forcing air in. Shaking with tears. Tight as bows we sat. Faces hanging over the stairs. Our evil house Ringing. There are banshees here.

Right then. Right the pair of ye. Do you see what you've done? Are you pleased with yourselves? What did I say about forward rolls? What did I tell you about keeping your knickers covered? She is jumping up the stairs. Take one and two. Crack my eyes are bursting from my head with the wallop. Blood rising up my nose. Drips my head forward. Drip of that. She gets my hair. Listen. To me. Listen. What you've done. Shaking me smack and smack my head. Dirty brat. Shivering. Sharp with rage. Get away from me and push me over to the banisters.

You. Panic. Mammy sorry that I sorry I didn't know. Your hands can't keep her off. She knows all the duck and weave we've done before. And hits you on your ear. On your cheek. That hard. Ah Mammy sorry. Sorry. Sorry please, all you say. She have you by the jumper. Slap you harder. Slap and slap and slap. Push you in the corner. Mammy. Mammy. Getting red face. Getting sore face. Slap again she. Slap again. Screaming. You imbecile. You stupid. I cupping all my blood nose in my jumper. Crouch. You. Bold. Boy. You. Stupid. Stupid. You'll never manage anything. You're a moron. He's right. You're a moron. Hail Mary. How hard can it be? Hail Mary. I've had enough of you. The pair of you. And you. You'll have to go to handicapped school. No Mammy Mammy. Slap you. School for morons is where you belong and you can live there and you can do what you like and I'll never have to put up with you again. I've had enough of you. Both of you. Selfish spoilt brats. Do you hear me? Enough. Morning noon and night and this is what you do to me? Handicapped school do you hear me? Slap slap. Your nose weeping while she pulled you by the hair and then a hard one. A really hard one. Hard down straight upon your brown head. I hear it. Mammy my head. Mammy my my don't Mammy hit me anymore on my head. Holding it, your head, all bent down. Feel it throb you. The shock like sacrilege. Mammy not my head anymore, putting out your palm instead. She didn't then all at once. Pushed you back on the floor. Went into her room. Went into the dark closed curtains of it and shut the door on us.

We standing and hunkered there on the landing. Me intrigued by my bleeding. Pump skull and brain around is what it felt. You turned your face to the corner. Glowing red and white with welts. Stood there until you managed to pull down all your sobs. I heard you grasp your breathing. Still it.

Took me hot hand to the bathroom then and water on my face. Gentle wiping, saying there now it's alright. Cleaned blood from me like I saw at school. Head back gulping the thicky flow. Now, you say, we'll be good. Now we'll do what we are told. Maybe she'll forgive us if we'll be good. Alright? We'll be good now. I said stupid shit fuck piss cow bitch frigger shiter fucker bitch pig. Stop it, don't say that you said. You have to be good. I said, she can't hear you now.

Tomato soup we made. You opened and only tipped a little on the sideboard block. I wiped it in the darkness. We were keeping still as still. Didn't even turn the light on while you lit the gas. Poured such red soup into that pot. Set it whisper down on the stove. And stirred it with the wooden spoon so we would not scrape. Poured in a white bowl. With a slice of bread. Some kitchen roll folded on the tray. A proper soup spoon by the side plate. I carried it although you were bigger. Not to drop it. I was careful and your hand might slip. Put it down there. On the floor there. Just beside her door. Then you knocked it. Very gentle. Saying Mammy in a whisper here's your dinner that we made. We had a talk and we'll be good from now on and do everything you say. All the time. Please don't send me to handicap school.

Then a wait. We heard her walk across the bedroom floor. Quiet. Foot by foot. And she opened up the door looking all tired out and white. Bent down and lifted it. Saying thank you children. We'll see in the morning. Go on to bed now. Good-night.

5

Get up from that bed. Come on we're late. Ah Mammy. It'll do you no harm Madam to show the Lord you care. But I feel sick at mass. None of that please. There's no fresh air in there. Get you your shoes on we haven't got time for this.

Grannies rap their hearts. I know that from hot mass when they say Jesus's name. My feet hurt, knees hurt on the kneeler where someone's foot left shoe dirt there—sorry will you let me through. All the people up and down saying Christ has died Christ has risen Christ will come again. Mammy I can't see the altar. Lift me up til my legs go dead.

It's a dangerous place for smacking mass. Any trying to run up the aisle. Get back here. Climbing through the seats ahead. Sorry. Sit down. Sucking tissues or getting under the pew. That's a good thump in the back. Stand up here and it goes right through your lungs. I like that, to make men from sucked toilet paper. I have plenty and I never clean my nose. Stop that dirty thing. You get it for G.I. Joe man banging on the floor. But he's jumping. Ssssh. But Mammy he's. Ssssh. Jumping off Niagara Falls. Stop. That. Now. Ow. Be quiet I said.

And when we go out all the old ones saying would you

look at that, and aren't they great at their age you can get them to behave at all. At that age mine were up to all sorts. Sure they had my heart broke. She smiles says they're a handful, but you wouldn't be without them would you? No. Thanks be to God.

Do you like coming to God's house? In the car home. Careful. And for this the answer's yes. Would you not rather be watching the telly? No Mammy I wouldn't. No.

She offers demure love now and saintly head. Sign of the cross. Kissing beads. And bible stories every day and night. All the eating locusts I liked. Hair shirt sticking in the skin. Devils in the wilderness and stones for bread. A good suffering Jesus. Lank and ribs, tats hanging in his hair. Sore and sticking on the cross even more.

On my own, draw marker on his picture flesh. Quiet or it would be a slapping. Don't you dare be defacing Our Lord. But I. Blood from this eye. In my own time on the sly she never catch me. Lying on my belly singing When creation was begun god had chosen you to be mother of his blessed son holy Mary full of grace. Stick it in him. I like it hurts so much. His mother is crying to see him. Lovely blood on thorns and scourging is the best thing though this picture doesn't show his back. Holes of wounds for stabbing in lances or nails. That one is infected. It would be worser than this if they stuck a knife in I'd say. But I didn't have red felt tip. That got squashed in Tiny Tears's eye. You did it. Still, good to see him going bloody to death, though pink. Busy I was with a million gushing cuts to draw, make them worser, giving scabs. Where's the pain in that one? But I'd like to hear him crying, screaming most of all. How bad was it Jesus? Mr. Jesus Christ. I thought Christ was his second name. She all the time pointing him out in pictures saying Jesus Christ.

Mr. Christ. Mrs. Christ like Claus. You gone all strange, saw me, said I see what you're doing. That makes Jesus cry. What? Drawing blood down between his legs. I amn't. You are. So? It's dirty. Don't tell though, sure you won't tell? I won't do it again. Alright but you have to say your prayers and remember to tell it when you make your confession or. What? You'll be going down to the hot place.

6

Down the road had farmer girls who were my class friends. Grease on their lunchboxes they always had. Smell of salad cream. Cheese biscuit stink of a house if I went down to play.

Me and the stink girls when we are playing. We do something else at all. For badness if I stay the night—ach leave her here she'll do no harm. We're donned in finest vestments Mickey Mouse or Donald Duck our nylon nighties. Reverend she and Father me. Our altar decked with cotton-bud candelabra. That chalice mug with flowers on, the cloth the mat and Jesus wafer cheese and onion. But first my children confess your sins. I am confessee. That is. Fr I do the cornflakes ad. Wag my bum like dogs with tails saying oooooo lovely cornflakes. And cornflakes cannot be a sin. It is though here. Do. Not. Wiggle. Your. Bottom. Like. That. It. Is. A. Sin. For her that admonition was the one they'd use and for my penance didn't hit too hard. Me. On my legs. But sometimes pull my skirt up because that's what priests would do. In front of all the people. Then they'd see your knickknacks. Ten Hail Marys and a Glory Be.

Now my children it is time for mass. Sing that song. Through him with him in him in the unity of the Holy Spirit all glory and honor is yours almighty father forever and ever. Say it, this is the body of Christ and eat your crisp. This is the blood of Christ and drink up that thick ribena blood. Don't spit out. And on her mother push the door we quick disband for blasphemy's the fatal sin.

But their mother sent our one notes. Give that to your mam a ghrá. Saying we're the Charismatics. Doing the good work. Doing the good work for Christ Our Lord. And she came one Sunday evening sat praying on me—a great haul for the fishers of men. They were talking for an hour and she said every Thursday then. Six o'clock? Yes. Fine.

They come with fruitcakes. There's a few little scones there in that tin. She says tell your brother bring in some tea. Put the tray down on the coffee table there, good boy. Isn't he great? They're click-clacking by the time you come in. Oh you'd go mad sitting in the house all day on your own. Look at that isn't he great? Haven't you him well trained?

Doing great. Are you delighted? Of course you are. He's a great lad godbepraised. Like mothers they know all the questions and answers before. Knew to pat you. Knew to ask how's school and who's your teacher? Making your first holy this year? All that.

They polyester tight-packed womanhood aflower in pink and blue or black and green coats if the day has rain. Their boots in the hallway, crusty with cow dung or wet muck. If in Sunday skirts, every pleat a landscape of their grown-up bodies. Tired. Undertouched. Flesh having run all night after the cows. Flesh carry sacks of turf up lanes from the shed and spurt out child and child and child. Son he has wanted. Girl he did not. Making frys at all hours and smell of cigarettes called fags by them. Lily of the valley and vaseline. This country's awful in the winter. Brown skin nylons. Leatherette shoes. And they'll just have a little cup there in their hand. Good for them they like God and Jesus the most. That's what they come here to say and do. There's in their bags holy books and books of it. I picked up this one. I'll lend you that. Now you take this I read it and thought of you. Hold out their palms out and let the spirit in. To save them and to set them free.

Some most are women. In a blue moon a man. I like to eye. Sitting in the corner jugging as I can for all they say is interesting to me. Dress undressing no-neck cindy. Not stopping or I get look at little lugs there listening in. Oh taking it all in that one. Doesn't miss a thing. Spelling I know but too quick to understand r.u.n.o.f.f with the s.a.c.r.i.s.t.a.n and they are living in s.i.n down in such and such a place. There's stink girl's mother and her sister with women's troubles so peculiar all pointed down and asked and how's ahem? Ah she'll not sit down for years. Apparently the smell of it is something wicked but god knows it's not her fault. Their brother's second wife—ach the first died leaving five behind. Tell me where's the sense? They're wild as wild. As bold as brats. The PP's housekeeper—God rest her late husband. A lovely man. She gave him a hard life but sure. Mrs. one whose husband ran the AIB. Uppity up in herself—behind palms in the scullery they whisper adding a splash to warm the pot. Great red hat she wears to mass. So we have a look at her and where's the humility in that? Ah each to their own, they say. Then your woman who bought a knitting machine. A hundred and twenty pounds now where did she . . . Her little boy. Downs. God love him. She does school jumpers so she can get him toys that are ed-u-cat-ional nod nod. That's right for God helps those who help themselves. The politician's wife they'd normally spite but God help us her heart is broke. He's running about with this one that one. She can't look down on them. Her vows were sacred and he'll not get her into mortal sin. Her heart may be pierced with a thousand spears but she'll offer it as penance that's a bit proud don't you think? And the one whose husband's a desperate drunk. Like his father before him you know the type, vicious. That'd kill you in it by mistake. Her blue eyes. Her black eyes. Is he on the bottle? they say and pray for sometimes giving up and the forgiveness of his sins.

When they get down to the business rosary. Circle. I feel the Holy Spirit close here. Among us. Healing our wounds. Filling us with Christ's love. Put down that you and come and say your prayers. Speaking through us like the apostles of old. You and me sitting back aching straight in God, thinking cindy's boobies lie out just there on the floor. Sometimes I'll do you a foot dance. Jiggery. But you're not for laughing anymore. Bow your head. You take it for real—I tell you that boy has the makings of a priest. But I will not bother til apparitions approach. Our Lady of Medjugorje's message says those awful secrets near. Her vision girls bright views of hell. Their family's falling in. Those pets those friends. Cold worms of fear. Will that be me? Leave if I can. Run. Sit down Miss and bear witness to their blessed truth.

Picture how she comes. Our Lady in white, when you're not looking. She beckons you to Christ. Pray to be chosen. To bear her secrets for the world. A dying world. Please don't to me or catch her floating on the stairway. Reaching out. Howabout stigmata instead? Worse though you'd never go to school again or look at my hands in case I see it. The Holy Spirit's in me. Not a punishment. It's a gift. No not like the violin. Any eejit can do that. I feel it aching in my palm but when will the blood burst? Now please Jesus or not at all. Lickety lips of the praying wouldn't mind if I was one. But they'd all like it for their children. A visionary born from me? You'll only be able to tell the seasons by the trees Malachi prophesied or Colmcille. And they say the last secret of Fatima is destruction of the church. The Vatican won't say either way because that'll be the end of days. Gulp this. But we'll know anyway from Medjugorje the day before. Shiver I purple terror high in my throat. The dead will knock your window. Deadly bony spirit hands. They'll beg for you to save their souls. Open the latch they cry. You will not. Can not. You must turn from them. Away. Shut the curtains. Light a candle and pray for your salvation while the apocalypse blows your door. And if they plead they love you, so much the worse for their souls. Those poor souls howling. Sucked into the forever night. Will you save us Mammy? I'll say easy children close your eyes for this world is coming to an end. But Mammy it scares me. Well better behave yourself then.

They pray to God and pray and pray for God's sake to be saved. They're swaying rolling. Palms out rigid. Letting in the Holy Spirit. Come and make our lives a perfect sacrifice to thee. Russians blowing up the world. Pray for them. For all the Chinese going to hell. For the black pope that's the last one. Him as well even if he's next. I nudge. Could Satan be talking through? No. There's holy water eejit and not much terror in you. You are filling with redemption. But I am for it. Me and my sins. Listen as they do it speaking loud in a thousand tongues. Could Germans understand it maybe French? Sounds A la la ka leash a na to me.

But when they go and it is night I'm a bit heart stopped. Gives chest hurt fright. Make the sign of the cross and I'll be fine. You'll be got because you drew on Christ, dirty thing.

No if I die before I wake I pray to God my soul to take God bless you me Mammy Granda and Granny and don't let the end of time be tonight. You say thank you god for being so good and are not afraid of the dark.

If it's summer before the sun goes down I sometimes leg it from the holy joes. Mammy I have to go toilet and go and run hand-washed to stare into the sun. That's a good job. That'll make me a strong one. I heard three times makes you blind. But mine's in secret so I stare fine for it won't ever blind me. God holy holying you though. He might be some kind of saint. They have never met your like. Manys a mother would've given up hope. Her arm on your shoulder. Her gentle stroke your head. I don't know where I'd be without him.

I'm just bit on the wild, bit of a pup. Nothing interesting to prick a curate. Not like Hail Marys you say as well as Glory be. For fun Father and the souls in purgatory that they be saved—he said to me—now where did he get that but God?

Still. I can leg it down the drain. Inside under Jesus I make my dash out in the rain. Slap mud sandals. Slap mud all up my socks. I'll skid it. Scutter it. Holding thistles for fairy soup or foxgloves bad luck teacher calling giddy goat or I will tell your mother you were saying shite. Making out curses and people die. I can. Being magic. Saying fucker Christ. Into the fields. My bad words best collection. All the things my mother never taught me. To shit in a field or run in from the rain. So I knew it always then and do it all the time. Oh crouch. Dock leaf. Plopped. True I could be killed for that. Such elicit outdoor. And a white one too. Should not have been licking chalk. I couldn't bide the loud Do not. Theeverysooften crunchy crunch. And white guilty gums.

Poison I know. I'll die from it. But a little one. Ah a sneaky one and Oh I quail to think of that. You did something you should not have. Chalk's your downfall. Chalk's your crime. Day in school I. Didn't lick the blackboard just my hand. Smacked it palmly on. And sweet chalk powder licky to my tongue. Swoon through lunch know I'll get caught or Who did that disgusting thing? Where's the glantóir? Teacher roaring. Who'd dare violate this board? She better confess because I always know. Panic runs lines across my face. I won't raise my hand. She'll kill me stone dead. Who did that? Nets not cast wide. The pair of ye, get up.

They trup foot heavy but will not confess. Did you do it? No teacher. You're lying. I can tell. Ye little tinker bitches. Itinerants, I know to say. Not in my house will you call people tinker Mammy says. No one's tinker to you Miss. But our teacher does. Always smelly tinkers. Tinkers sit over there for living in caravans and get more walloped than anyone else. There. Always back to ye she says. Troublemakers. She knows them well. I sweat hands knowing I should tell. That love of chalk. Those smear is me. She crack their foreheads hard to each. Crack. Pulled to by the pony plaits with neat grease ribbons. I'm shame to that. They stand gloss-eyed and rub their heads. That'll learn you. Get out of my sight she says and they reddy stare over the stone school wall. Looking at bushes with snail trails on. Snails at their noses. Snails in their eyes. No Daddy theirs will say don't to my child. I know that. No Daddy mine. Go on ye so, and trup them down to snuffle lie sore heads on their desks. Noses dripping in their cuffs. Teacher scrubbing hands on a j-cloth. Don't touch them little scums. I tuck my white hand in to lick at later on. Later. Alligator. Cat.

. . .

Not there, I walked around and around. That house had up hill down dale. Steps and mud. Those wellies red. Umbrella. Wondrous being dry. See fat drops plop and run like a river down for flies. Spiders. That time it was always raining. Summer. Spring. I don't know though when we were or where. Puddles and puddles very good for sailing peanut barge shells over. Like over and over the sea. Or this is Lough Corrib or this is the Nile. I'd like littler men to sail them but. Your soldiers aren't mine.

And sometimes you have schoolbags. A tie. Little sisters are. Yuck. I hate girls in the schoolyard. But still lie belly on the stairs with me. Who zooms quickest? Face first? Feet? Would you ever mind your brother's head. Boys on bikes are better and I am left boat floating behind. They always ask what's the scar in your hair? One threw a stone at your birthday that cut your ear. She grabbed him by the jumper. Little fecker don't you ever do that again or I'll. Everyone thinks our mother's a bit and desperate because where's the man in that house and who will teach those children right from wrong? Up to all sorts and in my day we were la la la. I'd say that's what they say.

Strange. Pushed out to the ocean of school. Wave back occasional to her shore. Hi there, Mammy. Never see me more without my secret life again. I spy boy's urinal. Kill red things on the wall. Snap and broke the elastic waistband of some girl. I'm telling. Her Mam. Mam. Mammy or. You'll get a thick ear for being noisy. And I never learned times tables. Scaldered to the spot. What's seven times twelve? Never learned that. Thicko to the front. Face the class. Now for you. Have a smack. Was all that happened for years. And my head is good for secrets. I can bang it on the wall. It takes the nervous out and no one bothers for it at all.

So. This as well when no one looks. Go n'eírí an bóthar leat while the wind be always at your back. Run up the fields. Blink to the house. Go sun blindness. Turn my arse. Lift to fly. Balloon across the earth. Puff ball keep your knickknacks covered. Belting on the wind me. Beating me at my own game. Scup there skirts and give us a dance. Be pelted by the dark rains. Feet wet like trough. Soak them blue to black through flesh and bone. Scratch my arms on fairy blackthorn. Knee cut rocks for learning how to fly. Whip grass cut hands and lips on a scutch pipe. I'll call all the fairies and ones living underground. For I know they're listening. Will give me thorns in my pockets and thorns in my bed. I'll jig on their houses til my lips turn red. I'll give you a whirl twirl. A smack on the paddy whack but Get in this house. Get in this house you, always, always comes.

Skating on the beach. I dreamed it. Empty sort on a yellow sky day cliff. In the evening of it. All alone though gulls are there. Cormorants I know. Chicks and hens. Buttery throat calls squawks. Dipping fish out. Wheeling in it turn and dive. Flutter like a panic wings that they would all fall down above me. I hate those bird feet hanging. Rubbery storm air though blowing over the water. Coursing I think. That clouds and wind skiteing sand spray floats of it up. Catching at the back of me. In the bad time of year. This is. Roller skates. Tying-on ones. Butterfly screw and lace-up ones. Heavy and leather over my shoes buckle red ones on. Rollering on the sand front. Going foot to foot to foot to foot. Spinning wheels round digging. Crunch as glass on the axel rod. And then water heaving up behind me. I hear. Fling itself at my legs. Giving a howl out. Drag across the stones. Dragging at me. Drag me in. See the sand dunes. The sting sea grass whipping vicious in the wind. Waves purple chocolate. Snaking at my ankles. Trip me up. Falling on my hands and face. The ocean. Am I drowning? Red knees in my red tights fallen on the foam. I am in it. Gushing back for more of it. The waves are more and rolling over. Back up me. Over me. Soaked and leaden crawling on the dust. My red coat. Sogging. Face down and shrunken in a hood. My faceful of sand. Mouthful of sand. My hands clawing under water tow me out. Heavy head. Heart going mad panic stricken. Saying out. Names. You. You. That type of lung screaming out. Raw and whistle-ish screaming no sound. Expel. Expel it. No one hear me. Struggle. Help me. Gurgle. Glugle. Salted mouth pit. Salted seaweed tongue. Drowning. Gasping. Filled up to the nose and the eyes and the brain. And going cold now. Going under. I am. I am. Going. I am gone. Stop. Up. Breath. Breathe.

Mammy. Cry out. I had a terrible dream. Shush now. She comes. She sits with me down. Those aren't real love. Just made up in your head that can't harm you really, now you're awake. Now there. There now. Nothing bad will ever happen you. Mammy can I sleep in your bed?

In her mother arms I lay feel now and then her jolt awake. Leg jostling. A little snort.

A little choke. Her eyelids flicker in the night. All such usual things to me and good to sleep against. She that always keep me safe. Our nylon nighties static cling. Tiny ribbons on the neck and hands. Matching roses. My sunshine. Only. But Mammy leave the hall light on. I need to see it through the dark.

PART II

A Girl Is a
Half-formed Thing

1

The beginning of teens us. Thirteen me fifteen sixteen you. Wave and wave of it hormone over. Like hot flush cold splash down my neck. Spilt with new thoughts, troublesome that is and things that always must be said. Spill it out. Spill it down.

Where's that father? Mine? Who belonged to was part of me? I think of. Where is he? Imagination of fathers sitting by me on the bed. Stroking my hair you're my girl, belong to me pet. I have heard of seen those things somewhere on the telly. And I say will you ever tell me what he said about daughters before I was born?

She says I've something to tell you after all. Your father's hmmm. Your father's, sit down. What? Shush. Dead. A while ago I got a letter from his mother, once it was over and done. She said he took a stroke. Quick. Probate won't be long. But you never told us? Why didn't you tell us? There wasn't much I could say, not like he loved you, us I mean, and now he's dead. You're provided for. It's time to go about our business. What's that? Moving house. Why? Because he bought this and I don't want it anymore. But I don't want to move Mammy. Don't start. But we've always lived here.

We're. Moving. House. Because. That. Is. What. I'd. Like. To. Do. And. If. You. Don't. Too. Bad. Because. I'm. The. Mother. And. You. Will. Do. What. I. Say. As. Long. As. You. Live. Under. My. Roof. You. Will. Always. Do. What. I. Say. O. Kay.

We scour a house. Sniff all over. See if it's a good bed down. I don't understand marching around thinking upstairs downstairs toilets good bad indifferent, that is fungus that's not foam. Are those rotten windows is there a draft under that door? My ocean insides wallowing about. Look at you you not that bothered, calmer but hear at night you pound the wall saying where'd he go? Where'd he fecking go?

Pack up. Teeth feeling itchy in my head. I've eczema, a load of spots, then a bleeding, Jesus, period one day. Thinking, walk around the house at night saying bye to you thing and you and you.

You ripping bookshelves off the wall. Crash it. Throw it on the carpet. Snap. Stop that. Accident I pulled too hard. I'll pack these, snap these knitting needles of hers. That stinking wedding cake ornaments she has. I'll break them stick them in her drawer as if she cares as if she'll see and wonder where it's from.

Pack it. Throwing out this bike. Was that his? I ask you. Yes you stupid bitch and whose else would it be? Can we keep it? No. His umbrella and binoculars too? I want. Something. Like you knew him, like you know anything or ever saw him even. Give you a slap scratch. But you'll give me bloody nose if you can, you can't I can run away.

Box it she says or in a black bag. That his briefcase and letters and magnifying glass and this pen. Whose is it? I ask. Chuck it away she said.

She said I like this place you will. You will. There's your

room. There's your bed. And don't you give me a face like that. Get up stairs and make up your beds. Rumble tumble.

Have this yours mine his hers whose that and what's the matter don't you care at all?

I'm sorry if you feel. Tell me something good that he done once? Your bloody father's dead and gone. Much good he was he left a will oh don't worry it's all for ye not me. Feed you clothe you all that stuff oh yes you'll be fine but there's no good old story. I haven't that to give. Your bastard father. Your bastard. Yours. You and him. Get out of my sight and don't forget to say your prayers.

Hail Mary full of grace the lord is with thee. Say it. Blessed art thou among women.

And blessed is the fruit of thy womb Jesus.

Holy Mary mother of god pray for us sinners, now, and at the hour of our death. Amen.

Do you like that? Do you like the look of that school? There. That's where you'll be going. Both. Now. For the first time. Isn't that nice? At the same time. Yes different years. But still. You'll mind each other. You'll mind each other. You will. My family is love.

We sliced through that fug school bus. So misfortunately new. Thicken soup-ish teenage sweat and cigarette boys slop always at the back. Held tight my rucksack filled with rattling tins of pens. Fat drizzle blotch through the polyester skirt I sideways slope to walk in. Felt my hormones long to slink quiet out of these hard eyes. Do not be seen. Do not see me. But I must turn myself to the great face of girls.

Raw red in the cold snow air. Blow puffs of exhalation in tea smelled breath up the windowpanes and gaggle. Birds and beast they. In damp army jackets and sweat-sunk skirts.

They'd be faggy if they could. Full of perms and baggy T-shirts. They may wear their shirttails out as I may not. Cerise talons itch for. I am homestyle hands still cleaned and trim. Neat on the cuticle. White at the tip. I may not be that girl. And I may not say there are rosary beads slipping in my pocket on my thumb. I have them talisman against all wrong they'll do me. I know they will.

I be new girl. I could wish to be dead but for the wrong of it. To have to be saying again again where I come from. Who I am. And I'm from someplace so much littler than this. That redneck culchie. Backward. Farmyard. I am all these things to the great girl face. Those herd. Such bovine singing heifers. Come don't hate me. All your walkmans fizz in tune, in time with conversations, pointing graffitis on the bus, love this one that one. New girl stinks.

I'll let my heart walk away. I'll think of home. I'll feel all their smells converge around me to that bit I can't attach. That's the inside of where they all are. That they have smelled each other all their lives and know the way. And know the way it is. They say I'm proud. Stuck up. I'll dream myself up above there. The roof of the bus and looking down. I think I'll see them down there where they fart and blame some other one. Where they itch between their mucky legs. Where clammy thighs catch their tights right in and give them sore spots little ingrown hairs. I see you through those eyes. Antennae. Newness. Shocking as a stranger. I see you. Back, unaware meander arms and legs into the pool of sharks. See them stretch out to snap you. Chew and spit. On that bus. And shout come down here new boy. You, I see, see me but pass off. Climb the ruckle of schoolbags. Balance yourself on the backs of the chairs. Your feet are drowning when it sets off. Gunk you. Throw you over. With a hard knock on your face. On your knees. Hefty drop from which you can't get up. Well. No escape from bus muck on your hands. In a slobber on your face. They're roaring sniffing. See your blood pouring down the aisle to them. Snapping. Chewing at your hands and feet. Ha ha ha breathe out Spastic. Spastic fall over. Can't Spastic walk? I feel you on the inside, that blast of it. Done wrong. I ponder will I help with those new girls around? Their great faces birch derision down. Scalder up my neck my throat to me and my head. I say are you alright in the muffle of my coat hood. Where I can hardly be seen to feel you matter. And you say—spring up—I'm fine. I'm fine. You laugh away think they won't know it was not fun for you to fall sprawl. Bus bumps. Bus grind over the bridge look out. Turn my head from your catch of throat of tongue, on the wrong part of the word to be free and easy. Hear you shuffle on down to at the back. I know they have you off down there. That you'll be butt and crib of jokes. I leave you there to your fate and soon. I hear you going all the wellie, telling—no one laughing—tales of where you're from. They are leery. Laughing underhand at your frizz hair. Your little gut that rolls a bit on your band. That does you down that you don't see or worry, will be against the cool of them those pitchfork farmer boys with their green wellies on. With their rank stories of strung-up cats and slit-ear pups from that big litter had last spring. They'll throw a bat against the wall to see if mush flap squeal or die. Stick a blue tit in the range so it will squeak burn. You said tit. Burning tits they like that. And say that word to all the girls if they can. How's your tits? Have you any eggs you fucking bitch. We are. What are we are doing here? In this place that is full of that. Is overbrimmed of torture.

I feel it gone, my fucker Jesus self. It weep away like

longed-for wound. Take off that bandage. No nothing there. No badness to keep me. Prop me up. In this place I am as slack gut. Nothing inside to keep me up. With all the coldness in the rooms. With all the people breathe the air around who think me strange and odd. It empties me. It throws me out. Dirty water. Dirty cup. I think for moment I'd rescue you. Say how scum it is. This place. Like this. And do not. Leave you to do your standing. Run for cover. Feeling the earth come down around me after thousand-pound bomb's ripped it up. We are transplanted. We are the new now and the wrong. The lost. The done for. Ever. I see I am sliding into years of this I think. And you. My lost then brother. You'll be strung up.

Hey you two. New two. Yeah you two. Here's your stop. Get off.

For all of that I wanted to be out of it. All of that. You wanted to be in.

One day I saw you. That prefab shadow on your eyes. That gravel on the playground under your foot. Four or five ones there with you. They sat. Coats roped under their chins and eyes filled with fag smoke watchfully. Teachers come round the corner just like that. Laring they do always. Making fart noise hocking spit. Snort up clumps of guck from their lungs. You do not. That's to fall foul. You will not do what you're not allowed, even for them. For the comrade nudge of adulation. But you'll find other intimations of their special cool.

This day I see you sway foot there. One foot to another. Kicking the stones. All these——some red-haired acned, some blond-like wispy thin hair their blue eyes freezing, some raise a stink in every room of the school. I hate the stunk air after their class has been.

Smell German classroom their deep BO. These are swinging on the fence chain by you there, standing left right swipe a pebble with that black striped runner toe. And they say joggling each other, what happened you there? Where? That big scar on your head. I wince in my slink hole see. The question never answered I know by you. I. Shall I think of some diversion? Come over and be a center action? I do not. I do not no. You would not thank me for that.

You say, and shock me, a knife did it. Silence. For the first time impressed. They cannot delve you all a sudden. Something cool they cannot know. For country boys are beat by dads or priests around the head or a teacher in fury with a big maths book. But not with knives that cut their skulls up. I see them. Sizing now your magnitude compared to them. Them thinking you did not always live here. Must have happened when you were young. Must have happened at another school. Is that true? Who'll disprove it? Not I. I'll not. They do not ask when? who? but Did it hurt? A little bit you say. Were you really cut? Yes awful deep is why my eye's not so good. A great assimilation of all your school-bound woes now up in one knot. This healing vast equivocation. You throw all in the pot. Its lid on tight. And was there much blood? Yeah loads of that. And hospital and people passing out? Oh loads. And did they think you'd die? They did. Somehow I didn't, you say. They never knew anyone nearly dead before but grannies and grandfathers. Did they go to court? They got away. With it? From the country, thickorwhat, you say. Oh right. Oh right yeah.

I smelt it go around the school all day. In crannies in whispers in home economics behind me, before me, to right and to left. Hey dimwit shitfit what happened your brother? What happened his head? Is that true? You so full of shite. It did not. It did not. Sweat me down my polyester pinafore. Don't want to get into it. Don't want to say Aye Yes nor No if I can help it. But I don't want to burst your lie.

Bus home you were not tripped up. And no one said thicko fuckup shitehawk. And you did sit at the back of the bus. I went over and over each bump in my stomach. The luck of it. Bad luck of it to tell that lie. Of all. About that. That thick meander line below your hair.

She always tug fringe over it. Hide all the memory, says please grow it out a bit long. You will not though some reason of your own. It's my scar. It happened to me. I say it's too short. Stay out of it you.

We jump on the verge from off the bus. I heard what you said in school. Such a liar you are. Shut up you say and it was a knife did it anyway. Don't say that, you know what I mean you know it well. And your schoolbag buckle graze my cheek shocks my stomach. A not what I expected. So I threw mine at you. Making myself a show to neighbors if they're watching and they are. You missed me you are shouting. Steaming down the road ahead. There'll be skin and hair flying. There'll be wigs on the green. I shout I'm telling Mammy. Baby squeal. See if I care. What's she going to do? The earth is rumbling. Things are splitting up. So I say nothing at home. But hold it in the air so you see what I have got. Like, what were you saying to the lads today? And. Really that's not what I heard. What's that? No nothing Mammy. See, I can level the blow when I wish. If I wish. Might or might not. You live under it. Defiant but under all the same. But I did not mention it again and you sat with the cool lads on the bus.

2

She driving. Me in the passenger seat. Bringing the statue to
the next house. It's rotation because it comes from Lourdes.
Have you a good hold of her? Yes Mammy. Blue blond gold.
It sits plaster baby on my knee, crown in my teeth and I like
the great green serpent coiling all round her feet.

  She drives so higgledy piggledy down the road. Bump.
Don't break so fast I'll drop her. Don't be a cheeky brat. Quiet.
She sings amazing grace. Says hmmmm. Says anyway. What?
Your brother. Aha? Not so well at school the teachers say.
And? I say to them he studies every single night. I tell them I
send him up to that desk. And what didn't I buy him, books,
copies, everything. I think I'll not be interested at all in this.
So I say sooo? My head throbby boy thoughts. My nose big
with blackheads. Hair and grease normal. Staring out the
window balancing the virgin don't chip her there and does
she have ears in that golden mane? I think and make display
of my disinterest. It's important she says there's something
else. What's that? Umm I don't know what you but teachers think he's a bit subnormal. Just. A little bit. Not under by
much. What? Going round and round my. I don't want to. I
don't want to. I don't want to. Hear that. I shout stop that.

Saying. Believing that. Always saying stupid things about him. She says will you calm yourself. No I won't. No. No. He's fine. That's awful to say. Well that tumor could've done more harm than we. Stop. I belt young Virgin Mary on the dashboard. Take it. Take that. Take that. Wobbling the car. She. Swerve it. What the stop it stop it stop. I don't want to. Hear. I don't want. It in my life. Stop the car. She stop the car. I must get. Out. On the roadside. Stop it. Let me out. Pull in.

Fuck that virgin onto the tarmac. Take her head does she like it? What's the. Don't tell me. Don't tell me that. What do I do? Aha. Aha. It makes my head run. Makes my face run. I fall in the grass. I graze my hand. I feel lungs closing up under the breathless. No. No. Breathe it. Breathe it. Put down your head. She says. Just sit there. Head between your knees I'll shut the car door. She pulls it over. And puts on the break light. Sssh.

Sorry I broke the statue I say wet with cry. Don't mind. Don't mind the statue. Don't mind that. I don't want. Shusha shusha. I. I. No. I don't want. And I feel a sinus. Feel a brain erase. Feeling limbs feeling. Pins and. Shock and. Needles. Get in. She says leave that. She says it's alright. She says he's fine. She says sure they never know what they're talking about. Now. She drives us home.

And this means we are eating dinner stew. I am sitting. And she there pass the salt.

Thump. In my. Thumping. Face and neck. You busy making at me ape face. Big jaw. The funky gibbon. Shuffle kick under the tablecloth. Ugh what's so wrong with you? Saying so and so teacher saying such and such. Saying la la la. To me. It comes like river up my throat. Puke on my dish. Chunk dribble my plate. And again. And retch again. She pat my neck hold my head go on. You shouting Oh that is so disgusting can't you get up to the toilet. Such a retard. Quiet you. She pat my back. She pat my head. It's alright.

No I'm not going to tell anyone, I say. And you shouldn't either. I don't see what's to be gained. Well they think he'll get along alright she says. Ds but fine. He'll find something that will make him happy. Are you going to be telling everyone behind his back Mammy? Think of holy joes praying and all they'd say. I'm not hope you'll not is what she says. You're a good sister and he's always been good to you so. Right? Ssssh.

He's coming up. Something else. Oh pork chops so were two a pound. Is that good? I say.

That school tread. Going over and over. Term learn holiday back again. My Cs. My Bs for not doing much, that much. She doesn't apply herself. And you get, you get upstairs to that room and do some work. Every night you're stuck up there three or four hours and you're bringing home Ds and Es to me. What do you think your father would say to that? He'd be ashamed his only son's so useless. You're just bone idle. That's your problem. What are you doing up there? Stop that don't be saying that. Why are you saying that it's not as if he can help it. You know. You know. Just what do I know? she says. Sure you're the one who told me. It's not like he can help it. No it won't get better if he does more work. Maaaammy leave him alone. And you shouting what are you saying to her? Why don't you mind your own business, if she gives out to me what's it to you?

But. Shut up and butt out. So nosy. She says there now son. That's alright. Your sister's just having a phase. Everything's my fault but she'll snap out of it soon. I say Oh fuck off. Don't talk to her that way. Then you can fuck off too.

3

Say hello to your aunt and uncle. You haven't seen them before. Nudged his jaguar into the drive or volvo or fancy I don't know about that. He black curl-haired she bob-cut wife. Our mother's sister she. To call. To come and stay. Better off than us and close I think when they were young—we played house snakes and ladders and little women. We hear her on the telephone every month or so. Now then youngster, how are you? Pass me onto. Is your mother home? Or go on and get your mother tell her I'm in a state. And she mentions every once in a while your aunt loves tea rose scents. She sends a check for Christmas and birthdays and now and then. And parcels of hand-me-downs from girls about my age. Auntie so with bottle-green tights. She's a hips woman they say with a size ten top. My God a broad and wing'ed arse. Nudge and jostle you me Shush. In all they're grand compared to us. Bags that match. Driving shoes. Leather gloves and a cigarette lighter in their car. Come uncle uncle and play your guitar. Come uncle uncle and smoke your cigar. Those are what I've been told they do.

Come and smile and give us hugs. Ah he'll not be tall like his Da oh should I not? His father was a tall man after all aunt adds. Hmm we've all sorts our mother says with her arm across your back. Take your auntie's bag upstairs and your uncle's while you're at it. I look at him. I look him back from looking right at me. His eyes flick a switch. I'll stare you dare you and don't think you're posh than better than us. Come in and sit down and you'll have a cup of tea with. Ho ho look at Madam, can't get over how she's grown. I'm thirteen now and nearly more. Soon.

Sit smile and give bottles of bubble bath and packets of crisps and jigsaws theirs already smeared with. Lovely girls. You might like it thought it might do. Your cousin loved that one. Oh lovely lovely. And secondhand knickers with butterflies for me.

Second-arsed. Amn't I the lucky one. Pink and green. For you a book of Jesus and a plate with praying hands. Yes I am fifteen a snicker splutter. We'll put them in our rooms.

At the table she speaks slow and loud like we're deaf. How's school doing? She's scared as hell of us young savagers. She's heard tell. The evil house and halfwit brother. Sullen girl and her forward rolls. I don't mind her snit one bit. My all-set temper might spark to it but we have a lovely awkward dinner of gammon and mashed spud first. I do love them more says she with a pineapple ring on top. Haven't you maybe one of those? No. A biteen then more salt. They're dry those spuds. Pass it. There you go. My girls won't touch it. Pork is such a, you know meat. Was the milkman was a jew? I say under my breath you wrinkle snotting. What? Our mother's eyes plop from her head, but they chew neat and cud-like and have not heard. Nothing I think, til I see him. Uncle uncle. Maybe you're no fool. I get the I'll get you later on look from our mother and jelly a bit. And how's your work? I made partner. Well isn't that great. Holidays in

Spain. Do you get away? says the aunt. No not that much. I
don't know how you do without the sun. Well. We're also
having an extension. Oh. How big's this house here by the
way? Three bedrooms. God how do you all fit in? We need a
new guest one and with the girls so grown it's en suites for
this one and en suites for that one. Hhmmm. Oh walls? I
suppose it'll remind me of my youth—we usually have carte
d'or. He says give it a rest would you, not everyone's as well-
off as us isn't that right? Yes my mother says looking greener
stewed-up cabbage. And I see he is watching me with this,
seeing how I am. I am champing inner lip. Inside us all are,
better or worse, for she's a bit this aunt, relentless.

Did you get the check? Did you get my check? I've almost learned to growl but you avoided it or did not think
she was rubbing it in. I could bite this hand that feeds for
parading the bill. Did you get that check she kept saying to
her I keep forgetting if I've asked? My little snarling yes you
do. Our mother says go upstairs and leave us to talk, or your
brother's watching telly why don't you go join him. I'll do
the dishes I'm saying thinking I won't leave. Keep an eye on
what's said about you and me. I'm unhappy aware there'll be
loyalty smeared somewhere there on our kitchen floor. Not
mine. Not to you. Or yours to me. Or her. No go make up
the camp bed that's what you can do for me she says so I do.

I sneak. I snuck. I listened at the door. I heard them.
I pondered you should send him to special school. Those
marks aren't fit for a boy that age. Oh such clucking and
glucking. Snob and preen herself. I hear my two are off to
the convent. Not a ladder in their tights or a pain in their
heart. Such brilliance. Unearthly. I snoot them. Aunt and
uncle. Chintz for brains I hiss and think. Listening listening.
Yes of course they got accepted so naturally I know a mark

or two when I see it. Compete it. I'm having bile thoughts. Great green ones of spite and their sloppedy daughters with tongues too long to keep in their mouths. Should we be that so we can be right? We're clear awful wrong the way we are. Yes they're having grinds and trips to the orthodontist. One should give one's children the best in life. Golf. Give them a taste so they can never live without. Shop at such and no sales. Grow them good and wanty. For bungalows near politicians and the captains of industry. Our mother I think foamy at the edge thinks I need this like a hole in the head. Yabber yabber put the teapot down and take out the biscuit tin. She treads it calm and forth with hmm and yes and is that right? No says aunt as long as they have their degrees. Shop-floor management or whatever history. Degrees the thing and tra la la—what are the chances yours'll do that?

I'm raging. I'm spitting. Come in slinging the door. Oh are they really aunt and uncle how was it they got in the convent when they only got Ds. Just lucky? Didn't you pay for them in? You shut up don't be so cheeky. Your aunt's thoughts are for the best. Is that so? Is it that? Why is she always doing him down? And me. Getting podgy! And you taking it all in. Sucking it up. You cow come here eat your tea and say we're all these sorts of things. Go to your room. Go right there now. I mean it. Straight away.

I'm flooding the hallway up those stairs to my room see their bags shout fuck off through the floor so they'll hear, they'll hear me and know what I mean. You snobs. Bastards. I'll say the bad words I have. Coming here. What? says you stick your head through the door. No-thing. Nothing for you to know. Go back to the telly and leave me alone.

I'm sitting for ages and sob and whine. Til the back door

click. They have gone out. And you went with them I know. In the room I sit alone. Quiet and listening to the groans of the floor and the rattle of water running hot through the pipes. Six o'clock now and.

I hear his footfall. The banisters creak. Definitely his feet not yours. I chew my lip.

Tap on my door. Tap tapping he push it through. Are you here? Are you alright?

Thought I'd see if you're. I'm fine. Well now. What? That's quite a moment to treat us to and on the first day. I know it. Can I come in? Alright, do. Your aunt's a bit of a madam gibbet. Hang 'em always. Hang 'em high. I laugh at him and his aunt stranger wife.

Meaner than true. Why does she? She doesn't mean to. Doesn't think it, never has, through well. She has to make a big competition between us and your girls it's not. I know that but. She's very fond of you, underneath. Nice way to show it. I'll have a word about. Sorry. Me too. And breathe in out.

Shouldn't we be friends? I am your uncle after all. But it's the first time that we've met. No, I've seen you before. When? When you were born before we went abroad. I don't remember. You were only small. Do you like England? I do. What do you do? All sorts of things and do you do? I go to school. I knew that. Yes you did. You've quite a lip. Someone has to. Why? Just the way things are . . . I see. I'm sorry to have asked. I'm sorry I shouted. I know she's your wife but I don't like her. Oh she's. Not that bad. So you said. You're a funny girl. Why's that then? Cheeky madam. Maybe I am. Oh you are. Well that's me. Good for you can I ask you. What? Do you climb out that window to meet your boyfriends at night? Shy me and do not say for no would be diminishment of some kind in his eyes. Smiling's best when. I do that. Watch him. Smiling eyes. And he just smiled at me.

We went to school. We went on that bus. In the cold lunch break they are kicking football on the muck pitch. You run. Run. Run. That bad eye I know cannot keep up with a ball nor does it see one of them and his doing you for the crowd. Behind your back. For their laughter is a mighty thing to invoke. Your little limp. Sometimes the way you shake your head. It's brilliant that the worst one on the whole field doesn't know it. See him do it. For their roaring. For their great lads fun. He does your voice like a thick tongue. Pass it here lads after you say it. They kick it to keep you to and fro. No one's playing. Only you now but you don't know. Round of laughing. I see you stop then. Something twigging within. Look around. To the clumps of them doubled-up in two quaking squealing. Happy pigs getting fed on you. The way your hand hangs down or you stumble on a rock. He smears a muck bit down his forehead for the scar that you've got. Jesus fucking spastic Christ. And you were saying, what is it? Hey lads what's going on? The more they look the more they laugh. You now getting all het up. Can smell the joke descend on you. How did you get your scar again? A knife. A knife? Oh was it? Very funny. I heard you got your brain cut up. Did not. That you're brain damaged. I am not. You're a brain-damaged liar. No listen you said. Handicapped. Ugh they're sticking tongues in their bottom lips. You stumbling toward them. Not thinking. Thinking how to stop them say at this. In the mud you stumbled over. Caught yourself. Stood back up straight. Listen. Listen lads. All they say is uuuuuggggh. I could kill them for this or you. I could roar.

I could cry. I do not. Anything at all. Just stand feel it worse and worse.

Thinking of the scald and full of shame. Was it yours or mine? Think please just leave the pitch. Please just walk away. It won't be worse than standing there. But you're still trying. Fumbling red for words. He's doing you even as you speak now, to your face. My throat. Is blank. Is sewn up. You shouting what's so funny? I nearly died. I still could. It's still in me. It isn't funny and then, for pity, say why are you laughing about me? They are and laughing more. Your anger permits. Gives goals and goals. Your face red thick.

Bulged indignated. The bullish face fat with humiliation. Handicap. Handicap. One from the back gets the ball. Kicks and aims. It strikes your face. Bleared with mud. And knock you over. Laughter. Laughter. Never ever will it stop. Not ever. Not ever again. The bell rings and release for you from that place. I close my eyes and wish this day had never been or you or me. I walk back and will not help. Pretend I didn't even see. Did you see me? Look at them hear them talking just a bit embarrassed about it. About what they done. And I will not think of your feelings anymore. For it's a bit too much to know.

I ride the bus. It's condensation. Smother. You sitting just behind. And quiet. You don't say a word. I'm turned from it. That did not happen to you or me today. I think. I will not think of you. I think. Uncle. What would you think of me sit thinking of you? My head at work and turned away from everything happening here. Their cigarette smoke roaming up from the back for you. For a way to spit in your eye I think splitly. It gives me. No.

Turn from that and turn away. The eye go in. What? How

much secret pleasure to stare at uncle in my mind's eye. Think of him come across the room. I have him. Scrutinize. I am smiling. It is from. What are you laughing at? as we climb off the slime bus. At nothing why what's wrong with you? I let you walk ahead. I don't know. Let you just. What's in me? There's something twist. Must move or shake him. Uncle. Think. I must give him some surprise.

And in the kitchen I see him there. You go drag foot. His eyes go with. I go ignore him. Stuffed throat as I walked past and could not think of how to shock. Hi aunt mammy. Their hellos to me. I going. Keep going. Not my single word for him. Not for him a lift of my eyes. I keep them locked. I'm going to my like a light went off I am going up the stairs.

Later it ran up me. Legs stomach knees chest up head. Like smoke in my lungs to be coughed out. I'd throw up excitement. What is it? Like a nosebleed. Like a freezing pain. I felt me not me. Turning to the sun. Feel the roast of it. Like sunburn. Like a hot sunstroke. Like globs dropping in. Through my hair. Spat skin with it. Blank my eyes the dazzle. Huge shatter. Me who is just new. Fallen out of the sky. What. Is lust it? That's it. The first splinter. I. Give in scared. If I would. Stop. Him. Oh God. Is a mortal mortal sin.

Our father who art in heaven hallowed be thy name thy kingdom come thy will be done on earth as it is in heaven give us this day our daily bread and forgive us our trespasses as we forgive those who trespass against us and lead us not into temptation but deliver us from evil amen.

I sit bowlegged Encyclopedia Britannica on my knee. Sex Sexism. Sexuality. All the words. I know it's something. I've looked in there before. Since I was ten and since I knew what men and women sometimes do but I am something else. I am. Going to the bad. To the somewhere new.

Prayer time. She called and I went down and we're all sitting there. He is sitting on the chair. You face still bit red your head hang down. Your head. I don't want that. I see him. Smile at me. A reading from the gospel of St. Luke. My own face. I flower a tinct of what I've read alone upstairs. It course me. Whipping blood. And Peter remembered the word of the Lord, how he had said unto him, Before the cock crow, thou shalt deny me thrice. And Peter went out and wept bitterly. Amen. Now there's a lesson for all of us isn't there? The aunt's a little hoarse. Now a decade of the rosary. Shall I give it out? Do. I feel the more my inside lie. If I could just be pure. What would I do? His shoe. His shoe is there beside me. Don't. I want to look. I struggle want him watching. I will ignore I will ignore. Him. If thou oh lord will open my lips my tongue shall announce thy praise.

'Incline to my aid oh God. May the Lord make haste to help us.

Two stairs. Three at a time if I can. Leave it. Sitting room. Watching there the telly all of them. I'll on my own. Be quiet insides. Don't be fucked up. I will wait. This out. He'll be gone. Quite soon. I'll be pure to then. I will. It'll be. It'll be. Fine.

Are you hiding from me? You haven't said a word in days. We're going in two. Are you still upset about your aunt? No. Not about that. What's wrong? Nothing. I start to cry.

Don't. There now. Don't. There now. It's been a bad old year for you all I know. A lot's gone on. It'll improve though. You know you can think of me in a father way. I'm only at the end of a phone and we'd love you to come and stay. See your cousins. They're just about your age. Where you going? Come back. Hey! Come back here please.

Oh sacred heart of Jesus I place all my trust in thee.

On the last night before the last day I'm over the hill. I see pastures open up for running free from him. They'll be gone in one more day. I'll dig it out. Intemperate. Something this. What? Intemperate something wrong. To look at your family and think of something. What? Something else than just hellos. That's dirty. Something night.

Sit down here. They're gone to the shops and someone's mother who gets messages in photographs. The Virgin Mary hiding round the back at Knock or Maria Gorretti saying cheese visiting Lourdes he laughs. Blasphemy but I'm not one for the fires of hell are you? I don't know I wouldn't want to find out. Hedging your bets then, a very wise choice. Blood swirl and swirl. My thud cheeks up. You're not talking he says. Not saying much. What did I do? Nothing. Did I offend you? No. Quick with your nos aren't you just a bit quick? I think you're too shy of me for comfort's sake. Sorry I. He says I see you. What? I see you very clear. I see you. I do. So come here. And I can't help wondering if you see me? You see, I think you do.

I'm invaded in my ears by pulse is going round and round. Pumping in my fingers. His touch my face with flat of hand. You are. Oh you're a strange one. A quick one too for all your age so don't think I think I'm not a fool for this. Little madam youth and vigor. Little madam knowitall but I see you. For. What. You. Are. And do you know there's no one home?

I am sweating here. Ready to give and not. Not at all ready for what I think I'll get. But I give it. I'll give it. Take this cup. I'll drink I'll not. Thy will be done. Let him kiss me. If he wants. I. Drink it. But when he reaches I turn away under his thumb. I want to kiss you. He. Turns my face to him. Dissolving fright under his hands. He put his mouth on mine. This is kiss to me. Then. Wave of. What. Lost. And he says. That was nice but don't you want to kiss me back? I. I'd like you to open your mouth a bit. I. Do. He kisses me. The deep again. With lips and teeth and with his tongue. Touch me soft there I did not know would be. Fill my mouth with it. He says. Open your eyes. Is this the first kiss you've had at all? Flexed and on a wire I'm. He knows something I don't. About me.

That I am naïve. Do that. Don't do that to me. I. Feel I might begin to cry or sink or fall. I want. I want. I cannot say. I'm almost. Ready or not. Got to leave. Don't be angry with me he says. I'm very very honored. He touch my face. Kiss me again. And I touch his cheek. I touch his chin. I know now. What it feels. That mouth. His stubble. Grating.

Think of cheese and not my skin blooming rashes. But it does red and pink alive and specially for me. The burn of it. That smell. That deep in his neck like warm and rich and far away. Like memory I might have had. Will make from this. Have made. And sound of kisses I did not know. Lapping. Thinking me of being at the shore and breaths like breeze going over my head. He tasted. I don't know of coffee. Right. He tasted like dinner. Like something deep.

But I am waiting for. Something with his mouth on mine. Something touching down below. There's not. He not. I am what I should do? My hand. On his trousers. I feel.

What. Stroke. He breathed out. No! Not for me he says.

I stop that. I am not. I go red. I'm not that man. And I'm ashamed to have. What he did not want. But his hand on my chest no my breast. He says that's enough. For me? I am scalded. For me he says and too much. I am. I. Stand up peel the skirt from off my legs. The back of is stuck there. I'm clammy sweat. And legs are wrong. Excused and dismissed. What I say is You fuck off.

This night is a restless night. Turning in my head the. Wish I could tell you until the morning came.

Come running by the lake. Fall down. I am almost too old for that I should be smoking drinking now. Taking hands up my jumper. Fingers down my skirt. I should be. I should be. I am not. Yet. I stand there. Eyes mist to the wind feel the fresh rush past. Up my nose. That sting. That new day it's so early in the morning. I see the white and clear.

Rising up of the waters. Running round my feet. My gravel feet. My earthbound feet that feel the sway of it. Water. Of the world that's changing now no changed. It's changed and this is looking back. The past a flash front. That mix. Knowing what how I should do be say. That's going up. That flock of geese is rising. Rising to make all the noises. Honk like cars and wings beat hard on the air. Battering it. Cutting it down. They're going up and up. Feathers and fat young breasts rise and rise above me. I see. I see clear. And the trees there, glassing the water making it jump in go under. Temptation for the tips of my fingers. For the soles of my feet. I step there. Cool and cold and colder. Outside the leather. Coming in over my white socks. Feel it rising. Catch my ankles. Send me tremors. Send me shivers. I know what I'm doing. Mud suckering round my toes. If I stand. Still. The reeds glass bend a little. Shiver winter. There's a soft cold breeze. I search the quiet out for footsteps. For the armies. Coming. To slither under water here with me. Those spirits smell and see them I do in my sleep. In dreams of all the things that in my life will come to me. Take hold. I fear not. Hear not. See not. Feel the rap on my knuckles of the water going in. It soak my coat up. Up my leg up. Feel it there inside my thigh. So cold. So ice and glass and see though things and friendly hands. Between my secret tight shut legs the water. Lurking brownly seep inside me. Drag me down. I do not. I know not. I know not what I do. It is not that. It is not drowning I have come for.

Not for death or any other violent thing that I could do to myself. I am here this hour for. Storage I think. Cleaning and cold storage. I will gush myself out between my legs.

Whoever let the poison in. The dirt retreat. The thing I want I should not get. I'll put my head in for discreet baptize. It makes me want to, feel like laugh. Out loud and crack that silence. Hear the curlews and the gab of swans not far from me. A wee way off. The sun is coming. Much more warm now than I wanted or had thought would be. This crevice lake could be my ocean if I was. That duck. That bit of scum. That bit of tree there floating. I sink baptize me now oh lord and take this bloody itch away for what am I the wrong and wrong of it always always far from thee. Ha. My nose fill with that bog water. It's run a long brown hill to get into me. Its salt its bits and dirty pieces in my eyes and in my lungs. Ah. You are not here. In this world deep and brown. Filled with rattle gushing noises. Sounds. Unearthly water bubbles rise the top. You are not here. I am free from love and that cold pain shooting through my forehead. That's a good thing. It's a fine and right thing. True to what it is. Gurgle. Swell into my bronchioles. Fill that space. Push each air drop out. I let my feet float up there off the ground. I know I am a puffed white shirt floating on the water. Face into a different world. Where are you? You are not here. I am free. To not hear spastic fucking spastic. Feel the slither of one glob of snot or spit at your head. Or don't touch me. Cool the ocean running through me I wish waves were over my head. I'm floating downside up and wrong side down. Hmm help me I am drowning. Look up. Look up. The day's begun. The cold and grasp. Retract now my wish for wading going in. My hair a cling now on. Sticking to my face and that rust smell of lake. Put my feet back on the bottom. Slipping in. The silt and grub of it. I think are here pike Jesus they bite I know bring some children down. I've heard into the murky depths. My insides feeling squeal now. Yuck this filth. Yuck I have done. The circles snapping circles of the I wade water out to the bank. My heavy clothes and slipping grapple blackthorn bush to pull me out. The silence. Keep the moment. Panic slipping I get out.

I'll catch my. Death of. You know. What's it. Here can't be a leech. Not in this country. Too cold here I'm sure. The other side now. Cows are lowing. Lonely ancient bovine cries. Their teats are turning over wanting out relief of hot milk. Let it all begin again. My body cold reflected back up to my face as I stand there. Look down. I see my sorry self.

That girl. My wicked. I see new ripe ones. Interesting eyes. Purged off. Cleaned out for sure the stings and bites of. Those things that happen in your head when you are young and cannot fathom never being clean again. The house will still be quiet. If I go there.

Drip the floor. I felt this morning strange beginning. I know. I know I won't tell. Yet. To whom. I go. I see the heron fly. Dart of it over my head. Heading are you out to sea? To the newfound world old now though. To a sudden death or a happy mate or a quiet circle or a quiet nest. I watch it overhead. That heron flying. Toward unknown. I don't think I will be clean now. Think instead I'll have revenge for lots of all kinds of things. The start is. That is love.

The house is dry and creaky. I am sopping on the floor. I hear him. No. Aunt or uncle rolling over in the bed. I'm not at peace here anymore. Now today. Glad. They'll be gone. Still. I hear something. I know that step. Forty-one just like new. He is coming early down the stairs. The smell of water waft about it must be. I think. And he will see me in my clothes wet through. Teeth running motors in my head. My bark and twig hair.

I look at him in the door as he see me. No surprise. What have you done? You look. You're wet the whole way through. I am. What did you? Fell in the lake. I walked there early while it's clear. I see and you. Yes fell in. Don't worry. I'm okay.

I know that look that vicious look of him to me now. And the usual inner throb in me. Knives in heart in lungs come a spoon scoop me out. Scoop me out for what he want. But I go past him still. Feel the busy silent want of me. Know. I know that, see that, know it now. How strange my baptize renders me. His want me. Fuck me if he could and I and I and I and I. I have that. And I do not. Do not need. Have something else I need to do.

There'll others. Some others. Some day more who want me I want to fuck them too. Thanks uncle for sage introduce. I left him dripping in the door. Ha. He did not get me after all.

Oh but he did. I'm lying. I am not I am. By the cold range in my white drip shirt.

Caught me. Went about me tooth and claw that I wanted. Felt within the time has come. No Christ here on the kitchen floor. Against the back of the kitchen chair. Pull my skirt down by ankles. Shed. And it was so quiet all around that I could hear him open me.

Graze me opening my legs. Take me in. And that dark body unwashed night and thick pajama's smell of week worn. Someone else's house and their daughter taken over. Under his hands. Full of sweat and passages of skin where he has touched his wife now over me. Her shreds of her. And hard he is I think. For what I know. That's a thrill of me. That I am. Feeling running rivers over me. Running falls. I'm splashing falling into it. His cheek on my head. His dark hair. That I am warm in this. Full up. True. Here we are. Here we are. We eventually are here. Go let myself go down in this. He has a mouth of me. His hard hands. Touching and pulling me under the water. Alright now? Yes. He ram that. Oh God. It hurts me take it out. It. My heart thump on top of him and feel it shaking through his back. No. Take me. Take me down under. He is goding goding goding. In his breath. Like a great surprise has taken place. My legs and thighs and ankles. He will have them all of me in this. Done and done to. Doing. I'll do all of this. Dance with the pain of it and I would do later for many bleeding days. Sting and itch. Not from disease. From new stretched and snapped skin. Up inside that will not fit in time. Expand and let him lurch there. I want. And this is what it's like after all. After all I've heard. It hurts me. And kissing choking me. Almost too much of my body taken up. The air squeezed out. The air pushed to the edge. Coming out my eyes. My ears. Too much. Where is the room for. Too much so much. It. Is too much then. I'm taken over buckled onto him. Light and pulled up off the ground his. Fastened stung. Being small then suddenly just for him. I cannot cannot take this. Pain. Scratch him. Pain of it. Keep clawing at his skin. He does not.

Does not know this. He is digging into me and me to him. He's. Push it home as far up. In that tight spot. He is. He is. I will feel it bruising pains. And breathing deafing out my ears. My back against the chair wood. Rubbing to the bone. I. Feel him filled with. Now. He filled with. My pain. He is coming. Off inside me. I think and I think of painting houses. Streets with. Painting the town red. I must be almost I am dying when he does it. With the pain. Suffocating. And his cheek. My nail my nail. That's it. I've done to him. What's done in me. Jesus Christ he says. His lungs a breeze. His catch up. Breath up. Fresh. Like it's new to him. Still jostle in me. See my knees up at his waist. A sight. Alright? Come back to earth with lungs inflated. Come home now. He reach between us and pulls it down out of me now. Come down I think. Feel no more pain. I am dripping water, him, out on my thigh. And clicks my brain. As though the house moved. Who turned the sounds back on? I feel that daylight in the window. It's caught me. Rack. It's blanching me out. Bathe it. My hand unseals his cut. My face my Jesus. Fucking face. What have you done? Jesus. He put me down. Are my feet? I see it. My nails duggened in. Peel the skin off. He's bleeding near the bone. Quick. Put his thing back in. Men's trousers. Strange how it works when I was little always wanting to pee standing. Oh. I must be. I think I'm filled with blood. I'm wet and wet the whole way through. I'm sogging. I'm. Viscous lake. I. Sway. My eyes back. Jesus Christ he says you better sit down. Are you alright? I am. I am pure white. He says I'm I'm. Do you feel sick? No I say I'm. Watching his neck beat. Blood around blood around. He says just breathe in deeply. You're going to be fine. It's just a shock when. He can't say. The first time. His face is unusual now. Listening for the stairs. Eyes all around. Just be calm. Just be calm. Pat me on the back. You're fine. You'll be fine. At this time I should not smell of drying weeds of scurf of lake I think but do. Not to him. Maybe. Then anyway. His deep night unwashed creases smell. Why don't you go and have a wash he says. I'll put the kettle on. Make some tea would you like that? Yes. Sorry about your cheek. It was a sorry. It's fine. He push me. Fine fine fine. I laugh he's worried now. And am laughing all the way up the stairs.

Quiet bathroom. Everyone rolls in bed. No one wakes. It's a weekend. Only we are up. And now's for peering prodding. My fingerful of goop what is it I know sperm. It looks like it I know I know. Like snot or phlegm. Hock on the street. Sniffs strange.

That's good and exciting. And there's a little blood there. And it hurts like mad. It's a lot. Blood. Clot-ish. It's an awful lot of sore. He rip me. No. Just feels it stings to touch. I heard it could. Had read but thought I climbed trees a lot so. That's broke. It is surely broke. It did like something wicked. Burn. Sperm sperm sperm. It's inside me. I hunker down. I washed it out. And pubic hair that's longer blacker thick than mine. I'll wash me. And my hair and everything to be clean. But butcher's block. I felt between my legs would look like that.

When I went down there were cornflakes toast and jam for me and tea and anything I would want. He doesn't look. I'm shy I'm shy. He kiss me said I'm away today and you make me insane. I've never done that before. God what's that hey that what we done? I don't like to hear him speaking wrong. We did. What we did. Him anxious. Not at all like. But I am happy. Satisfied that I've done wrong and now and now. What now? Calm sliding down into my boat and pushing out to sin. He's on the shoreline getting small. His hands on my shoulder. Brushing past my head. Are you alright? I didn't hurt you? I'm humming my toes beating time on the lino. That's alright that he is off. I'm off into the world of something and have something knotting in my head. Not school. Not thoughts of you. You yes. First to come to mind but. It's not that place. There's not room in this part of me anymore. Relief. I think. What's next and next? It's surely coming now.

Good God what happened your face it's a right old state. Is it? What is it? Was it a cat or what? Wife aunt said. I went for a walk a branch swung back and got me whack in the cheek. Really dug in. Really stings. It cooks in me. Hot and boil my face. She does not.

No one knows what he and me have secret. The dirty's done and when he walks past me I'm sure it's burnt across my skin. I look at him think you've fucked me. What if they all knew what. We. He and me. That's something very new.

Then later in the day. They just went. Got into their car and drove away with some, well hopefully we'll see ye soons and give us a call when you get home just to let us know you landed safe. I was. At his peck. Fairly passive. Say it. Bye. Following a voice in my head. My tongue. Cleave to my mouth. Think of his. His bending brush kiss on the bone of my cheek. Bye then sweetheart. Filled with shame. Take care of yourself.

Whisper. Then. And Good-bye to you.

. . .

We are days. Watching telly drifting by. Coiled in front. Bored and always is. The evenings after school. But it comes over still. Whizz and whiz. What was that I did? I think of it in bed at night as. On my own I. Think will it always hurt? Will I always bleed? When things are fit that tight how can there not be bruises? I did think about it too at school. To fill my head with something new that's not this. Blackboard chalk and slime in the loos and the always stench of boys' feet and impulse off the girls.

He didn't write or ever phone as aunt did often. Again again and how are you? Did you get that check? Your uncle tells say hello. That's quite an impression young lady you made. She like me now. Strangely. I don't know. I wanted to ask you. Someone. I knew you wouldn't know. What this all this is.

We were moving off now. From each other. As cannot be. Helped. I didn't help it from that time on. You know. All that. When you said sit with me on the school bus. I said no. That inside world had caught alight and what I wanted. To be left alone. To look at it. To swing the torch into every corner of what he'd we'd done. Know it and wonder what does it mean. I learned to turn it off, the world that was not my own. Stop up ears and everything. Who are you? You and me were never this. This boy and girl that do not speak. But somehow I've left you behind and you're just looking on.

4

Fifteen sixteen. Eat coleslaw sandwiches with ham on top. My legs tucked up underneath my skirt. Tights stretched tight that I hate for they rub. Coffee. Me and my friend on the mitch. This is neat and clean where I can be. My growing-up. She smells like biscuits.

Crisps. Old fags in her oil and her hair. I think her knickers must stink down there. It wafts up sometimes when she crosses her legs. Or is it tights too. Skirt rolled-up polyester. But I like anyway.

She and me. Like to lurk here in the day. Those gossips we have are the very best and we read and read. Quote quotes back forth. That's good for sharing books of this and that. Word perfect. We snick snack at each other. Correct each other's grammar. Chew gum and talk and think of sex. I do not say but hint a little. That's a powerful thing I know.

And we go on travels. Great worlds to our minds, like interrail from here to there. Slum it downtown Bucharest eat cheese in Paris fall in love. Take boats in Venice to Constantinople by the train. Where speak good Russian Portuguese. Know people. Flit around the world to New York parties. Kandahar. We don't know the world but want and want and want and on the very tip of tongue I'd fly away if I could. With her. It is our love affair. How we'd be. Who we think we are beneath royal-blue jerseys and pleated skirts. Icon in the making me someone new tell every single one at school to go to fucking hell. And sometimes we sit by the lake. An early morning or some after school—in the daytime monitors drive there to catch whoever's on the hop. Read Milton and feeling moved discuss the heavens and the earth and film stars we'd do with a chance. It's love. It. Is.

Love. Or love waiting for a man to come and take her place. But how would someone fit, I don't know, in between us two.

She is sufficiently hated by all at home to make the escapade worthwhile—having a friendship outside that womb. Making it an empty shell. Escape of me. We don't say lots of secret stuff but good for a laugh and that's enough. Who is better? She or me? Quick quickest. Fastest putting down. I belt her to the canvas every time. Still. She has something I've not got. That's. Everyone else on her side. This is being liked at school. She sway there here and there to this one that. Can I borrow your copy? Can I have a crisp? Always smells like cheese and onion for it at the break. Too looking in her books I find how square roots done I never bother learning that. My brain isn't. I'm up for Art and nothing else. Strict in it I'm on the outside of these schoolmate mates, being drawn in somehow by herself. Working so hard at working the room. Having people say hello.

What's that? What's that? I learn.

For a change now I wear my skirts high. Rolled up to the arse when I get off the bus. A new thing. Where's it from?

Seed. Is this. Is in my head. We are going toward a new and I'll tell when I get there. It's not straightforward yet. But when it comes she'll know.

You are behind. You are way behind in this. I see you lagging. I can see you limping off at the back but I'm getting very tired of looking around and in a bit I'll leave you to the fates. She knows you but she doesn't care and we are speaking less and less because. In all that you make me want to get away. It's too much and you're much too. Young. For me now. Is the simple truth. Where I'm going you cannot come.

That I am turned fifteen is true. You three years more than me. At eighteen Leaving Cert. Is due. You're almost there. I do not toil nor do I spin but you do. That upstairs every night. The light on scribbling, dream away you must so your results always say. But you're polite and getting by. They wish the best said teachers all to our mother who can bang her head on every wall. What will you do? Where will you go? She says almost every night. I think you'd like to stay at home. Bring coal in. Clean the fire. Stoke the range. Find something living here. She cannot see you doing out in the world. I see. I agree.

I see you still at school. The sometimes butt but always desperate eager to be one of those ones. Of the boys who lurk smoking. Who wish they knew the insides of the girls and say so often. Say out loud hey Miss I think I'm so good, come here and give me. Oh fuck off. You're not like those boys. Don't go looking up to them. You do. Too obviously for me. They don't want you. Can't begin to know what you're like inside this you who's still good at falling over. Walking into visible things. And I do not either. Consumed with all my dreams and shames.

What's wrong with your brother? He's a bit. You know.

You know. What? Well he's a bit you know. Know? Ahem, a little bit strange? He looks a bit. Is he a bit slow? No.

That's a really stupid thing to say. Jesus who are you, saying things like that to me? You're a fucking bitch sometimes you know that. I'm sorry. I didn't mean. I heard someone say is all. Heard who you better tell me now. Heard who say what about him now? I mean it, fucking say.

She did tell me after that. Once I'd made her feel ashamed. A rumor going round the school that your brother should be in some mental school for retards they said that in class he doesn't know to properly read when called out loud and never answered questions right. That when he failed a geography test he told the teacher she was ruining his life. Doing him down before the class. He shouted and pushed her and they had to pull him off. That he's a psycho. Blaming everyone for being thick. Oh is that what they say? Someone said your family is all fucked up. Blow-ins weirdo's born-agains or something bad as that. And about me? Go on. You might as well I'd rather know. I was proud of being brave. I thought that's what I had to be and asking it was showing how.

You she said well they think you're weird and really up yourself. You're always wearing that long coat and never talk to all the lads. That you'd be something if you tried. I know not I do not understand but think and think on after this of ways back in and to revenge. Not take any notice they can see but bend myself in secret til. What? Til I can lift this.

Fury. Out. And get them. Really well and get her for. For. All kinds of things. For the good word in my ear and thanks for that she was too kind and liked the telling just too well.

On a spring day's when I hop the world in this new way I'd never done. We take off early she and me to down the lake on the chance school gaelic match keeps all monitors at their bay. It's usual too and she and me are not the ra-ra going kind. We snicker over them at that and buy some biscuits on the way. Sophisticated we think kind with blueberries were rare. Blueberries are the great unknown and must be something in New York like muffins lattes and ice-tea. We see the television. We know here is not like there. And I am reading Scott Fitzgerald know that I must drop the F. Think American twenties just divine and I'd be Zelda if I could. Think suffering's worth it. To be mad a fine exciting thing to be for those short times in those mad years. Wearing pearls and drink champagne and bob my hair and show my knees. Be daring darling simply wild. I'd be if I had a chance I'd be.

She. Feeling more pre-Raphaelite has dyed her hair an orange red and keeps Rossetti in her bag for reference always to be inspired by love and nature and dying young. Her choice is poor compared to me I think but nod and smile along at every quote. Think her a little behind and all that cheap to be admired.

So blueberry biscuits and bottle of coke we go sloping in the backstreets down to the lake where the sun shines waters lap and all the birds sing. And we sit in the grasses down beside the water's edge. I will not put my feet in though I'd like to if I could. But it's not cool and I'm too old now for that I'd say. We talk. All that usual that we do. Lie take the sunshine on our eyelids consider why this makes see red. Think beat of blood.

Guts and things. An almost hazy day but for nip on the breeze a bit. Shredding grasses with our thumbnails. Throwing grass seed on the lake we look for fishes come gobble up. They do not. They are staying low. This lake's as bottomless as the pit she says. Goes down into the middle of the earth.

Everyone knows that that's why so many people drown here and their bodies never pop back up. I think I'm listening to this but off in the distance over the brambles are sounds of boots. I prick my ears. The lads approach. The boys I know them by the sounds of hoarse laughing and shoving push. Ssss she says it's the lads they must have mitched the match as well. Prick up. Sit up looking around.

They see us shout girleens, girleens! Decide they're coming down to sit by us in our hidey-hole. There wind'll catch their fag smoke and take trace off into the sky with it.

Oh you two. I thought it was someone else. Oh right. But now we're here lads shall we stay put? We laugh at that, she and me. And kind of rippley felt within for no good reason but this was something new. Some attention's what we like. Noticed and worthy of these cool boys staying down with us.

Hey what's that book you're reading there? God how can you read books at all? Look at that three hundred pages an awful lot to read. Ye two are always really strange. What? You know using all long words. Sure you don't know either of us I say. When did we last speak to any of ye she snippedys and not at all pleased to be made up posh or strange or anything far from their fine herd. Anything too like me. Well you know you don't go out at all. Ye're never down here with everyone else are ye? Oh drinking on Saturday night? When the guards come and chase you all away? I can't resist. Hiding in the ditch sounds great craic. Ha ha you're so funny says one turn his face from me with. Mumble mumble. At least we're out having it instead of sitting home reading books thinking you're so great. And how do you know I think that? But they're not interested, saying to each other, have you them maths done and did you hear yer man got his hand broke in the vice down the woodwork room last night?

Fuck. They cracked his knuckles. At least he won't have to do the tests next week. Ha ha well for some. I'm going to be bollixed in Irish.

I'm needled now wishing they would go away. It's enough and I'd like the quiet back. I turn. I start to read. I leave her for she loves to flirt it seems. Shallow stupid bitch. I'll save for later suck-up jibes. Didn't know you always had to be everyone's friend. I suppose if being popular's important . . . leave the rest unsaid. Annoy her. It's her own thick fault.

In a while of mouthing I get up and walk off. She calling what's up with you? I'm just going for a walk. Well don't get caught or let us know. Cough loud if you see. Yes yes. I stroll. Feel the grass slit through my hands when I tug trail it. Sharp as ice inside the deeper finger and thumb crease. I am warming up the fire to think of him. Of my legs round him. Gloss and embellish. Gasped my name. Broke my heart. My longing longing. Not for him but I think so. I let it be. If only they knew it'd be revenge for everything.

Pick a primrose. I like the touch it has the soft and smell and crush gently gives the best and lasting perfume on my fingers. Squeeze pollen falling on the ground and wipe that off on my skirt. The muck earth slithering under my feet. How would they ever understand my life is more than cider? Complex than that. Fuller deeper richer. Irritation that. Something. Not as good as me in the back of my head. In my silent they're not so clever not so quick and rule the world anyway as if it's fair. Think I'm too good. I am but would not say it to their face. Lucky for them. I'd annihilate. Champing at the. I would. Such. I would. Hey aren't you the sister of yer man in our year?

Behind me in the thicket. Standing up against the light. I cannot see him very straight. The fella with the head thing. What? Yeah you are his sister I know you alright. Bristle bristle hair on my spine and on the back of my neck. You go on the bus with him or sometimes don't you? My brother's got a little scar on his forehead if that's what you mean. Except it's not that little, and all that bullshit story about the knife he says. It's not. What? Bullshit as if you'd know anything just because you're in his year. I wasn't having a go. Yeah right. Yes. I see. Well. Don't be so uptight. Oh fuck off I know what you lads are like in that year. And what are we like? You know. What? I know what you did to him so don't bullshit me with you're all interested and nice. All I said was you're his sister nothing more and nothing less. Oooh defensive too. I amn't. Yes you are and you lot should be ashamed. Why? I didn't do anything to your brother if that's what you're saying. Oh didn't you? I didn't. I turn. I sit down. Let the morning drizzle in its shush I think now. I don't want to talk to lads like him. The purpose is? I close my eyes and let him do the work if he wants. He can't I wouldn't. I would not. I'd almost sleep here but it's much too cold. I'm sick with churning round the things ever said of you. And listen for him beat retreat he doesn't. He must stand and look. Hmmm this one with his big ears. To win I sudden streak. I'll be dumbfounding. And out of my throat comes a voice I don't know that says in words my thoughts out loud. The lads in your year are fucking scum and bastards and thicko pig-ignorant culchies. What? They stink of hair gel on too thick and biactol that doesn't even work. Your friends. The nice boys of your year.

Pimply faces white as never seen the light and crusty lips and dirty hands. Think they're all so cool and can piss on me and my brother but really they're just desperate for someone anyone to give them a wank. Just leave me alone.

But he didn't answer. That voice already burning in what they don't know for all their talk. What am I? God. Is that right. How would that be? But there's some bit feels savage. That doesn't know the wrong from right and sees the way to venge. I might. I am. I will.

I open my eyes. Do you know how to fuck? What? His red face. So it's like this is what it's like. What? Easiest do I ever did. He run scarlet. What? Spit settle on his lip I say let's go for a walk. No risk for what will he answer ahhh and never no for sure.

She's turned and looking though she didn't hear but she knows something's. Not like me to walk away with some lad and I know I'll tell later to wipe the smile off her face when she says soooo what were you at? Go on give her one shouts one of the lads. Little does he know.

I tell her I took him farther to the trees and pulled my skirt up. Opened my knees said come on. He was almost died of fright. Tried to kiss me, press against me. Saying something sweet and nice. Like you're sssssh. Take your trousers down. I'll only touch his tremble cock. Red and small and scared of me but looking forward all the same. Go on then I say you're a big hard man. You know don't you know everything. I don't he says. Oh don't you? He tries. He cannot get it in says I. I twist myself around. He did for a little while and it feels like nothing inside me. He gulp say sorry sorry at the end. And I say I didn't think you'd be a virgin. Jesus. Well someone had to do it for you. Booky booky me and pulled my skirt down pick bark off. Walked away feeling calmer now that that. I told her that later when she was. Startled still. I suppose it didn't leave much room to say things about it. What for? Why not? Weren't you scared he'd say no? No.

I pull my skirt neatly under when I sit back with them.

Don't want grass getting up my bum. Jingle jangle. I can be lots of fun see when I start to talk. I never knew you were such a laugh they say. He came too sat beside. Put his arm around my waist. I push that off. What are you doing? Am I your wife? They roaring laughing ask and what were ye up to in the hedge? Nothing much I say.

He was the first off. Worst off. I begin. Now I know full well what I can do. For me and for you.

Now I had two or three behind the prefabs. Consecutive days mind. Them boys. Muck to the great knee high. Slip my boots in it. Their knees ache with bending for they don't know what. I won't say I don't either. Building building numbers up. When the rain comes I will not postpone. It's now or never. But there's a lookout for the vice deputy head who looks for smokers in the break. Not this. This no one's ever seen though it runs round the school like wind.

One in the Ha bike shed. Handlebars dig in my back. He's all embarrassed I should know the fat spots on his thighs. I have no eyes for that. No ears for any sound emit. I'm thinking counting ticking off. The great work. It's my great work.

At the lake then two more on the late Saturday nights where they would pass me hand to hand if I would go. I would not. Maybe next week maybe next time. And swig of vodka pressing up my lips. That burn me down. I cannot see their faces or hips that bounce ready for me. I lie. I take my share of them the whole way and there are other girls here. Each one for herself. We don't look her in the eye. The lads are here for what we are. It makes me laugh. That guzzle and the useless whinging come of them. Some little squeak rat caught in a trap.

And in a car the best. Warm and parked away. They'll do what they can to me in here.

On my knees I learn plenty—there's a lot I'll do and they are all shame when they think their flesh desired. Offer up to me and disconcerted by my lack of saying no. Saying yes is the best of powers. It's no big thing the things they do.

When I go home my brazen flesh lets off the sound of doing something I should not. Our mother careful look and questions, cannot understand the alteration. And she'll not let adjustment be without a nuclear fight. No going off to be another girl than I was before. No. There must be confession. Explanation. Close the bedroom door and bathroom. Keep my body secrets in, hers out if I could. I do not, will not be frying down in hell. My mind is blanket clear. It's hot inside and not much breath but no one sees me where I am. It's good not feeling pure.

We sat in the kitchen my friend and me. Drink instant coffee hot now tell me tell me what's it like? Does it hurt? Are you sorry after? Do you feel ashamed and I encourage her to follow. You'll like it on the other side. I'll tell you how to do it right. She me laugh about I imitate their squawk Oh I'm coming coming coming. Makes us laugh hard all the more. But how do you dare and what'll you say if you're caught? This are boring. Better saying why it's great.

I think she slipped away to other huddles back at school. Did not come around here so often. Quietly made a getaway from me and my many sins. Tarred with the same brush all of that. And after I wasn't at all sorry about it. With her orange hair and love at first sight glued to her snout. I don't wish I'd kept my big mouth shut.

. . .

There is no Jesus here these days just Come all you fucking lads. I'll have you every one any day. Breakfast dinner lunch and tea. The human frame. The human frame. The human frame requires. Give them something. A good hock spit for what it's worth. They'll say my name forever shame but do exactly what I say. I'm a laughing skirt up round my knees and feathery boy rosen cheek between. I found the shell I'll rap until it breaks. I found my new blousy blazen face. It makes me. Laugh. The shininess of it. Of say so.

Follow tremble and obey.

The word go round it get round soon and soon I was to overflowing everyone could ask but I. Pick my moments when to strike. Say, come here and do your best.

Those girls' heads turn in the class. Flick flick ponytails. Wag wag at that. Natter natter look at that one. Dirty hoor. For I was somehow up the ladder. Above a bit of tongue or feel of my tit. Could say for sure this is what it feels like. To do. But I wouldn't. Not to them. It's mine alone. To replay on my own. For I am a woman now.

But that one day. A Saturday. Click click. I stood with my forehead on the glass. Thinking I can leave a grease print unappetizing as it is. When did my face get like this? All that bloody fuck and sweat. It's cold. The afternoon. Then on your blue bike you come breakily up the drive. I don't know where you've been. Into town I now suppose. Back door squeal as you opened. Radio upstairs chortle to itself. She's out praying with the nuns. A holy hour offered up for? Us. Exposition of the Blessed Sacrament. That means two-kneed genuflect.

At the doorway where you stand. I say your nails are

really black. Are they so? Yes they are and I go back on thinking of my skin and still you stand. Ignore my ignoring. So, what do you want? You're wolfing back air and words and all sorts. Beet face boiled up ready to go. What? But you can be consternated for all I care. As if I care. As if. Well you'd know about dirty things you say. What? What's that supposed to mean? Your face embarrassed me. That it took so much. And quietly like glue stuck in your mouth. Please tell me if it's true. You know. That you.

What would I do to be dragged into the floor? Go plummet down please. Hell open up and take me in. Do all that? you say. Dirty stuff. Dirty things. That you did the it the thing with one of the lads from my year. That you did it during lunchtime in the bogs with some other. Shut up. Stop it. But you're keep going on with wart toads popping from your tongue. That someone saw you down the lake. Who told you that? Is it true though? Is it? Is it? You are almost start to cry. Fuck off I say, you say that's not the answer. Go on tell me if it's true? And you're walking coming crossing. Grab me by the elbow. Is it true? Is it true? I know you're stronger than me now. First time and push me to the wall. Don't you lie. You don't lie here. Is it true? Bang me off it. Go on slut say that it's so.

What do you want? Is it true? It is! I shouted pushing hands and might against I sticking fingers at your eyes. You choke me. I expel splode fight against. Kicking at. Struggle.

Whack for I'll be screaming in a minute. Push me on the ground. It is disgusting whore sputter filthy disgusting wrong it's wrong to. Do. Fucking bitch. I curl up miss me kick the floor. The stub of it. Rolling.

What's going on in here she shouts. Caught you by a scrag of hair. What in God's name are you doing to your sister? Stop it. Stop it calm down. I mean it. Stop it. Dear God in heaven stop it. She struggle. Struggling with you. Struggle while you pull her struggle off. While you push. Shouting roaring off your head. She saying this no way to behave. You'll never make a priest like this. And pushed over. I see she fell. Jesus. Jesus all I say getting up. Putting hands out for blows. And she and she too. Stop it Jesus calm down. She is saying if you in carry-on this way they'll never take you in. You give her other push. I don't want to be a priest a fucking fucking fucking priest. That's no way to talk my boy as though you're on TV. I want to escape you say I want to get away from the pair of ye. And strike out. We're not struck at all. It's going in you. Beating up against the walls. I want to be in the SAS. And you turn. She. Hit her between the shoulder and the neck so she cries. I. And then you ran. Out the door. Out the hallway. Out the house. Running to. Running like mad.

That's a lash I'm quiet under. All the night you were away and she me sat and holding hands or piece and jam or cup of tea. Is that him knocking at the door? Her neck blacken and red. It was not you at all. Where were you? And when she had gone to bed I locked the door in secret. Let you stay out there.

But the next night you came home. It was a very quiet way. Say not a thing. No one say and that was the end of that.

Wander about the months sucking my teeth that you hurt. Touch and touching-up my eye. Packed in and up that life between my thighs. Keep it now for alone at night, for my thoughts to blister on. Can I meet you round the back at lunch? Just fuck off. You all can.

It's only ever going home. You watch me. Crucified on

the bus to hear them going Ah I wouldn't mind a bit of that or the fine thing's arse or I'd do her raw and red. For now taking it away they have me. I am at their mercy. And you push me down the bus steps.

Push me out the door, saying see now see what you are? Everyone's embarrassed at what you did. Everyone thinks you're disgusting like a maggoty pervy type I'd kill if I went to war. That's the job for you. You're very sure. But did you tell? You'll never say and she says nothing. I don't see so I don't think you did.

The last day is off school and you're finished. All your exams the same. I don't mention but I'm aching for the moment you'll be leaving. The summer's come. Something's good in that for me. It dry up each my wounds of nasty thinking what I did. Now very nice do dishes for Mammy or rake the fire out instead of you. You never note, for that's that now. Dirty beast and go away. Alright. I will. Leave or. I would. If I could.

And you are gone for army trials. Up the country. Long weekend and say yes that's the life for me. It took two months. For your exams. For army invite coming through. That's a loose summer working in the shop for you. I think you might at stacking shelves. It's boring but you never say for August's coming. She says prays for the right thing— please God a vocation—whatever that may be.

Remember O most gracious Virgin Mary that never was it known that anyone who fled to thy protection implored thy help or sought thy intercession was left unaided inspired by this confidence I fly unto thee O virgin of virgins my mother To thee do I come before thee I stand sinful and sorrowful. Oh Mother of the word incarnate despise not my petition but graciously hear and answer me. Amen.

August comes.

And when you come back that last day there's envelopes. Two on the window ledge get damp with condensation she says exciting look at this for you. You tear them. It's the start of the end of this life. Well it seems so. Then. Maths F Irish E English E History E Geography E Chemistry Incomplete. Oh love I'm sorry. It's not that that counts you say. So that one's that but one the next. Oh Jesus. From the Irish Defence Forces. Stamp.

We're sorry to inform you height weight IQ and eyesight are are but we wish you the very best.

You there staring across the table. Weeping mother press her faces into hands. Oh what. Oh what. What will you do? Eighteen years and no exam. You mumbling things like join the navy. They'd soon teach you to be a man. Not soft as shite with all the women in this house. Stop that talk. Conspiracies walling in around. God will I never get a break you said. What's waiting to jump out and be reason for your failure? Ha ha ha.

Not you. Never your fault. The fucking army. No need for that filthy talk. Who needs all that anyway? you say. They'll never be their own man.

Slinking I if I could past. I don't want to talk about this. With her. Near you at any rate. It's your problem. Hers to fix. But your brother. Don't tell me. He would make a lovely priest. Fuck off off that. I'm still your mother. True. And don't talk to me that way. Before there's anything else though I'm out the. I'm out the very. Quick. Quick.

PART III

Land Under the Wave

1

Back to stacking shelves for you with all those ones you hate. Shot to the ground they'd be if you could. Still it's sixty quid every week. Twenty for her. The rest for you for buying sweets. More packets every day that you conceal. Up your coat pocket. In your sleeve—when you're walking through the kitchen. But my job's the bedroom bins.

Color foils off been all stripped. Plastic twirled in tissues but I saw I see it. Ever pack of Murray mints. Scoffed them when us two weren't around. Glut glut gluttony I decide to say if I decide to. Out you. Stick you on a greedy spike. That's if I need to. If I will I don't know. Yet.

So we're doing Lent this year she say we've been too lax now look at us. And all our groan was no effect. Giving sweets up. All things sweet up. Yes and literally good for the soul. Oh my god those magic words. Set me to flight. In my secret world I'll find some way to rebel. Smiling offer up my fudge for Christ and for all the angels and the saints.

Hey presto or Olé! And give up sugar in my tea. And give up milk. I drink it black and eat burnt toast for indulgence of. The dead. I like this very much. Sacrificial virgin self I seem to be.

Much dourer you than me. This is such a waste of time you say. We've swapped places for these mortifying days. Say effing praying what's the good of that? I said my night prayers every night and look at what they did to me. Who? They did. They all.

Didn't want me to succeed. I see. Good. Oh yes? You just have it so easy look at you. What? All the things you did but your life's always so. You're always doing well, you say. I am, am I? Just leave me by myself you stupid dirty sow. Cow.

Morning mass at seven o'clock up the convent every day. Trup trup trup St. Theresa echo wax parquet. Say prayers for your exams she says to me. We'll see what's to come. So here's to holy acceleration but all I see is the wall ahead. And you say alright I will too. Liar faker. I do not look at you your eyes when I can manage not. Think about your daily sweets.

Clap. Trap. We go on slugging chest and head when we can. But I always swerve from you are so fucking dim though that's what I prize now the most. Not for being clever gets you what you want. Just where you are, I won't be.

Mad lust of it you get for computer games go blip across a screen. That's your eighteenth birthday gift improve your mind with. Further education she says. Thinks of analysts in rows in shirts and saved up tokens with the milk. You blip it often. Your room at night.

Going. One another and another one after that. From the morning til you went to work and after tea after rosaries after watching some TV. The new love take up all your time. Eating sweets and Jupiter Landing. Come on and have a go. No. I don't want to. It's killing all your brain cells. So?

. . .

And after one year. All the same washed over. And after two. You are all calmed down to stacking neatly every day. Getting on the ground floor. Cursed and resigned. To something. What? All that stuff you go on about. I am keeping it clean as long as I can and see think you've forgotten all of that. That thing in the past lake shed prefab.

Everyone's quiet. They're moved on to greener fields. Are grazing there on someone else. Just feel a scald of it now and then and think I'd like to get away. But look those boys out in the eye. I know it. Worse things. More than they. Spotty little dribble spittle. But my head goes half wild. Turning over my new leaf. I live to work up other days. I peck out of this school bus shell. Get the wind pouring through my hair. Moving to my own flat. Live on my own potato bake. Far off. Far off. Leaving you and her. Away. Turning tide off.

White out my eyes. Ears nose and throat. That two years sitting in the gap. Exams come and go and soon I'll soon I'll not live here anymore.

I do. I get my As and Bs. I am ready to leap. Go then headfirst. On the train. I stand with my socks up. With my fingers sticking out. Wave away. Go on away. To the two of you that's groggy from crying. She. You're putting one hand on her shoulder. Take care of yourself and give us a call. Bye then. Bye. Pulling off pulling off for the city. Leaving that. Go back. All you behind. Put breath back in my body. Right now. Next now. What I'll be?

2

City all that black in my lungs. In my nose. Like I am smoking am not but still. I'll have a creaky bed up in some woman's house. For too much a week, that I don't guess. Will do. Maybe soon. Unpack my socks and. Oh. That's being lonely. Lying here. Head and feet not knowing where they've come to. The rest and. Both of ye. And shocking. That.

Homesick. I am. Oh God. Between my eyes spat new sparkle pangs. Give a leg up here. Give me a chance. I'll be dwindling over baked beans every single night and see some Murray mints think of you. Oh terrible. Such an unexpected. Slip.

But with all that I begin. On the very first day. Going in the college door hello. Oh I am. Yes. Just over there. Fine thanks. Yes thanks. Fine grand yep I will. There. So so we are just the one of us now. Me. God everyone's at home still doing the same why am I here? Think of her in her rosaries and you at the shelf.

This room smells of chalk smells bad to me. Go on. Jesus. Loads of people. Strangers coming going here. I see in this room rolling blackboards is a new thing. But grills on windows is a what does that mean? I don't. Never seen that before. Ha. A wicked city I have come to. So all kinds of things must go on. I know.

And another one comes in and another one comes in. Is it sixty people here? They talk like all this is the same to them. What things have they done that makes them easy and right? Saying yeah yeah yeah when I was in the States or I was in London this summer. They know the world. They know what levi's proper tops and shoes to wear. Am I I am dowdy or something with too-long hair. They speak out loud and I am wrong wrong wrong.

Some girl with all nice clothes on wearing makeup as it's alright to do. God isn't.

Never—desperate that. I must. Oh. Something new. Sitting down all the blue stuff on her eyes are laughing looking round. Crossing her legs like she should I do not. Giving ankles crossed more than enough. Hi and how are you are you here for this course too? What? Oh yes aha I am yes too. Oh good thought it was the wrong room never understand them accents them Brits have got. Your woman in the office. Yes I understand enough.

This one's talking. An awful lot. She's got me out of all the ones. I don't know. I have my red dress on? Are you living near? Just around the corner. I'm from here she says. Oh right. I just thought it would be a laugh you know. I know. I don't. God look at that she says. That'll be him The Big Cheese. And in he comes in. Fella sparkle-eyed with a plomp load of books. My heart go bang at no go back now no go back. Some new education begins.

Coming coming? What? For a drink you must, course you can go on she says. Na no thanks I don't na no well alright I will. But when we get there I don't know what to do. Not never been to a pub. What'll I. Go on. Go on iniquity time again, it'll go with all that smoke she is blowing up my nose. She's done this lots before. I see settled on the barstool drooping out her chest. What'll you have then hey what to drink? Em thinking I'll have Guinness for want of knowing what else what. Jesus that'll give you guts. Go on well I'll have what you're having I say. I have lager, two please and sit down there. I'll get these with my held pound note out or two.

Bringing over giving a bounce. Big red gums. Her pony-tail flick it back forth in my pint. So then there's some kind of talking going. She and me. I've drunk up that. Stinking still she smoking silk cut red, look at them so small. I do not know smoking ins and outs. But good for giving Marilyn Monroe face. Puss. Droop her eyes down. Look all. That. In my mouth and in my hair. Saying her family and crazy dad's a famous writer I haven't heard but then but then. Grog-geldy when they lived in Sweden fighting over opera seats and drinking schnapps. I fresh bewildered, ripple thrill of it people who. Oh God. Oh God. That's it. And her mother's orange hair and black lace skirt she wears when she talks on the television. So boring she says. Always going on about her family in public because she is Therapist. We're nearly in America with that. Like Hollywood and I am gob impressed. And me? Nothing really. No my family's just the. You know. Like everyone else apart from you. And we'll drink another and brain go down til seeya tomorrow. Alright then. I will.

I take the bus home reeling over me. That's a feeling. Frighten brilliant new. I am just head on the pillow when she phone. The bring bring. It's half past nine. I'll sleep but landlady whack. You. You. Your mother's on the phone. She's been calling half the night don't let me say it again. Sorry.

Hello love and how are you? I've been calling half the

night. Just wanted to know how you got on? And are you settled in and is your room damp is it fine have you managed to find your way and is the church nearby? Yes Mammy. Don't forget to say your prayers. For Jesus loves you here or there. I'm fine Mammy. I am fine and you are are you well? Is that the right words I am using? I feel big and vast and my head's buzzing all round my voice. And every stuff. Hmm everything strange. You sound a little. Are you drunk? she says. I'm. Are you? I'm. Holy God you are. Have you no. Have you no shame? No more than a week gone and already come to this. You listen here young lady. This is not how I reared you to live. I want you to promise. Promise this'll be an end to that. You know drinking's the devil's work. Now stop it. Promise. Say you will. You will. I trusted you. I'm saying Mammy I will. Never thought you'd carry on like this. Oh crying. Mammy Mammy Mammy. Don't be crying. I only had a few. I won't then. I won't then again. Promise me. I do. I do promise I won't. I'm sorry Mammy. Now don't. Cry plunging sickness waves of home. Go on my drunk brain encircled feeling my own badness sticking in. Oh how I'll be sorry again. So breathe now. Ha. Ah. I do. I'm done and down. I won't. I promise. Drink again. Good well that's all I want to know. Your brother sends his love to you. Right. Love. Take care of yourself. Good night. Good-night. Strings of words. Strings of words. I go upstairs. I go up to sleep.

I keep my promise until the next day and the next day after is gone. I smell this is some world I'm in with loosed-down hair. It is my mother cannot see. Cannot see into. I am glass no more. My body gone opaque so one hundred miles far. Won't know won't hurt her. Not ever can you say. Not ever you can tell tale tattler on me.

· · ·

We are bad her. She and me. My friend I'd call. Run wound to each. Going. Going. Thither thither. Places. Going all aware. Going to no good. Perhaps. Fling. Think never ever thinking I'll look back. Nor do I don't I. I don't know what or I don't know yet.

See here this party. It's a mad. I had never been. I have only seen and thought films were like that. Music hurting on the innards. Door. Lungs. People pouring noise out front back of this old house. Some glasses beakers. I have cans. In my bag. Where do I? Out them there no don't put down or they'll go you'll be sorry. Money spent. I trup trup off behind her. Think I'm new and white. In the garden. In the wet. For grass still sucks it up all day. Where's this? Just some fella I know she says. He said come and bring a friend. Him and other lads have this band. Oh. Brilliant. Good too. They squat here. Christ. What do I know? What do I know? People living mad life but I'm around it now. I can be in.

I'm. What I'd say to those girls in school if. No. I won't. Won't be going back in there. I'm going just to say hello she says you stay here. And I sit under this tree while. What type's it? Apple. Mortified at being alone. Drink up. Watch. She seeing them. Says I'm black now am I? Well then give us a kiss. She slather their hands on. Blankets wet full mouth smirking aren't you pleased to see me? She knows all the right stuff. Right things done said brings the. Going house in. What is perfect on this lawn, there is no shame.

She. Looking over her shoulder. Roll her eyes. You know what it means. I'm going. Off. Nod. Laughing me and she'll tell later on whatever he has done.

I am fine sit and drink and watch. All this harlotting go full on. Twist to look like I'm in here not just sitting by myself. Lay in the grass. Foots trodding dance around. See up skirts. In trousers. Music pumping ground under my head. I think some poems I'll write. About. Sights. Remember. This wood smell of. Damp and. Dandelions stain on my bare leg. Sip up my. Sip and slurp it drink. Think of being by myself. Here. In this stranger's downstairs flat. That. Whirl. Some fella coming up. Do you mind if I sit he and who are you then? Who are you? Do I know you no I do not. I turn my head is very slow and.

Some strange man he is to me. Some man with black hair combed strange like balding but not. It seems. Will I talk at all I will. He chatting my name and all those things. I falling into that. Suppose I am here on my own. Will you another? Thanks for that. Will hear him tell me he's how old a lot oh God lotter than me. I am addling but good to be seen. It's very good to be seen.

Hello there and one of these. You want some? Smoke. Never do. But will. It's something else. No I don't know how. But. Go on lassy you inhale and hold. That'll do. That Jesus rips the tender throat out. Jesus give the eyes a very stream. He is laughing with at me but about my whirring head. I don't like. Do. He lie beside. Stick his fingers in my hair. Aren't you a lovely lovely thing. And talking to he's talking still. I curling poems cannot listen. Smoke in again and in again. Feels hours and hours him and me. Our heads on a root. Benutted tree I see London. I see France. I can see your underpants. I hear him singing put his hand between my knees. Go way think I'm laughing. Spin the brain away from here. Ha you're tickling. Don't do please. Come on says he come on time to go to bed. Time for us to be out of this fet air. Where we going? Come on o human child. I singing oky ho-ky do-ky. Ha ha help me down from this wet earth. I'll come. I'll. Now I'll come with you.

In the morning peel up eyes sweat shut. Cracked ceiling somewhere I don't know. Doubt. See. Thinking what's the wherm I? Who? Lying. Man beside. Breeze whistling from a mouth.

Hello. Wake up. Sorry. Who are you? And I think I remember. Someone's lap. I sat on. On a bus. And I see. And in that chair was. God. I know. What's the worst thing that I done? He poke it in. Oh yes. Yuck. Going inside. And check myself. Feel I yes I know he's done. Inside. This I should, I do know. Do not do this. It's all that bad and could be worse. A lot lot later on. Worry then. Who's he but? That man there beside me. Wait he rolls and I can see. Sweaty eye paps fill sinus guck. And he is balding in the light. Time to go my separate ways. Good-bye tra la la la. Get in the day. Into the street. Quick. Thanks yeah bye don't call.

The sharp light. Picking at my eyes. Needle shafts of. What have I begun or ended? What I've done. Sex as. Go to mass. Confession. And I thought I would not this again, is it the same as? Now I step. Pebble under toe. Think about. Kick. Not again. No. Stop.

What's. See it spin. Look around. What if. I could. I could make. A whole other world a whole civilization in this this city that is not home? The heresy of it. But I can. And I can choose this. Shafts of sun. Life that is this. And I can. Laugh at it because the world goes on. And no one cares. And no one's falling into hell. I can do. Puke the whole lot up.

Wash my body on or off and think I'll be some new a disgrace. Slap in this alley with no doubt rats I am leaving. Epiphany. I am leaving home. I've picked up and left. Fresh. I'm already gone.

3

In the new world I am do this every single time I can. Don't take them to my own digs for my landlady I'm not having that going on in here. Instead become myself in rooms of cold familiar, for to me they are the same. Blankets in the window. Mattress on the floor. Same as last night same as weeks and weeks ago. No just leave the hall light on and take my trousers down.

Crumbs on the carpets and insects bite my back I don't care for. Nicer is not what I am after. Fuck me softly fuck me quick is all the same once done to me. And washing in their rusted baths and flushing brown with limescale loos amid the digs of four a.m. before I put my knickers on. Say stay the night but I am gone. Down back stairs fag glued lip sore on and wait for, get the night bus home.

We're in this. She and me together. Doing all the things we could to make us mad to make a tale. Dancing up upon the tables. Unbuttoning our tops. Throw our knickers in the air. Get out of this pub. Don't have your sort round here. Fuck you. Suck you. Ha ha ha. Chucked pub to another. As though we care for we are we are Boo!

And tell me what you did? Did you do him this way that

I. That's rank. Disgusting. You dirty slut. We drink to that we'll pour it down our gullets and go hunting for men.

Win the day and scrawling all the things I write on cigarette boxes in my head or in my hand. And flicks of it and stubs of pen with just about the ink run out. We're going madly she and me and all this time and I can be. Can do this if I like and if I want and no one's telling tales at home. I love the. Something of it all. Feeling ruined. Fucking. Off. I'm ready. Ready ready. To be this other one. To fill out the corners of this person who doesn't sit in photos on the mantel next to you.

At Christmas. I come home. Down train forlorning what's going on. All the things that I will miss going back to the ground. Stickly conscience. But I won't. For I'm not doing that anymore. But. It's something. Peeling on the off the mask. Which? I don't know. Sorry. Which way round. So she'll see me. You will see me soon enough. But you won't know. I am very sure of that. I know I smell like cigarettes. That's one thing. And a rest?

Hello. Hello. How are you love? And how are you? You alright? Was that. Train journey. Tired now. And how are you? Long time no see. It's good you can. That's all my bags. Thanks for that. Yes I dyed it. I don't know I like it something new. Good to keep me on my toes. You didn't recognize me. Your own girl. I haven't let it get that long. It needs a clip you're right I do. God it's raining. Yes. Go in. Don't stand in it. Did you park oh over there I see it. And what have you been up to since I? What. Not. Does that mean. Sitting at home on your arse sorry on your B.U.M. Ah don't worry I'm only messing. Are you at the shop? The still. The same? Still the. Oh right. Up a floor. I. Yes. That is something. Yes. Just pop it in the boot. Thanks. Right and. Hmmm. And. All the way home.

Those mash potatoes I like. At home with mincemeat and peas. Burned. I like those the most. It catch me in the throat choke good. You're so sullen I say what's up with you? The computer game's stuck in the tape thing and I can't play again until it's out. It's boring God how can you play that? Stuff. Numbs your brain. Can't help it. Just like it. I'll show you later what it does. No. None of that she says. I don't want your sister getting all sucked in. What? I won't. Sure I'll have a little look.

And do and you talking like wild. See this fella he does that. See this fella he kicks him. See now. Hit. That button. Go on. Now. Now. Now. A backflip. Isn't it mad? Isn't it brilliant? I say. It is. And my lips. Addictive in my mouth. Definitely blanging that one down. Bash him hard into the floor. You saying left one right one that's it now and more forward get the hang. I. Hours of it. Hours of fun. Like we were Han and Luke again.

Piddle fingers in the puddles. It's stupid game. It is. It is. Is it not life and death. We roll about the floor. Getting awful kick from this. I'm above I am not. Not tonight. Together. You. I.

She's narking though. I don't notice first. Business of wearing my skirts to the ground and makeup. Then the jits I get from going without a drink. A little sup is what I'd like. I must not. Do not here. Go on a bit of Christmas wine. No. I hear her saying. Not you too now. Off at that. That nonsense. What? Every night. I never see my daughter now she's upstairs. Playing computers thought you had more sense. I thought I had one with the sense they were born with at least. What? How do you mean? All that rubbish up the stairs. I bought to be writing programs or whatever it is. Not for that. For fun. To pass the time. It's a waste of it of God's good fruits. I don't think commodores were hanging on the tree Mammy don't start. Don't you be cheeky. I know you look down on me but I'll not have irreverence from. You especially. You're not too big. To? To what?

To. Leave the room.

And again. Something else now. Salting her. What it is? You and your brother. You're not babies. God knows I have done my bit. What's the problem Mammy? Say what's wrong? Well. You know. I'm sitting down here on my own. I'm on my own here. Every night. I'd think you could spend some time with me. But. Mammy. Oh you're your own woman now. What does that mean? Well you know well Miss. Makes me craven sudden. Double up. What has she heard? Ah no. She'd say. If it was that. Sure. Yes she would.

She would. She'd go spare. She'd not miss me hit the wall. Oh you don't think much of me. What I believe in. But you need not give your distain. What? So blatant. Bad as that. What? Like that. Brother of yours. My mouth pulsate guilty. Why what do you mean? Oh nothing. Nothing. Who am I to?

Growl about it all the weeks I'm here, she does. I can tell. It's to push me off your side. But. Still. I don't know. We are not the same. We are something else now. Shift. Allied in other places than we were. Games and stuff and fun that. I see it first then soon so much. And she is saying more than she was behind your back. There's a flea now, for your ear. My ear. I think about it. Bed at night. I'd justify. I throw. Mercy mercy God on me. There's so much. Dredge up so much muck. I'd drown in that much shit. I couldn't put a face on that. So listen, I say to myself. Listen careful to what she says. Listen. Hear it. What the words are. What's going on under them. Don't fight her. Hear that. God I know. Go on. This is it. She wants. I will do. She want that I'll rifle through your flesh. So now go. Ask her. Mammy? Say it right out. Is something wrong while I'm not around? What's the matter? Oh. I hear.

He's got this job and he won't drive but won't get a lift with yer one and he won't give me his pay now and won't move to his own and he won't help around the house and he won't fill the buckets clean the fire and his bin is full of sweets and he's getting tub now and he won't go out and he has no friends in and computer games morning noon and night and he won't make the dinner even if I'm at work til all hours and he won't even throw his laundry out and he won't make his bed and he gets raging if I say and he kicked my washing line pole in two and he won't clean the drains and he won't put up those shelves and he won't take the hoover out and he is eating curry noodles late at night and makes me wash his dishes up there's something wrong he's so un- fair and I always did my best for you and worst off he won't come for prayers or on Sunday go to mass says Jesus shove it up his rear I never reared ye to speak like that and what shall I do with him what can I do he's a grown man he's twenty- one and sometimes I wish your father hadn't died that he'd had enough gumption to be a man it never would have been like this I know we've had our difficulties but you're such a good girl that I know I know I must have done something somewhere right what did I do to deserve this treatment?

I did try. I did try first. She won't hear. She will not. You know Mammy something's wrong. You know there is. And has been. She turn her eyes from me. I am not supposed to say. We aren't. None of us. A secret that we. Must not remember. I can't do. Say that. And I do know. She won't bear. It. Somehow she think that's not the truth. Better so lazy than. What? That's a trap. Leave it undone. Unsaid. It is true. But then? And so I say. Not. Nothing on this. Yes maybe nothing's really wrong. That's an excuse. Yes. More. I like that. It's, has been a lie I carry. Yes. I made it all up in my head. It is not it is. Yes it could be. Very well. How do I know? It was a long time. Broke a statue so what? She could have said anything then. Do I remember? Do I? Ha. So. Maybe not. Maybe not very well. Now. Some inside revolution I made. Turn the world about. So. On this day. I begin again. Again. It's easier and I breathe it in. Yes I will not know you very well or what inside's working right or wrong.

Cluck my feathers. Puff them up. Think. Right so. You're a fucking bastard. Actually. Fucking useless now I think. Carry on. Your rubbish. As though she hadn't had enough. You selfish fucking bastard shit. Just make her life misery and your own and my. Think I'll brave you. Tell you where you're wrong. Shall on her right side knight against you.

I am in your room. Saying. So tell me. What's all this about? All this shit of you not doing this and that. This room's a pigsty. It's a hole. The smell of it in here. The stink.

Your feet and you. Dried-up food. Jes. Us. Open the window God. You turning. Say what's up? What? I. Look at this and all your clothes you know. She's not getting any younger. You're the only one at home. You're not a baby. I know. Then what are you going to do about this carry-on? She can't be running after you all your life. You so bone idle. Does it all revolve around you? Sitting playing computer games. There's a whole world out there you know. You show no interest in anybody else. Not a civil word or help around the house. You know. Bring in the coal for her. Do the dishes.

At least your own room should be clean. Is it you blame her? You were too lazy at school, is that it? Is it? You're not such a hard man now. No one to blame but yourself. Self-pity. Self-indulgence. Get up off your arse and do something with your life. Read a paper now and then. Or. Are you stupid? Have you no friends, little wonder. Who'd hang round with you? The state of this. Get yourself a girlfriend once or will you spend your whole life stacking shelves?

I like it you said. Running out your eye. I just like it it's fun to watch them doing kicks. I think I'd like to kick like that. I practice it when there's no one in. I hiyah'd the clothesline and it broke. But. By accident. Not. On purpose. I didn't know how to fix it but I tried. I propped it up. It was all rotten inside. I'm sorry. Sorry. I'll do better. I will. I. Do it then tomorrow. I. Don't be angry with me. Eyes in tears sniffing. You are so dissolved. Sop of them sitting hiccing in your mouth. Now's not supposed to work this way. Just thought you liked it kicking too you say. You and me isn't it just? Like when we were little playing all that stuff. Before. Clap. You know when you were thirteen but I remember we did have great games. Oh God. What have I said? Wilt guilty my own badness swilling up to my head. Bleeding through. Don't move. I can't. Anyway. Just get off your arse and pull your weight. That's it. Jesus. What have I done?

That night sitting sitting room. Her knits. Floor balls of wool. You come in. Quiet as any. With the Irish Times. Sitting back against the sofa. Doubled over and knees bent. Flick. Flick through it. Your eyes. Turned about. Think. Talk. And look at me and say.

What do you think of that? And see this picture? See yer one? All the things out in the world. And fill your eyes up. Fill your nose. Then looking back and flick again. I saying

Yeah or no or so? And pressing on. You. Here what you think? Your opinion of the thing? Aye yes and maybe no not me. Not so interested. Think nice to be left alone. You're trying too hard. Rubbing me the wrong way. Ho. Sniff. She says and what is that? Read the paper. Since when do you? Who got you up to that? And quiet cross the room you said she did. Point at me. Had a word. Put that flea in my ear. Did she now and what gave her the right? Turn. Now miss. What are you playing at? What? Come back here splashing orders saying who's doing what. Oh thinking you're so grand. Off up there at some college. You needn't come back here to be upsetting him. Your brother is your elder and you should respect that. Are you listening? I am. Almost to the floor. Gobsmacked. Right down there. Excuse me? All these weeks you've been giving out saying what a so-and-so he is. He's not doing that for me or this or this. So I had a little word with him.

Told him what to do. Oh you did did you? Well aren't you great. And who asked you to or told you or wanted you to? You self-righteous Madam. Looking down your nose at me and your brother. I can tell. We get on. Just fine without you here. Fine without you. And I'll thank you not to inter- fere. The cheek. The cheek of it. Snapping snapping. So I got up. Went. Packed my bags. Left next morning by myself. I've had a fucking nough of this. Good-bye and then good-bye to you.

I went off back to there and my best friend. Come on. She me go gallivanting. We'll run riot. Run the best. Ourselves and everyone else into the ground. Going on with. A project we like. That likes us. Bite and chew.

I give mother letters a miss after that. I'm not calling. Com- ing home. Being good and nice girl as I should. I know. Don't know what's the rub of it. And your birthday. That came. So what's it to me? I think I'll not. I'll not bother at all. Who to say I should.

You're twenty-two. Too old for me to give a shit anymore.

After that she and me go back to our work. Drink this. Go here. See him. Do that. Lie across each other's beds we tell each other sorts of things. It makes us such close friends. No bits pieces left unsaid. And truth now tell the truth we say. Her father felt her up. It makes her red and cry. Daddy still loves her the best but he wouldn't want anyone else to try. That is love. Her mother's milky bag of gins under the cupboard. Her sister is a fucking bitch. Always trying to get her in shit. I tell her. Kinds of stuff. About you. My brother's shy. Patterns of the truth but not it. I. Hold on to that. It's for dwelling in there. If she wants to spew it out, that's for her. Not me too. No need to say. What is there to say?

When it was my own birthday. On the day. I am broke. Bloody. I. It has to be said. To turn nineteen. No cash under your wing. She says sure check your account. There could. You never know. Tenner. Fiver. Something you forgot. The wind clip my knees on that street. I stick my number in. Balance. Press. And guess. Guess what you know. There is in one hundred pounds. For me. For me. Hmm. Ssssh. I know from where. So thump my heart. Jesus. He did not. He didn't. Oh God. He did. You did that. She's leaping click her heels. We're grand grand hip hurray. I didn't like that much. Pilfer pursing my tenners. It was not so much fun knocking vodkas down my trough. I've a bad head. About it. Still now. Thinking you made the effort. Look what I did. Not. Not such a nice. No. Fuck him anyway. He's sucking up. Thinks I'll get all melted. I won't. Yep. These are my guns and I'll stick to them. Yep. I'm sticking. Creeping. I wish you hadn't. Or I was. But I'll still spend it all.

I met a man. I met a man. I let him throw me round the bed. And smoked, me, spliffs and choked my neck until I said I was dead. I met a man who took me for walks. Long ones in the country. I offer up. I offer up in the hedge. I met a man I met with her. She and me and his friend to bars at night and drink champagne and bought me chips at every teatime. I met a man with condoms in his pockets. Don't use them. He loves children in his heart. No. I met a man who knew me once. Who saw me around when I was a child. Who said you're a fine-looking woman now. Who said come back marry me live on my farm. No. I met a man who was a priest I didn't I did. Just as well as many another one would. I met a man. I met a man. Who said he'd pay me by the month. Who said he'd keep me up in style and I'd be waiting when he arrived. No is what I say. I met a man who hit me a smack. I met a man who cracked my arm. I met a man who said what are you doing out so late at night. I met a man. I met a man. And wash my mouth out with soap. I wish I could. That I did then. I met a man. A stupid thing. I met a man. Should have turned on my heel. I thought. I didn't know to think. I didn't even know to speak. I met a man. I kept on walking. I met a man. I met a man. And I lay down. And slapped and cried and wined and dined. I met a man and many more and I didn't know you at all. I saw that then. It happened a lot. You putting money in. Here for you. Little bit. I but I never say thanks. I never said. Sorry for that now. I don't really know what I was up to.

So she called me when are you coming home? We haven't seen you in an age. Now you will. Come home now. Ah you will. It's your home. Where you belong. I'm praying for you every day. Ah come for Easter. Ah you will. It's been a year. Do. Ah. Do. We want to see you. Should do. Should do.

Sure parents drag you in the muck, through puffs of fag ash on my bed. You'll make her happy. Why don't you go. It's no skin off your nose anyways.

Clippedy clop. Ah train. Going back down there. Those fields. Going through them just like then. Drowned over. Filled up with rain. Even cows drown here. Even sheep. Even people if they're lucky. Children falling under every year. All the suffocated grass. The world's submerged in raining. And feel old lady rosaries crossing over me. Like music's going in my brain. Against me. I would. Push. Away. Get off this shore. Let this chalice pass. That old prayer. Not forget that. Me. If Jesus was here he'd have gone.

Running. Screaming with his sandals all flapping in through the cow shit. Oh God get me out of this. No not my will but thine be done. If they could see me saying this. See under my skin. Awful know. The knowledge. Jesus. Poison that. Their lives and minds. Impious me. But see. But see. I'd give sacrilege a good go to be shot of it. Free of it. What? I don't know what. But it knows me. Give me a good bite in its jaws. That'll break my neck in time. That'll have me eventually where I am, it wants me. Crunched and obey. All over. Over there. Those houses passing by. Those bungalow dot dot my conscience. Shall I not do right? It's a cesspit. A suck pool. Where all dead go. Am I. Will I. End up like them. Live and drown here. Filling my lungs. There's no escape. Get out for likes of me. Gurgle liquid up. Hold my nose. Fall in. Ah God. Shut up. You're only fucking going home. It's not that bad it is. Is. Not. There. Go on. Give over with all that then.

That station I know it. It's here. I'm yes that's fine. Hello. Hello. Lovely to see you. Yes. Something. What? What is it? We had some news. Yes? Your grandfather's. Died. Oh. In his sleep. I know it is a dreadful shock. Oh terrible. So. We'll have to pack the car. Go north for the funeral. I haven't seen him in a good what fifteen years. Oh Mammy.

And true she looks dread. Hug her. Think well at least I'm glad I've come for something even this. She hic and cry. That old bastard. Get me all stirred up. Riled. But still. But still. Hello. Yes. To you. Standing. Strange what was that? Off a bit from her. Something of your look gave me. Something. What? There's a bit. Something. In there. Anyway.

Hello.

At the house. That's the same. It was a year ago. But calmer. And my eye catch dust.

Some giving up or winding down? I can't decide.

Pack it. Yes pack that have you got black? With you. I always have. Just as well. You must you know she says. My family. Everyone will be on the look. A good gawk. Sure you know the type of them. Always something to say. Who gives a fuck? Don't show me up she says. And none of that foul mouth if you don't mind. It's just a word. You father was a well-spoken man at all times. Do I give a. Don't please don't just not today. We'll have a fight another time. Just check your brother's packed his bags. That fella's memory is shot to hell. Are you packed there? I am. Are you sure? Yes. Are you? I said I'm sure. Throw that in the car. I did already. Good for you. You two. Please just stop it now.

We're driving off. We're going. I think well Granda's dead. What do I care? That's crept in me. Listless. Quiet. Dead inside perhaps me. I'm not. I am not. Who's he anyway to me?

· · ·

Hours and hours. Here we are. Sea wind slit breath. Salting in my mouth. That's a sharp sharp air. Give you ice in the eyes. Sea pitch pulling itself over and back. Greenish blacky. Drag off groaning rocks. I close my door. Lock it tight. I haven't been to his house. Take out the bags from the back she says to you.

He lived looking out on that. Cliff ahead. No wonder he was such a strange. The front door opens. Inside people there. Such aunts and uncles I've not known before. Even you. Bewildered by all that lot of them. That's a whole ocean of cousins alone. Hordes. In a shipwreck I would chuck the lot. Go in. Go in. Hello. Sit down. God years and years. Is it? Years and years. They pockle on us. Make up some tea. Can't you see they're froze?

Will you have a sandwich? Ham? Egg? Cheese? Sure this lovely one with salad cream that make me retch, bit of lettuce and corned beef. I will. I'm grand. Well just the one. Bite into that as introducing's begin.

Now this is so and so. Seen you in years and years. And shaking all their sweating hands. Get kiss off the aunts. Some of them. More leather looking than our own and dyed, made up this one that, with great precaution for their age. But I can see her off their eyes. The browny almond turn at end. They're not so friendly. Maybe are a little bit on the sly. It's much too small here for us all they say but two in a bed couch and armchair, you'll be grand. I. Glare at me. I won't complain. He would want it wouldn't he? Yes I suppose indeed.

Some of them smoke some of them drink. A whiskey at the table. Ice up there in the fridge. Do not you. Mammy just a little one. As though I could stop you. She's that headstrong. Go on.

And uncles. Now with my mouth full of egg. I have not thought. Oh God. Of. Right.

Here. Knock it back now. You'll be fine I say. You never did. Any wrong. So.

Not this one. He's a bit small. This one taller and too fat but gives hugs like he knows me. This one. Not. This one. Isn't him. Not him hello how are you? Not. God where is he where is she? They haven't got here yet. Their plane's not in til very late. On top of that. A long drive here. Awash that is relief for me. Just now. He is. But later on.

I sit crossing my legs. Wish I could smoke. I cannot. Oh just the one. She'd kill me.

I'd be killed for that so maybe later on alone. Hear all the recalling going on. Well he went quick at the end. I'd say he would have liked that. You know he was always scared to die. So that's the best. God rest his soul. The bastard. No now's not the time for.

Amongst themselves. The varied factions. Good for keeping well away.

And off across the hall I hear the sobbers too. Taking it in fits. Go howling. There now. Don't do that. On to the next and on and on. I didn't think he was liked like that. All cousins staring past each other thinking who's this one? Whose one is that? Evade the meat press parents going talk to so-and-so. Now you like computers talk to him. Poems you say. Well that stumped him for a moment til bright bollocks spark came scurry back with see her there? She's a one to meet. She writes for the local. I'm fine thanks where I am.

Such a long time listening to all these things. Blistering blister so proud of us. Tape measuring everybody's life to the wall I realize he's up the stairs. Grandfather. Stretched out lying there. In bed. In state. In his pin-striped suit. With his hair gelled back. Hmm like a red rag. I have to go up. Take a little look. I'd like to. Innermost in. I've never seen a body properly dead before. I bide my moments. Then. Quick. They're merging on the fruitcake. Out. I slip off. Should not? Isn't he is mine as well and doesn't just belong to them.

Stairs are creaking. Much more cool up here. Turned off the radiators of course I know. The pale light spew the landing underneath his bedroom door. Is it his now?

Whose is it then? They're laughing downstairs. Great wild roar haw hawing. Covering me. Covering the sea sound.

I push it little stiff. Small feet he had. And very shiny shoes. The leg. His jacket tucked just neat around him. Very clean. A candle burning. And his hands pressed Jesus in the garden. And white and white as hell. His nails the color of his face. Translucent let the light go through. The cold room. Jesus freezing. Where he did not expect to die.

So Granda. I don't talk to the dead. So now. That's strange to see him here. Dead. I could give him a kick if I liked. But it's not worth the hassle now. I could undo his flies for shame. I know he wouldn't have wanted me to. Or kiss. Poke him. Squeeze out an eye. I'd lift it but. Maybe. No. Better not touch. I haven't seen him that to this. He's looking so unrumpled now. Just not that angry. As he could be nice. I doubt that very much. I know they've washed him. Stuffed his throat. And packed his arse with cotton wool. Two p's something on his eyes. What else. Stretched him so he's straight. The eldest daughter. Did that. On her own up here. A nurse or some kind of thing. No undertakers in this house. In this house we do our own postlife stuffing. I splinter at the sides. To think of it. That fairly strange. To do that to your father. That you like or don't, depending. I don't know so well. Is it not unhygienic? Still. The doctor said fine. Signed it all and all of that. So Granda.

I put my finger in his pocket. What have you there? A sweet. A toffee chew. A scrunch of wrapping. Lump of dust. Well Granda not so bad. And into dust you shall return. I eat it. Glad. It isn't stale. So quiet in this room and cold. As cold in death I'd say. And nothing new under the sun at that. I got up. Looked from his window. All the sea going below. Strange at all this going on. Last night he didn't know he'd be dead. I didn't think I would be here. That his daughter would be stuffing things up his rear end. What would you make of me hey if you could see me now? Having a good look in your pockets. In your bedroom all alone. A photo on his bed stand. Some woman's face that I don't know. Perhaps he loved someone once. It can't. I can't tell. But not his lot of family laughing way down there. Does it it doesn't really matter now. I'll sit here. I will sit down til long after everyone's gone to bed. Look at you Granda. Keep you company. For no one's praying for your soul. And no one will sit with you tonight. Doze beside the corpse. Not a head look in. Distract my vigil of sleeping or poke about his room. He's as private as he'll ever be right now. What's all that to him?

Three or four cold woke me up. At last in the night they have come through the door.

I hear umbrellas shaking down the stairs. It's raining out. That's right. Them clomping into the kitchen. Their daughters exasperate the cold. They clunk the range and stir the turf and turn the electric kettle on. A few still up who have been drinking. Saying fruitcake? And over there there's butter cheese a bit of beef. The aunt is clucking. Pass the knife the plate a round of bread. Now where will my girls stretch out the night? I'm listening til I hear him. Nothing. Don't hear him say at all. For ages. Must been slurping. Tea up. Whiskey. Warm the bones. I almost debate go down and join them. Think. I will not. I'm a mess. And so much family around the place. I'd see him if I could. No. Why'd I want to? On my own. Now that won't happen. Such throngs of all above below. And only two days. Maybe three. I give up. I creep. I creep. I go up the stairs to the five-cousin bedroom I am in. Get in the two-cousin double bed I share.

That morning. Blowing breath across my face. Cousin hair in my eyes. Younger. White to the touch and much too close. See her eyelids going I feel the sun thinking it will get here somehow through. So get up. Cold all round me. Going up my feet. Somewhere in this house is. I walk there look out. Brave day for all the clouds. It could might be sunny later. In here. Downstairs. I'll get washed and dressed. Go on out and up the beach a bit. Across the stones. See if there's a view. Be out. Be out a lot. And so much people clatting clatting downstairs. They're all get ready. Make the way for visitors condolers and drinkers of tea. I don't want. Roped up with that.

My face tight. Washed out. Fine I'm wan. Whey. Even mascara can't do plenty. I go down. Wearing my best frock not the black. Soon's soon enough for that. Too soon. I'd almost say but banging heart stops that. I am. I should be. There's an awful lot that's going on today.

I see you hunkered by the fireplace. Giving it a good rake out. Morning. Sleeping? Did you have? Some wriggling little farting one who wasn't sleeping half the night. We played gameboy after that. Well just as well you brought it then. True you say. I go on in now. Don't be nervous. Don't delay.

Go in. On in. To the kitchen. Blazing it was heat and lights. People stoking up the range and crossing over teapot stretch to pour a pan of sausage out. Plate of fried egg black pudding. Cigarettes a thousand to one. Legs crossed. Knees out. Reading the news. Radio going and chat chat chat they're racing over and fro. In the corner. In the corner there. Turn my eyes on that. Turn away. He is standing with some uncle. Smoke a cigarette. Talk. Smoke a cigarette.

Look now there she is says Mammy. In her element of family here. She'll do the talking. I will let. Not too bad. We've been waiting on you for you to get up. Where did you disappear to last night at all? And would you ever look at the time. Your aunt's been asking after you. He. Stop that. Looking. Now then. At me. Catch that. Strange.

Surprised. Smile. Messy hair. Creases running all around his eyes. I would not have known her, he says.

Well my girl says his wife come in. Well you've grown. You're all grown up. She gives me a kiss with her thin lips. Has a little stroke of my hair. Well look at this. That's changed a shade. Out of a bottle no doubt. I can always tell. Say hello to your uncle over there. And I do. I go and kiss him on the cheek. The skin. That bone. Which he lets me. Says do you remember me at all? Nod to that say yes. Cunning game but. You haven't changed I say. No you haven't changed at all. See she's still the Madam that she was he says. And laughs. And hardly looks at me. They laugh. Approve of saying. And I can't tell what's the. Join up. What does. Makes me uneasy. Guilty somehow. Is that right? I. Laugh. Ignore. The banter. Fade off and let them get along.

I make my breakfast. Eat that. Don't look. Don't be letting my face get warm. I've done worse much more times again but. Drink up. Say I am going out. But love. But love. So much to do. Sandwiches and cakes. All hands on deck. Too many Mammy in here.

Anyways you know well I can't cook. I'm going for a walk. I'll be back soon enough and do the few bits when I get in. Well now. Be sure you do. There'll be loads of people your grandfather's neighbors he was a well-respected man. The strange this. Coldness. She upset. But what for I don't know. For him it must. Feeling bad for the evil house and all that stuff. Go on time on. I've on my mind. The other things. I'm out the door.

That air. That air God save me. That wind going so hard on my back. In my frozen mouth. What is it the uncle bother me like that? What would he say? Remember other kitchens we have known? Remember that chair or the scratch in my? What's that man to me? Fucked me long, long ago. Hurt me and not well. It's not in me anymore. A thing that happened on my route to here. But him? Sure maybe guilt's the thing. I should say rejoice uncle. Remember what we did those years ago? Could be my aunt knows. And that would be something worse again but no she doesn't. I would tell. I'd see it on her. Who cares forget. In two days I'll be gone. Resolve to. What did you expect? The surf coming. Jumping up on the sand won't catch me anyway. I'll go back in. Just laugh at it for Christ Christ sake.

Flurry. Jesus they are bump him down the stairs. Two uncles. In his coffin. Granda. Toes first. Without doing well. Oh you're back now. In the nick of time she says. Throw over those sheets. In the sitting room. We're putting him.

Lengthways by the fireplace. They'll put the prop-ups on the mat. Is the radiator off in there? Well it's just as well it's cold.

Mind out now til I pull it round. Don't want them trip on it split open his head god forgive me I'm awful. She's chattering away. So I drape all the furniture with white sheets. And turn those pictures round to face the wall. Some aunt there stop the clock. You can pull the curtains to too. Not fully. Just in a bit. He is now. Set him gently. God he's heavy. Did he put on a bit of weight in that last while the uncles say. Now don't be talking about the dead like that. But still they're laughing all them taking the coffin lid back off. When did that come, I say. While you were out. Out gallivanting on today of all days someone's saying snappish just behind my back. I wonder that is. Oh who? Well fine whatever then. Now young lady, you will not. Lay out those mass cards. We already have some from just the neighbors. There'll be more. Christ it's freezing. Put out the silver candlesticks have we white candles? No. I'll go out and get I say. You'll have to go right into the town for them well. Well. I'll give her a lift I hear uncle say.

Walk to his car we're awkward. They are watching our backs shouting bring back Jamesons while you're at it. No. Bushmills. Something like that. Awful quiet. See him say that's the one there. With a hot smell in it opens of leather and air freshener. Rented so and no point looking for clues. Sit in. He says. Put your belt on. How are you? How are you? Long time no see. No. You're looking well turn the key. He take off down the road. I am awkward as I never was looking at my knees. Worser even than thirteen. Yes not bad and you? The same old the same. It's nice to see you. I sometimes wonder how you've been. Well fine. Go back to silence stay there let's stay there please. He drives then like he heard me. Only says Right! when he stop the car.

I come back with candles whiskey in my hands and wave for him to start up. He does. Would you say he'd like that? Your grandfather. What? Drinking at his wake. How would I know? You. I don't know didn't know him at all. That's sad. Not really. I always found him quite severe. I'm sure he says. When I first met your aunt . . . The trail of that. And we don't follow. Can't begin to guess, for it goes where? I say And my cousins?

How are they? I haven't been talking to them here yet. I heard one got married was it last June? Yes to some fellow. Do you like him? I suppose. Suppose? I don't really know my children he says. He says. You've grown so much. You've grown up. You're a woman now. I have. I am. I suppose I am. And beautiful. Thanks for saying so. He drive. Arrive. Pull in. The door. They come out aunt and mother too he says take this stuff. I'm just going to take her a run out the road. We were talking about where you and I met. I want show. Says the aunt curl. Fine. Now I wonder but. Away. We. Go.

We go up the hill. Like that. Look down he says. Great sweep on the bay. Lovely. Feel the car catch in the wind from the sea. Beat upon us. Keep those windows. What's this I am at? I don't know. I don't know. I cannot close my eyes with it. New or afraid. No not that. Not those things at all.

He stops. Pulling up. It's lovely isn't it here. A very fine. A beautiful spot. I walked down there this morning point. Yes. I know. I saw you go out. Right so. Stop up that chat. Silence now. We silent sit til. I have often thought he says. His voice bring me duffel coats school buses back. Drag me. Like it was. No I'm a long way off from that. He says About you and.

What we did. What I did. I did then. Twist my stomach. Look at the rain. I know I'm going in under with him. Where that is? Somewhere. But do this. I think do this. Whatever it is.

So are you feeling guilty? What? About what? About that time when you fucked me? Yes. About that. I feel guilty and I am. Because I was thirteen? Look you're no baby now. No. So stop with that. You know me. I do. Know you he says. Well. Go on say it while no one's here. Then. Look, do you think he says. You don't think do you that. What? I abused you? That you abused me? Well that's the question to end them all is here. Is here. I stop and going all around I know already but must see it first. Say then at last. No. I don't. Do you? Think that? At thirteen after all I was still a child. Quiet quiet in the car. All I hear is breath. I always wish I hadn't he says. All the time? Didn't you enjoy it? I ask. I shouldn't have done it and I know that. But you did. I did. Fuck me. Fuck you. And did you enjoy it? Yes. Why am I asking this? And this? Why did you if you knew it was so wrong? Squirm him. I couldn't somehow not. You were like. You were like. It doesn't matter he sighs there is no good thing to say. Well then. That's that. And that concludes this little chat. Your conscience is clear and I won't be calling the guards. I'm A-OK as the Yankees say. Yes I see. And I suppose there's been others? Yes. Plenty since? A lot. You haven't damaged me if you're afraid of. Haven't soiled my goods. You're angry. I'm not. I am not. I. You've got beautiful. Well you know growing up does that. What's wrong? Now. That's enough for him. I've had enough. Because it's all going merry round and round. In my head. And. But. Still. I won't say any more. I can't. But. Will you kiss me coming out of my mouth before I know what I've said at all. Will you kiss me?

What's coming next? There's a bit pause. He look down

at his hands sitting flat on his knees. He won't do I think. He won't. That's good. What do I want with. Shame. Jesus. Then he does. As he wants to. Now I see. He wants to. Now. Mess up. Botch this.

Conversation. Mouth on. Feeling bluster winds rattle the car. And the cold sea burning over in my guts. And he kisses me til my mouth is sore is red with it. Hurts I remember. This taste of his tongue I've not known. Remembered like this from anyone else. Bite me. All his mouth. Not alone. Kiss til. I. He touch me. Go on pull me. He could run right through me now. Riot. This is not like. Coming home. I feel that. There. His lips. I'm. It's too. Much. Jesus. Give my eyes back. Let me. See. My. Choke. Stop. Don't stop he says. Stop. No. Stop. I have to make. Myself. Sit back. Jesus he. What. His breath go. Like the clappers. Are we going to do? Go back now I say. What? Go back now. We should. Your mouth. Hurts me. Too swoll he says. You're sensitive to that I remember from before.

God. Be quiet. Just for a moment. Sit. Alright. Sit. Alright. Are you alright? He take my hand. I. Am. Shake. There. Calm down. We're going to be. I know. We are going to be fine. We should. What? We are not we. Go back. Now. Alright. Alright. Start the car now.

They didn't look upon us strangely. They did not see us at all. For all about the people descended. Slip in. I run up to the loo there I puke. I should have lunch. My face in the glass. Who's that I don't know. I do know. That's shite. But what happens now? Nothing. Don't obsess.

Come on. Bang the door. Hurry up you know there's a queue. I flush and wash my hands. Open. His daughter there standing there. She is older than me and my mouth reek of sick. Hi hello there I'm sorry. Didn't feel that well. I know the feeling. Yeah. It's all the sandwiches not enough sleep. True. I laugh think Jesus Christ. She goes on in.

By the coffin. You're sitting. Falling almost asleep I see. I am guilty. Sit by you. Say have a lie-down I'll take your turn with the body. And you do. That gives me time.

Catching my breath in the cold. Hello Granda. Now what have you seen?

The biddies are having their sup. He was a grand man. A lovely man. A terrible shame. Loss to the community. Still. It comes to us all in the end. True enough. But he had a good death and what more could you want?

I sat there most hours. Listen to the razzle of it. Watch him duck in and out now then. Give me a nod not a smile not anything else. See his wife. See his wife and she sits by my. There's a cuppa are you tired you look a bit pale. Nice for one moment but I don't feel guilty. I think your husband's tongue was just in my. His daughters, and they're sorry their grandfather's dead. I see him hug them and pat them now love, don't cry pet. Oh Daddy. Daddy they say. I don't cry. Not even a morsel. Dead and gone why should I? The pound in my throat not for Granda. Our mother snot quietly into her hankie grasp my hand. For I let her. She's dreading the moment they take him away. I'm not. See uncle moving. In the other room. Think Oh God. Something. Something's in me going on.

They carried him out in the rain that night. Made room on the sitting room floor for a gaggle. Bang the lid on. We processed to the church. All them carry him on their backs. Sliding coffin though they'd catch it. If it. It didn't. But he was well rattled still I'd say. I wore my black. Mother man-tilla and you your best suit looking solemn. As we cared. We did not. Neither you but still. I looked for him. He took his turn. One place strange for your father-in-law to be. Heavy. I saw sweat roll down his face. They all did. Fat bastard. Too many toffee chews or that. Dinners. For the likes of him. Now Granda. For all your sins.

In the church we were good. Said prayers and settled him down for the night. Corpse.

Night Grandfather and we all went back to his house. Eat and drink. I sat with whiskey thought his jam's in the press. Clapped into the corner and watched him uncle telling jokes for the laugh of them. They like. He comes quite popular up the ranks. His wife does not some reason. Her smoother brown hair. I think she's. A bitch. But still he married her. That. I don't know. That's something. But me and that's something too. I drink whiskey keeps me going and he gives me my fill. Have a little one. Do not Madam. Ach he says leave her there. And ever acquiesce she to him.

In the morning. Morning mass and the funeral. Parish priest says what they ask. A good man and a sound man and very continent. Carried up into the graveyard and lowered him down. Throw a rose on top. His daughters. More at him than on. Rub their shoulders sons and sons-in-law. He's buried. Under the muck. The end. Go on there get into your hole. Amen. And. Amen.

We troop back to his kitchen. And more eating more. Eating him house and home. Whose is it? Who knows? Who cares? Not me. But the biddies clustering. Have one of them ham sandwiches love.

So, that aunt wife says she says we're leaving. Early. Sorry about that. It was the only flight we could get that gets us back in time for work on Monday. Got to get back. Aye.

Well now we must meet up again not wait til someone

dies the next time. They all neigh and say the same but I go out. Look at me. I must go out of doors. At this. Go on, you knew, I say in my own ear. What did you think would happen? Funeral's over. Amen and again.

On the beach. On the stones. On the water splash. I'll hear it go right through me. Now see. Because he's going away. I knew sure. I knew that. But still. The ocean comes. I'll put my hands in. I'll baptize. I like again. That cold running round my knuckles. Catch it just a bit. Don't you start. And don't let the ice in. Don't you dare start now. A stupid fucked-up thing. Walk and walk it. Go on over the rocks. Put the air in your lungs. The fright out. You didn't want. Took it. But. But but. It's nothing now. Forget all that was nothing at all.

You're here he said. I thought you would be. Look you heard my wife. I'm going and. I know you are what do you want me to do? Why do I do that? Don't do. Shall I not then? No.

He's worried this. Face closing over with. Look. What? Jesus. I want. I want. You want what? No. He turns and thinks it. Want what? Tell me. He says I can't do without this. Without you. Again. I want. Have you a number? I'm over often I. Want you again.

I don't think, I say I don't think I don't know what is I don't what is if this is we should or, you know. So many things things things curling up in my head. Jesus Jesus.

Look. I haven't got time. Do you hear me? She's waiting. They're waiting.

Daughters. Yes or no he says. Yes or no.

I look. Flood my eyes. Because this is a long dark thing to do and cannot be undone. Will I? I say inside my mouth.

Can I? Do I want? I. Yes. I. And I say. Do you have a pen? Then. Here. Take it down. Because I have no idea what is right. And I know that he smiles. That he stands with his back to the house. And I look at him. And he strokes my face. And he strokes my hair. And he touches my breast. And says. That's my girl. I'll see you soon. And back then he to his own.

I'm as sick as I can be in the car back home. I'm as full of all sorts of things as I am. Was. Know that in the bone and race of me I am wrong different from you. Where is that from? Don't know. Still so nonetheless. I watch. She sniffing at the wheel and you your walkman in your ears. You'd be buzzing all the way home. She says. Come on children now. Let's offer up a few prayers for the Holy Souls.

Hail Holy Queen, Mother of Mercy. Hail our life our sweetness and our hope. To thee do we cry, poor banished children of Eve. To thee do we send up our sighs mourning and weeping in this valley of tears. Turn then most gracious Advocate thine eyes of mercy toward us. And after this, our exile, show unto us the blessed fruit of thy womb Jesus.

Oh clement oh loving oh sweet Virgin Mary. Pray for us sinners. Now and at the hour of our death. Amen.

PART IV

Extreme Unction

1

Jesus that. Stink of that. City when I got off the train. Get a lungful of that in you and see how you do, she says cigarette filter fraying brown on her tongue. Thoo pthoo. Looking knackered, alright? Not too bad. Come on with me. Thanks for. It's a good month is it since I seen you last. Is there loads to tell me? Ah there is oh loads. And aren't you mighty I say. Coming all this way. In. Not much missus. You are. Well fuck and I am.

Now I'd say, a good laugh's what we need.

Take the skirt off that one says your man. Some man. Later in the night where I am lying. My feet up on top of his bar. We're all laughing we are. Who. All of us here. Ah now lads my granddad's just dead. Shall we have a period of mourning? Shall we have a period at all? She roars. We shall we shall. And we'll drink these whiskeys down for him. A haon, a dó, a haon, dó trí down with it. Ah the neck the poor auld neck. Right in the troat she says. Don't be splashing they say. Go on lads. Do then. Lock the door. We do. We let them for we're having such a time. Sure don't mind the Gardaí they say. They can't see in. Switch them lights down. I'm dancing

dancing twirl my head. On the bar in my slip shoes. Pool and cake of it. Puddles and fag ash stink of sweat. This place smells like shite. Round the I do the rounds on the bar. Kick off that glass now. Kick that one. Into the wall. Would you credit it? One of them says stop. In my burl. I cannot see. Hey stop that you fucking. Fucking mad thing. Them glasses have to be paid for and not by my dad. Not my dad either I shout I say Jesus Christ. Skid the corner wood and almost fall off cut my knees. Easy now. I've got you. Easy now there missus she laughs says. Come on the lot of you let's go up the stairs.

In the dark we are climbing up where electric's not on. Everyone's feeling my leg makes me laugh out. Makes me laugh out more and she. Saying cut that quack. Sure we'll be playing hide-and-seek. And look for me and I am gone. Backing tiptoe. Moving in the dark. Put out my hand but slip and. Go on land. Shhh quiet slither I must. In the dark hands and knees. Find the bath. It's a warm spot there. Echo. Hands are warm.

Mouths kiss on me. Someone. Faces I kiss though they're cold though they're slimy full of tongues. Who. What's that? They'll get me will they up between the legs. Who's there? What's that? Shall we do in the quiet? Oh now. A mortal sin. You know. Go on empty mouths and tongues and hands and fingers pass me up. That some hurt me with nails on my face. Get me up. Up the. He. Up there. Jesus. What's that? What's that? Swig this there. Have it going up my nose sure I'll snot ribena that's not what's that. Ah springing like. Oh. No. Blood. God. Jesus. She's got blood coming out of her. What of her? Head.

She's a nosebleed this one or something like that. Ha? God yuck sit up put your head back. You know this is only the second time I've a had a nosebleed in my life. Gunk sliding. Get the ice you. Rolling in my throat. Go on. Fucking what's she on. What. Nothing. I never. Nothing like that. Fall back. Think I'll almost hit my head. He. Who. I'll go to. I'll go to sleep. Here. Wake you. Fucking state. Wake up. Get the fuck-up and get out of here and on my behalf she's efffing blinding. Fuck ye she says. Fuck you fuck you. What did you do to her in there? You pack of knackers. Pack of pervs. Well get the fuck you out of here too they say. Hoors and tinkers stinking pieces of shite. Go and Jesus Christ that one she can't take a drink. Joke. Oh. Good-night.

Drag me all back. All the way. Home.

In the morning. Stung my eyes. Awake now? Are you alright? I'm a. And what have you to tell? What? God you look desperate are you she says laying on my bed. Wag fag at me. What have you been up to? He? Who? Just I. I. Jesus Christ you know what. My grandfather died. Well that isn't the look of you you have. He? Who? Yes. Who? What? I just need a spot of sleep. Well there's a cup of tea there. Thanks. And I'm staying the week. Oh right. Bastard father did not pay my rent. Fine. Do you know. What? We should get a flat together. Grand so. I know. Tell me what you've been up to? Not a thing. Not a thing I say. We fell asleep teas in our hands. Nose full of dried-up blood tastes.

I sleep I can barely sleep next to her in the bed. She's roaring full of it. In-took breaths snorts all sorts wheeze and toss about. But my head's there on the pillow just in case I can. I am dreaming. What's on my secret face she sees? Lines of lies and things I've done. Oh what's coming down the road. Through the curtains. He. If I say no I won't no. I know. But I could but. I think about him. And it would it'd be like? This time. Now that it can't hurt. Now that I'm stretched I know. What could I do. Well we'll wait we'll see we'll. Go to sleep. Who? Shoo you.

And we do get our flat and we live just the same. Some days weeks time go by.

Hi there. You had a phone call. Who? Your mother oh. Call her again. Hello Mammy? Oh oh oh. I can't go on like this I don't think I can go on she say this way. What? Not. He. So selfish a child of mine makes me drive him pick up after this that and the other. It's an awful way to. In front of that TV at the end of my tether at the end of my rope. Sorry to hear that Mammy. Hung up before long. Not mine this problem. No.

Well now an exam is it whatsit doing bit of study here and there. About to slog about to slog I am. Why's he not called? Maybe I'm to forget again. Time. Time.

Ring bring. Chew off the side of my face. Well Mammy. Is it that bad? Do you think so do you think? God desperate. Look I'll call you next week. I did. For my conscience for my clean bill sake. It was bad for her when her father died. And she want to. Decide to clean the whole thing out. Wound of. And fester we and supposed to help. Not so easy. You must. You and your brother. Speak. I'll put him on the phone. Hello she's shouting, make some effort before it gets too late. But also often she says. Bone idle never does a tap. Make me wait on him hand and foot. Let me out of this claptrap. I. But. I go on in. Hello and how are you? Fine fine fine.

So off up there. City. She and I. Going mad. Back to the books to the fucks I forget we are going round and around again. Scald the mouth off you with that it would. I am listening though and there was no sign of him. Uncle. So we're in. Bring thinging this one that one home. Fella. Creep it ha ha up the stairs. Two by two of them not every. Spat out—at—after between us pair. Ah nice boy nice boy shall I have him for lunch? It's a roar. It's a laugh. We. For a laugh. Always are. No sign of him. Uncle. That's alright. And just as well. But she's always asking what happened you? Me? You're weird ever since. From the funeral. Something must have gone on. Say no. Always. For what would I?

That might be a little too much.

Fine fine I'll come if you want Mammy. If that's what you're after. I don't know what I can do. Sister be a brother sister fixer of her woes. Am I like that? Am I that thing it seems yes. So ho ho on the phone. What's this not pulling your weight sort it out please you sort it out. I'll do my best though I don't know. You say she give me all the blame. She doesn't want me play computers watch TV not sit by her or sit by her. Do something, I say, for she'll drive me mad. Sorry. And I hang up.

Then I visit see what she means. So much slackness. Sittingness. Sitting still. Sitting down. You always doing. Sitting drive me. Jesus. Spare. Something like. Are you there are you there? Is anything happening in your life? And I think. She'll be minding you all her days. Maybe yes or is it maybe no. Sitting nothing. Sitting not a thing at all. Watch the telly. It is all. What can I do? Instil. Some seed. For what? She wants me to. But I'm not your. Mother. Something. What do I do?

God I want to run. Make my run from here and you two at each other's throats. Day and night night day and on and on. She's on the nag at me. And to you she say, did you do that? Yes I did. Did you fix dry wash? I did.

Going to such and such? I am. And I say go on. You go and fuck yourself coming down here who you think are? Telling me what to do you're a fucking slut and all the world knows that. Shut up. Shut up. How dare you? Who are you talking to. Get away. Make me. Again and again. Spinning round in our good spew. Rancid. Rack of it. Such sweet family. I want. Please. Give a moment in this. Please. Give me a break.

I see sit by her crying I am so alone. I wonder if your brother's ever loved me at all. I can't do this I cannot. This does me no good at all. Screeching rowing. Every day. When you're not here I'm. Feel everything give out. Under me. Under this. He'll never do anything. My head whacking. Amount. And I wonder sometimes for her. Would you be better off dead? Don't say that. Don't you ever say that. I say it in me. But. That's forever now. Look. That is me. My thoughts. Are all shame.

I make off from it. I make my escape. Leave you cough it up fight it out amongst yourselves. Get away from it oh god. And don't. No. Answer the calls. Fill my ear up. Fill my mouth instead. Man drink do what you like to me. I am safe. I am free. In my own way I am but it weighs me, beats me when I'm not doing the rounds. Split and splatter my heart head. So I get cold in the mouth on answering her bring bring.

Do you know she says. This one's a big surprise. Your brother I'd say is going mad. Do you know he forgot to go to work today just forgot. What do you mean he slept in? No. Just did not. Creeping over my eyelids. Something awful in that. There's more than. Something not quite. Wrong. Have you made him go to the doctor? Yes and she says there's nothing wrong. He should get a pocketbook. Remind himself. But at his age. Do you know Mammy I think you should take it. What? Further. Do you? Yes. I do.

I do not want. I do not want to hear this. But suddenly it's clawing all over me. Like flesh. Terror. Vast and alive. I think I know it. Something terrible is. The world's about to. The world's about to. Tip. No it isn't. Ha. Don't be silly. Stupid. Fine. Fine. Everything will be. Fine. Chew it lurks me. See and smell. In the corner of my eye. What. Something not so good.

And I go out and buy you presents. The very next day after this. Knickyknack things I think I hope you'll like. Some postcards of films. Some tape of a band. Think I'll wrap them and pack them and stick them in the post. For that's a little. For a nice surprise. Oh my conscience badly. How is that then? I know. I send them. Those little things and I hope. They'll stave it. Fix it up. Put it off my little love. So it does it it does not do. What? Whatever it will.

2

The phone rings and on it she says. I think. I think. Your brother's going to die. I'm. What do I say? What? What are you saying? And the blood pumps in my gums. In my nose.

What's happened now what? Are you joking Mammy are you having a laugh? Say so. P. Please. No. He got a nosebleed forgot his breakfast where he worked fell over cracked his head I thought he would die. I don't know, I think, you know, it got going after, what, after all these years. I don't think that can be right. I don't think that it can do that because it's dead isn't it it's dead because. In his head because. They said, didn't they say that? What if my tongue swelled up in my mouth what if I just keeled over now I might. I'd like. Not that not that one thing. Take it take it. Take it away. Where are you ringing from? And she says soft, in the hospital, in such-and-such a place. Far from home. With you. Because. What do the doctors say? It woke. It woke. And it. Came. Split open your veins. Bleeding now into your brain. Such a. Toothless lazy thing to do. After all these years. Could it not have left you alone? Could not. I wish it was yesterday. I wish we were beginning again. I think. Back to the start. I'd be. Hail Holy Queen no that won't work. I'll offer something up. God. Mammy. I'll come I'm coming now I mean in the morning because. I. Because the last train is gone. I will though I will first thing. For you. For you. Nine o'clock. Alright alright there? Tell him I'll be down in the morning. Tell you. Alright.

And I put down the phone. And I go to her room. And I say. Something really bad has happened. Look at me. Something terrible has come. It's coming into me in to me. I think. Sorry. I think I heard. I think my brother's going to die Jesus Christ. Jesus Christ. I. I.

That long night. Loams my eyes. Burn. Lime it. I'll do. I'll. Reach out through it. Catch it before it comes. Quick quick. But it's gone like a rat. Burrow deep and dark where I cannot go. I have. Nothing against this. No defence at all. But. To fall on the spindle. To be turned into the darkness. To be turned into stone.

Swish swish all the hospital doors in the world sound the same. I am walking in out of the light. God. Under strip lamps and curtains and a stink of green. I am marching and looking. I am seeking you out. Try to find where you have been to. Where you've been.

She is sitting. Like I've known she does all my life click. In the chair on the ward in this petrified air and her face all that's stopping melting herself. When she sees me she's both hands. Oh thank god you've come thank god thank god. He's just being examined. You and me we'll wait out here. I expect prayers to come. But they don't. Just we'll lose him and I know we will. We'll not Mammy. Mammy we won't. Down we go.

When they've gone out we see sitting prop in the bed. You. With some bowl of pudding with your wobble hand eat.

Drop it look up say I saved you some. I. And you are, I know, look like five again. So I hug you and say now what have you done? Gone fell over like an eejit. Cracked your head. Well done. Sorry. You laugh all the same. Well done. I am smothered. Air bit strangled by that. So now how are you feeling? Ah not too bad. Not too bad a bit tired and they hurt my head. Touch somewhere a bandage and all around shaved. Ah that's nothing wait til you see what I do for giving me a fright. You laugh. That's calm now and I can do that. So are you truce for a moment? And she says we are. We sit. By your bed. Look at you. Think. Wonder. What is going on?

In time. In his time. A doctor comes. Young. Come in pull over your curtains. Sit on your bed. Cross legs flick give pen tap clear his throat shift. Come on come on. We don't know anything yet. We've to run a few more tests til we see where we're at. Where? We don't really know as I said. There is something going on. Certainly a shadow showing up on the scan. Ah that's old she says from his tumor before. No. Don't think so. I can also see that one. Somewhere else. This is different. I feel you must prepare. Zzzing in my ears. This I don't know how to hear. Must be for someone else. Not for him. Not for she or me. Yes no he doesn't mean.

There now that wasn't so bad when he's gone out. Looking. Spinning round. So they don't know. See you'll be fine she says. Did he not say said you. No he never did. Just wait and it'll be alright. I am nodding. Nodding dog.

In the canteen I. Sssh don't you say that, say anything to him. He's fine it'll be alright she says. I stir gravy on my mutton chop. Look you don't think perhaps we should.

Prepare. For. God won't allow that. He wouldn't do that to me. I've offered myself up and served him all my life. And I know He would not take one of my children from me. But the. The Lord knows. I wouldn't survive. Not that. No. For I'm not Job. It's time for our faith to be tested. That's all. Now is the time for prayer.

In the chapel. Down on my knees. Oh god Jesus. I beg you. I am pleading. See. I plead. But stones in my mouth. Lead on my tongue. You are not the praying person. But.

I. Not you. Not you. After all you have done. Good people do the praying and sinners go to. Hell. Thank you Jesus. Amen.

In a hotel room we sleep she and me side to side. I wonder at all the nights she ever slept. Think who saw her there alone? Her God her Jesus. And they always kept her warm. But the. Would she trade them? I. Don't. Know. And when he. Who? Father was sleeping by her what did she think of then? Him. Ah. Our father who cannot be in heaven. For the first time. I. I miss he's not here. Who then. Think strange man, what would you have done? No. Not that I know. You wouldn't have come. I know that one. Tell that tale. For all your love was what was it? Some early night, like going home. Doing nothing at the time. Fell from the earth face at the moment you were. Wanted. Most. Despic. I know. I'd kill you. If you were here. If you. I'd turn you in your grave. Oh Daddy Daddy. What have you done? Lie still and breathing. Go let traffic rock. It rocks me into sleep.

But not the morning when it beats inside my head. We cross the roadways snuff the thick clouds up and get there quick as we. As quick as we can. And catch you sleeping with your hand outstretched. See you simple as you have ever lived with all the raging peeled away. Soft face she has for you, I have for you then.

So hot in here to sit and sit. Tea drink. Coffee I'll buy

us cake. Take a walk down there. Have a look in the shop. There's magazines and we play Xs and Os. It reminds me when I was a little you say but not my head it doesn't hurt so bad. We say ah hospitals we already done all that. Sure we'll be out soon. Sure we'll get away. What'll we do then? Oh loads of things. Go to the sweet shop. You say. Get some toys. I. Yes we will.

Surely. If that's what you want.

No news for you today sorry. You'll just have to hang on. Labs back all of that.

Going on and on. I'd suck my thumb if I did. Stink of it hospital puts my spine on edge. Eggs me on. Tell us now. God don't you think you could tell us quick? No.

At the end of the day you shuffle with us as we leave. Down the corridors slowly and into the lift. Say good-bye. I see you dither and could never help being cruel so Do you know your way back? I say. I know where I'm going you said to me. Soft and forgetful is what I see. Red in pajamas. That white as walls. Face. Neat bites of stitches. On your head. Your forehead. Again again. I can see all through it. Getting deader I think no I don't think no. With your feet slop along the lino. Diamond green. If we were children what we would do here. I if I'd my roller skates. Zoom you and me out. Fast as lizards.

Fast as newts. But you limp and me in heels. I know the way back to my ward from here I'll be alright, you say. Good-night. I dither looking dither in your dither eyes thinking they don't know at all at all. What is it running mad up there? I put my hand. Hold your wristband down so you cannot see, say Which ward are you on? You say nothing. Going red. You did not know. Just standing there. Helplessly. The temper slugged with drugs looked out again at me like old.

I am not a baby. I am not a little boy anymore. Sorry well, I said, off you go.

Why did you do that? Humiliate him? I didn't. Did you not? He doesn't know where he is. He does. Does not and pretending won't help. You're a rare bitch when you want, you know that? Oh I know.

That night long night. Every rake of me sore. Raw. Hum good-night to you and you.

Good-night. That is all.

We are assembled. They come. They are ready for at last. Two and three of them. Leaning on the wall. Suck my cheeks in try to know what they'll say. Float it in the ether. I'll catch it by the ears and make it what I want to hear. This resurrection impossible cure. Go on. Maybe. No. I don't think.

Hmmm, they say now it's not good. Oh. It's not so good as we had hoped they say shifting by the curtains. Maybe hope to get out quick. I giving the quiet eyeball to them and the one giving his pen click click. I'd like to turn the sound down. Watch like they're silent TV. Would they manage to play this game? Not for you and me. Game for them.

Her sitting dead white in the corner. Don't think. Do doctors think of running off down the corridor? Slip. See nurse's bottoms patients drips go fly by. Run off til they can be Jesus in a quiet place. Placid. Raising girls up from the dead. The magic touch.

Concentrate. I feel sorry for this one. No who cares about them. They're caring they should be. Clipboard and sweat sitting his lip.

Hmmm, yes it is not so good. We think it's spread too far into the brain. What? We can't operate. For consequences. For the sake of a month. Or two. So his little chart is saying you exit now. Here you are. Afraid. Going down to death. It sounds like not much fun to me to hear my voice going wilter going vicious in my throat. What nothing can be done? You're settled in it just like that? No say no. We'll chemo it a little bit see what that can do. Might shrink. Might move it away. See what that was like. What? You never know. So what's the time scale? The big? Maybe. I'm sorry. Perhaps about a year.

And the blender go off inside me suck my heart lungs my brains in. Rip my stomach out. They mean it and this time. It's true. I looked at you. And you seem to me your eyes are glitching off and on. Are absent. I can tell. I can tell you have somehow not heard that bit. She gulping softly at the air. I think to her face please hold her in. For now. For a while. Until I'm able pick her up again.

The doctors doing telling do not take a note. For them death is always a matter of. Quiet. Fuck you. I do not say. Only going really yes? No. No. No. Burrow rat hungry in my voice. Chewing the arteries. Chew at the ventricles. Readying to turn me inside out. Clipping clopping behind their boards they see. The state of us. On the block. We present. If you can just be calm and I know it's a shock. I. Blood going racing round me.

Exploding through valves. Knocking my heart out of its whack. Going red and green before my retinas. Says doctor sit down. I do. We'll stunt its progress and get back some time. Some what? We will see what we can do. Vault my brain. It. Going over months. Enough time for. For everything? You look at me. Simple and sure I know what's to be done. Doctors. Thank you I say. Don't say anymore. I'll. I'll say it. When the right time comes.

In the aftermath we sit and rock. Sitting open hand in

the chair. Let what sunlight is come in. It must do surely. Keep on shining today and today and today. Going round the earth and all those places. It must. It has all my. All my life spreading now like a stain in front has not got me ready for the end of you. If I could lift this moment out of time. Rip it. Go back go back. Once. Please. Not for you this. Not for you. Your life must be a different thing. Not to face this. Not go through. Not be afraid in the dark of it coming on. Not see it between the slits in your eyes. But I. What did he say? Says you Did he say I could go home soon, now I'm alright? There he did. Yes he. Why don't you have a little sleep? That's right. Go on. Have a little snooze. You'll be fine. You'll be fine.

But on the outside I'd be running til my heart burst out. Walking through the gardens.

Storming through the trees. I'd rip their leaves off heads off if I could. I would flee the place and abandon ship. I would tear my eyes out nails out. Just. To stop. Just to stop it going in me, what I know. What I know. Will happen. Will come now. Soon. Get it.

There's no way for this. Not a single way. Out.

She praying praying. I'll leave her on her knees for good. Forever if she wants. If she likes to. Just leave her there. She knows the way. The truth the light of this? Does she?

Good for her and. Fuck me, I say.

I called him then in the hospital foyer. The want of like string on my hands. I. Phone pissing money coin p's away. Is that you? Then. Christ why are you calling me? he says. But. Pip by pip pip. I. Tell me what's wrong? Please come and save me please pull me from. What? Ten p's to p's pounds. My brother's going to die. He what? Clicks. Please save me.

Speak up I can't quite. Hang on. Hang on. I shovel them in struggling thick tears off my muck impure skin but. Purely too, beg. Please? I can't hear speak up.

Against that I give way. Against that I go under and he seems so suddenly. Far down the line. Besides what he could say with one eye on the kitchen? I think Do you love me? I say Is she there? She's not at the moment. It'll be. Fine he says. How can he tell? Can he see all about me patients miracling well? Are they picking up their beds to walk after touching which hems that made them whole? Let them. I wish you could. Or let them die. Hello? Are you still there? His voice tiny diamond cutting strips out of air. I want that to swim in, not pestilent here. I want us to sin so I may survive this, so I may hold onto my bandage of self if I can if I need. I'll come he says I. Just tell your fucking wife her nephew's going to die.

Get you hot chocolate her cup of tea. Don't burn your mouth on that. And listen to thee do we cry poor banished children of eve. To thee do we send up our sighs mourning and weeping in this valley of tears. I let what he said go over in me. It will be alright. It all will be. I think by keeping very still I'll stop time in its tracks. He can draw the poison out. He is talisman in that.

And in the hotel saying I need to go back up. Just a few days. Alright dear my pet. You go on there's not much for you to do. You're sure? I'm sure, we'll see you soon.

3

In the waves. I am in the waves by the city in the sea. I've
come out. To be in the cold. To see again for a long way off.
Out there somewhere is. New York. What if I could go? It
would be so. So far I cannot even see. Not from where I am.
Towers or taxis. What would I be there? I'd be free or. Looking from very far back to this beach. I baptize. Baptize me.
That I take. For I can't complain it's wrong. Free me clean
me and save me from. My brother from this. I have to. I still
have to go home.

I did. Quiet. All that house. Like the dust mites were noisy
like the rooks in the trees made more sound than you can
bear. Your ears tuning the volume like that she says. Whisper. Walk about balls of our feet. How are you, hey? How do
you feel? Good not too bad. Everything's loud. I think they
cleaned wax out my ears Mammy isn't that right? It is love
it is. It'll settle down. A week or two. I'll be back to work
you say soon. Stacking. They always need me. Always phon-
ing asking where I've been, isn't that right Mammy? Ah. Yes
love. And what else you been doing? I went to the hospital
I hit my head. Yes I saw you there remember? No. Mammy

she wasn't there was she? No love. Don't upset yourself have a little lie-down. What? I don't understand this wavelength at first view. He doesn't really remember she says Sometimes one day from the next so don't say. I see. I understand. They start the chemo next week and everything'll be grand. Will it? It will the Lord's told me so. I see but the doctors. And what would they know? He survived with the good grace of God before. But. Don't start with me. Have faith that's all I want. Yes Mammy. I understand. Make your life a prayerful one and he will answer. But I. That's all. Yes Mammy. Trawl through this while then go back where I came.

No sign of him. Oh God. And then. She says there's a message for you on the answer machine a bit weird, I don't know him. Some guy you done? Feed the tape. Listen over again and again. Hissing. Hello? I don't know if this is you. I'm going to be over this weekend. Hello? Shall I come? Are you there? I hope you are. Do you even live here? This wasn't the number you gave me. I had to. Never mind. I don't know if. Anyway call if you want. The hotel is tick tick tick.

Who's that? Someone special? Never mind. Oh now now aren't we the quiet type.

Sounds a bit old for you. Shut up. This not like that.

I don't know. Swallow it. And in this time. Is this the thing. In my mind. Shall? I do. No I'm not. But then. But then. I call him in his room. Hotel. And I say are you there? Is that you? Yes. What do you want me to? I. I want you to come to the flat.

I say my uncle's in town. Oh right. He's going to come over for a while. That'll be nice, to meet your family. Can't believe I never have. I won't breathe that. I won't breathe this. The shape of what's coming inside my mouth. Like rats.

Like scum. But I swallow for I am waiting just for him. Think this has been years and years. I don't know. Maybe shouldn't do it. How can I ask up prayers when. Look will you stay for a drink? Okay. For there's one part now thinking I should not at all.

And I let her even open the door. He is surprised by that. Hello. Hello have I come to the wrong flat? I share with your niece. Nice to meet. And. I stand just out of his sight. Is she here? Sitting room, go on in. And. He is so white. Threads there under his skin. Blue twists I could trace. Hello. How are you? I'd kiss him but. She says. You know, I can't stay. But. No. That party I forgot. Sorry to love and leave you.

She get her coat and leave me high and dry. Desert us to each other. Uncle and I and.

My fillet self. Full with marks of going wrong. Bang she shut our door behind and. We are quiet in this full room.

Do you want a drink? Yes he says. I'm glad to see you how's your brother? Going to be fine I hope. I. Sorry I didn't call before I. Didn't know what to do.

God his face like a pattern I have seen. Worked my way round with biros and felt-tip pens. Since I was younger. Since I was. Thirteen. I don't remember. Just.

I'm glad to see you is what I say. Something. I know. He will take me somewhere.

Will I make him? Come into me. Come into my house. Come in and stop all of the clocks for he can for he can and I know that. Give me a moment. Give me time.

I wanted you to come I say. My My My brother. I needed to. I close to cry. He says stop. I'm here now. Put my hand on his face. Put my hand in his hair I pull it. Pull to almost out he saying there leave it calm down stop. I'm here. Come for you. Dig his thumb in my sides. Fingers for claws. In my. I called you. I said. Where were you? For. What? This. He pull up my skirt. Put his hand between my legs. Well I'm here doing what you want. Put yourself on me then, in me. Pull all other things out. It's no interest to me and. Throw me. Smash that all up. Do whatever you want. The answer to every single question is Fuck. Stitching up my eyes and sewing up my lips. Will you do that? Say.

That. Do that. To me. Yes. Fuck. Yes. Help me. Save me from all this.

And he kiss me all over like I am alive. Take me stitch by stitch. Off. As though he knew and unwound it. All the flesh dirtied and tightly wrapped. Stinking smothered by life by. Encased where there's no need to breathe to think. All his body I cannot see.

Forced inside me. Clamp on me like armor was made of steel. I remember. Where the air is. Where is the air? We. The right word. At godforsaken last I am not on my. Stuck up alone somewhere. Go on. In me. Passing me going. He. Hurt. Somewhere beyond my tight chest my tight teeth my tight lungs my tight brain crunch my blood knowing where to go my heart stopping when it can let it go by. Have him. Do. And I give him. Such a wide space to fill. Such a great white and empty room. I am. Such a mess of blood and shame. I'll be killed by this. Perhaps not struck down. Don't believe don't believe with him inside me. Where I am? I don't believe anymore. Just. I'll walk out from this. Most awful sin and it won't make a change knock a beat from my heart. Go away. Go away thought. Him. I want you. There is something. I say Don't leave me alone. There is something going on in my. Please don't stop I say and again. Til I am hurt or I am sick. Keep going until I. Then you can let me die.

. . .

Morning is my worst. The bit of any time. Coming numb from sleep. And know again the world's happening. Tongue in my teeth and body of smells. Things in this day are happening to you. I thought of you. Of you. Of your waking-up eyes thinking what's today what's going on? And him sleeping on me. Crush. That face in my elbow. He in my bed. Well that's the first time we did it not standing up ha. Sssh don't say. I feel his body now like weights under water. Drag me down. I want. If I could be dead if I could be cut or broken up pushed underneath something feel my skin strip off. I would. Better. Must be better. I must be here. I should know. And what there is I must do. Living. Is something. Is somewhere. This man. I want. Something. Plunge from a cliff. Drag me backwards I must. I am so wrong. But. It's all the same. Go on go on you can go on.

By the afternoon when now he has his clothes on coffee drank. You know these are my eyes and you can look at them he says. Toast? It is a quiet and worse lie than I have ever told I say. Don't think about it. Never go anywhere near that. Put his hand inside my thighs. And don't mention him your name for here is not the place for that. When I am fucked and hurt. Where I go with my eyes wide. Shut. Open. It's all the same. Idle.

Smoking should you do that why because never mind me. And even if his daughters don't deserve. Look at their faces in my head. I don't. I do not. My aunt. Well to her anyhow.

Because this time I have got what I want. I would never ask for him to tell. He says lie down. I. He says Again.

In the evening when he can kiss me with all his tongue. With the parts of him that are quiet now. I am evened. I am done for this for this while now. He says he's got an evening flight. He is going home to my aunt. To his children. That his time's up. His time's up now. Thanks for I say. Kiss me. Everything. I'll talk to you soon. Good-bye then. Good-bye. Look what's done's done he says. Yes. Say hello to my aunt for me.

Don't. That the phone rings. That's my mother for me. Well I'll. Close the door when you are gone. I. He says. I don't know. Saying good-bye. Take care of yourself. Hello Mammy? Yes I met him for a cup of tea. Yes. For my number. He said. No I hadn't seen him since the funeral. He's looking well.

So what was that then with your uncle she says. He's just over on business now and then. Right. What? Well. The state you were in like he's you oh I see. What? After the funeral. And? Don't bullshit me. I. That stuff. I'd smell it a mile away. Funny families. Don't know what. Father's or mother's brother? Uncle-in-law. Well at least it's not that mortal sin. Ha ha. Shut up. He's worried about my brother. Pound. Bruise my lips while I tell this lie. Whatever you say but I know. What? There's something there. He's just someone to talk to. You can talk to me. I don't know what I'm doing do you? I say. What? What's all this, you and me and all the fucking and going mad I don't know its own reason or the point. What? These things. It's not right. It's normal. I'm so. There now. Sit down. Don't be upsetting yourself don't cry. I have to. It's alright. Get something out of me.

That night we're hunting. Pub to pub. Drink up that. Do you feel? Better now. Better than before. And some nice young man's mouth some nice young man's hands up my skirt in the toilets open up my thighs. Mind. All my life is hassle and all of this is fine. Singing toora loora, toora loora lay.

4

I come down to see you again. So now I'm come down every weekend. Do you want to go for a walk with me? Think you still can. And maybe fresh air as they say will do you good. Yes. But we go slowly and you rest on my arm. What if we were young, were small again? And if all this wasn't to be, what'd we be then? What I'd be. What I'd do. You say Mammy's making a novena. She says it never fails it never fails in reasons like this when asked with a pure soul. I am tired. Too full of stuff I've done. Where my legs hurt where my scalp hurts. I'll not fight the thing inside me anymore. Let it eat me up. Please God. I want it to.

You are saying doesn't it look like a when we were little day? High sky and snackish air. It does. We walk so slow for you. Hey look I say, what about that? Will you look at that? What? Up there. See where I'm pointing at. A load of ducks I see them. No. Geese. Swans. Yes. Honking. I like that. V over me. V off to some reservoir I say. To the lake.

Sure we'll see them when we get there. Fat bellies on them. Full of crusts and slugs do they eat them? I don't know. I'd say I would. Pâté they are for birds. Especially ones that swim. Not slimy like fish. Juicy. Escargot for them. Blather makes you laugh. I like. No snail shells. Not much fun that with a beak. Shards up your gob. Hurts. Did you ever think of it? No you say. I like them flying over a city but if one fell down. Going up to a reservoir or up a canal. I saw a dead one there once. Maybe it did just fall. Whack. That'd give you a quare crack on the head. Swanned to death. Do you know big restaurants serve them? For money you can hit them with a stone. Drag them back there. Swan's tongue.

On a big white plate. Full of grease and muck and shite. Disgusting. I wouldn't eat out of those canals. Scabies waiting to hop on you. Yum you say. Hundreds of pounds' worth of muck swan on your plate. Slurp it. Imagine, is that a wiggly bit there in the meat? It loves slugs you know. Imagine that. A diet of slugs can make you fly. Do you like them? You should try it. I'll make it for your tea. Do you still see them flying there? I do I do. Well they've gone off now. I hope no one will kill them tonight. Yes. Me too. Are you alright? I'm alright. Good.

Sting me to the bones to see you this way. To see you. There is nothing to say for the jaws shut tight when I'm alone. Will we all get better? Will we all be fine? Father in heaven. Father up above. I don't want my brother to die.

The telephone rings. I'm over next week will I come? I won't cry off. Just for this weekend this once and won't do it ever again. Gets the smell of me. I know. Even I can tell. The smell that I will always do whatever it is he wants because. Come I say.

I've missed you. Think about you all the time. Fill me over with. Stuff. In my ear. In my head. How's your brother? Here's some money. Thanks. Your aunt says hello. Oh? She says she might be over next time. With you? Me. Ha. To see your mother. Is she? Lend a hand. Isn't that great. Lend me yours he. I give it. Put it in his pants. Jesus. Jesus he says. Curl over me. And you're worried I'll tell? No. That you fuck me. She'd want to. Like to know I'd say. No. I'd tell her. Shut your mouth. This time I would. You won't. Won't I. Good to spill his cup. He hurt my arms. You open your legs. I. I've haven't stopped thinking about you for a moment he says. Shame I didn't think of you at all. Do it. Not until. What? You hurt me. He pull by the hair. How you like it? Does that hurt? No. Then what? I want. Words drown like water. Make me know what you mean. What? When you miss me. What words are when. Get. Jesus. Over. He goes somewhere else inside. Does that hurt? Yes. A lot. A lot and relieves me for a while.

There was someone on the phone was saying it's like fingers through his brain. Was it our mother, probably was, saying how chemo ordered administered make you puke like mad. They said though like fingers breaking down. Like fingers starting to bleed. I said it was an old one but. I told them it's not new. Mammy I. Because God you see. I would never survive. He wouldn't ask that of. He wouldn't ask me that. But I know we must wait a few weeks then scan. To see it all it will be peeled back.

For we're dangling by our ankles. When will I you she fall in? Think I'll spend my time going again. Home. Back there. Trains passing like teeth through my head.

Home. Knock knock. Well now, says the man, we came to lend our support. The ministry missionary fellowship. On the doorstep but right in my eyes. Praise the Lord praise the Lord above. We're not Christians you know, that way. The way like you are I say. We're Catholics. Yes but we heard about your brother? Brother. We heard of you and know you'll want to hear the good good news. Oh whatsit? Jesus loves you. Right enough and so and is there some more better news than that? The best news. See, the best news you will ever hear. I doubt. Don't think that's true I think chemo worked or miracle cure could be better even than that. Now see that's where you're wrong for only Christ saves. From above. From up the clouds where heaven is right? And the kingdom of heaven will come again. I don't think so sorry afraid don't agree with that. That's the problem. Why he's dying. You see the devil got in. What? In your house. Don't think that's true. Down the chimney, up the plug hole did he how did he get in? He's inside you he's around you and he'll drag you down. To the pit. I well know it. And your family too and is your father dead I heard he was. See see see? No. Wages of a Godless life. What do you know? Jesus loves you and he wants into your life. Let him come on in if he wants to. That's the wrong attitude to take. Invite him into your heart and soul. He was whipped and bled and beat for you, for you and all your grievous sins. Was he now, is that so? It is and so now so there. Did I ask him? Did I want it? Was that ever what I said slice yourself up so many years ago for me for ever for what I've done? Indeed indeed sharper than a serpent's tooth thankless child. You're Jesus's child. I am not. You are. Just let him in. Off the doorstep now I know enough's enough. So you're content to let your brother die?

What? For your pride and for your wrongs. He's cancer. But. There is no devil here. No Satan Christ in any manner. Crucifix to bow before. Figurines to kiss now. Get out. You need to get off this step. I don't want your sort round here.

Poisoned. Well God forgive you. And he can shove it. And damn you. He will. You too. Bastards. Showers of shite attend your every waking shitting prayer. So there so there so there so there. Bang the door on them that hard I'd shatter glass. Christians go and shite.

Do you know what's that was, you saying limping up the hallway. Born again. Not again. What? Yes you say, I think I'm getting too sick of this. When are they? They're here all the time. Yes? Saying prayers you know and lay on hands. I don't. Yes. I don't like that much. Sometimes. Too much I get. I get. Scared. Of die of dying of go to hell. She. For God's sake what's in her mind I don't. You're not going anywhere. At all.

Understand me. Listen. Don't believe that all. That nonsense rubbish crap it is. They're eejits. And I say, you'll be fine. You'll be fine.

And that day. Later on. I sit. With my feet tucked. Read some the book. Hear you listen. I think what's going on? Hear you, something, thinking what's. Oh God. Oh God. That retch. Ripping-out noise. I run up the stairs to you. Falling over the toilet you a miss all. On and on. See that now from the doorway. You hold the wall. Shake. The pool of it the force of it til I thought blood would come out. Your nose or out your mouth. Come out with organs swimming in it pool of sick I held your head oh help me over it. Across the toilet kneeling stroke your head go on go on I thought of him. Uncle. What. Want him to do it. Stop. Pierce me. There there. Lance the. And again. Take me save me from this as if. It's alright it's alright. He'd hear me there. Now. He'd know but he can't. Stop. How could. That's it. Get it all out you can. Must. I can't. Bear this. It is. So. There now there.

I put you to bed after that. Rinse out your mouth and spit. Tuck. Lie there. Getting your breath. Sorry. It's fine. There now there there. Calm. But. Again. Again. You. Can't be. Must not. Not again. What's left? You're falling off the bed. The rush. Help. Where's Mammy? It feels you could be dead. Of this. Of sicking one more time. Out at the novena. The rosary. Mass. At the first fucking Friday of Lent. The holy hour. The exposition of the blessed sacrament. God. Help me. You are you are. So bad. Just retching retching on my hands my clothes skirt it come out more than I think I would believe. The much of it stench coming back out more and more. Sorry I'm sorry sorry you said. I say it's fine it's fine don't hurt yourself. Try not to. You can't. Thinking oh my God what have I done? Not a little thing. Think of that. Not a thing. For the chemo's working so you must be sick. Good. It makes sense it makes sense of course it does. But. God oh god oh god oh god. You are you are. He is he is. Going to be fine. I wipe your face off. I want. The sick off your face your hands. Change the bedsheets empty that bowl. There now.

Lie now. Do you think you can lie down? Yes. Think it all could start again. Make the phone call. Shut up. But not this time. Now you're lying back. Give you a small cube of ice. Just suck a little of it and relax. That's alright. You're fine. You're grand.

You're sleeping breathe like a baby that has cried. Shiver of it. Shiver of your lungs.

And I'm watching. Hoping you'll be. Well. But don't think. Don't think you. Will yes you will. You'll be fine. I need to get out of this house. Sometime. Soon. For it's coming and good uncle's not here to. Stick it in. Don't. Not for this, this time my greatest fuck you daddy father in my need. Not. Shut. Emerge. Will someone help me? In time. In. Time.

Pray. Jesus. Please love me again. No one will. I wait and pick my fingers until she comes home.

And where have you been? Been with Christ. Jesus. Talking. Your brother will be fine. Christ Mammy. Ah. You'd do well. No. Right. Now Mammy I've got to go out now. Need a little break. Just. He was so ill. A little breather. Down the pub. I don't. Yes I gave. One two friends. A lie. A call. Well. See you later and don't wait up.

I go down and out alright. It's dark here and it is night. Orange streetlights. I know my way. For all the time past nothing's changed. I know the way. Know it. Know the way. Pinder ponder. It's a blister. I shall pop. Think. Buy me a drink. Help the medicine go. But. No keep going straight. I know the way. That road. Up that road and in. The quiet trees. The dark. I know what. I know where I come where I have been before. Before. What. This. When I was. I am. Young. Hello there you. Remember me. Lake. Rushes. Remember. Catch the wind. And I remember that and that. The lights move. Focus. Catch it. Focus down. Rip. I remember someone. Where they go. Where I went. Here. Here.

Someone burst me. Rendered me. Here. Scratched. Here. Keep me up. Aware. I am living. I am near. Is there someone? I'll find them where.

And do. In the thicket. The bushes. The hedge. Say. Just as though they always were. Probably. They are. Waiting I see just for. Come in fall among them. Not much said. Not much hellos. They are young. They are old. They know. They're thinking. Just the same. Sitting. Drinking. Vodka mouths for. Come and join us. Hey you sit down. I do. Fall that. At the edge. Thinking I'll go in. Just let them see me here first. And so much chitchat about football. Racing and

RTÉ. The fine. Always this. Is normal here. For me. The cold. That talking settles well. Fine for. And someone's leg. Thinking take that. Have it. For your own. Some man. Some person. What it matters. It's a damp night. For we're here and all the same. We're soft we're hard we're going down. True and I do.

He gets me. Hello Missy. By the wrist and it can hurt. Take me to the bushes. They don't care. Ra ra ra. The night's begun someone sings. Shut up. Haven't seen you before. I don't care. I'm here for. Kiss me slobbly. Let him do it. Wet and tongue. Lick the.

Squeeze me. Ah fine fuck fine. Something. Different and all that. Sliding. Variety's the spice of life. Go on get on with it. Part your legs missy please. That's all that we can do hey yes. Yes? Spits on his hand. Do. Grease himself. You fucking miss. Now. Ffffff. Open wide. There we go now hey. That. There we go. Ah. Sssss that. Come. Go on you fucking. Not. Ah. Something. Fun for everyone. There's it. That's it. Fucking. For a laugh. Ow I say. Ah ha ha ha. All this until blah blah he comes. My head bouncing nod nod on his shoulder. Off the bone.

After. Sore and used up. Is the way. Is the best thing you'd be if you were me. For you'd like that that solid feeling. On the ground. Full of stones like eating after fasts. Pull my knickers up. Tight. Go on rinse yourself he says. Where the loonies go. See a dead one. Gotcha. Ha ha. Go on slap it up you up your crack. Fish shit in you. Will you ever fuck off you cunt I say. Well. Seeya fuck you later. No. Fuck you very much. Ha Ha.

Go off. Leave me on the lake. Lapping like a shore. Reach for. Wash now. Reach. I can't. Touch. It. Ocean water puddle lake. Now. Put back my face. This is the last time here.

I went home. On the stones. In the pale moonlight. Nothing in or by my side. Full my mouth swelled. His guck between my legs. His. Horrible. Even better if it run down.

Skanky. Laughs. This is the way I'd like to be. If I had a chance. To start again. I wouldn't. I'd do this. I would. But every day. Every day.

Red lights red lights one two three turn the lock and turn the key red lights.

I look in at you sleeping. I have never been away. She asleep too. Praying. Bible at her head. And I get into bed when I've washed my thighs. Whisper. I. Thank God. For you. For it. Tonight. Amen.

5

These journeys. These train journeys they are always going on. What I. Am I doing? Rolling over the country. I'll give up going soon. Where? Here or back or. Enough. Thankless pointless things I'll learn. To. But. Like it matters now who inspired who and who. Fuck that I don't. Care. I. And your other one. Stupid cow out running friend. Drive my head round the bend with all the oh my life has troubles too. But I better do, have got to. Just stop see and cut the cord the thread with this life and I'll be alright. Give it up, uncle up, that's the way. No. And it sounds easy. It sounds not. But what I want. Not to be this. Ripped. Ah I see. Not. To. Do. This. Any. More. What. Nothing I don't do a thing.

Few fucks here and then and who's that to do with? No one but myself. See. See. In the future I'll decide. If I must go home. For good. If I. But now. But now. I'm doing fine. Like you. I'm. Doing. Fine.

Bring bring

He looks at me. Wonders what this is but I'm. I say. I can't wait for you anymore. Hands. Mouth. Take me backwards into that dark room. His. He rip me open and hurt because I say though I don't want, he beg. No that's all I ask. And take for yourself. Whatever. You. Want. Because I know there's not much left. When he kisses. I am. Strangle. And he pushes me down. Something flooding. My face my hands with. I. It's you I want he says not all this shit. Fuck that. Just hit me on the face. No. Then get off. Get fucking off.

Alright slaps my face. That's all I'll manage. Some more than. Please. Take off my clothes. Stand in front I of him bare. Isn't it just like what you did to me when I was thirteen? Didn't you like that, when you hurt me then? Don't. More. He hits hard. I say don't be done. Don't be done. I don't want this he says I don't want. Just til my nose bleeds and that will be enough. So he hits til I fall over. Crushing under. Hits again. He hits til something's click and the blood begins to run. Jesus he says. I feel sick. But I'm rush with feeling. Wide and. He thinks he's bad when he fucks me now. And so he is. I'm better though. In fact I am almost best.

After he says my little girl my little come here to me. Kiss me. Sore face. Wipe my nose. There. What the fuck? I can't say no. I can't say no when I'm with you he says. I feel the penis on my leg. Ever he keeps me under. Sleeps on top of naked. But my guts are free.

What the fuck is wrong with you? Morning after pull my hair. Look at your face.

Look at the state of your face. You want that done to you? Why do you want that done? Didn't stop you I say. He says I didn't want. I did not want to do that. Kiss the bruise on my cheek. Bruise on my eyebrow. Beautiful beautiful thing. This is the closest thing to love.

Jesus Christ oh Jesus Christ she says. Oh Jesus what happened your face? Did someone beat you up? Were you mugged? Fucking hell. No. She smokes mad now. Drop ash on the table on the carpet. Did he do that to you? Did he? Did he do that? He's not coming here again, you hear and don't you ever ask. I don't care close the door in her face.

I stand corrected at the edge of the street. I stick my face out in the wind. Bursts of air-condition heat groaning up the sky. Faraway jets above. I know where they'll fly. If I was on I would. Go like that. Outside my door I walk under the scaffold. Not the same as ladder. But bless myself all the same. I didn't for a long time and look what happened then? No what happened you isn't all my.

In the mornings after he came. I couldn't do. Did once or twice go hunt with her. Just lighten up she says. But fun's gone out of that I'm lost. In the deep sea. In as the saying goes over my head with what. With what. Salt on the brain. I have done. Do think of you. All the time. When he is here. When's he coming again?

He says he is. Not here he can't. It's not your flat. I'm not going out and I'll call the guards. I asked him to. That's worse. You are fucked up in the head. Do you hear me? I'm not going to sit and hear you beaten to shite. Muster all I can. I can do what I can do if I want. I don't know what to say. I have to do this for. For. For. What? You're not the only one with problems. So wrapped up in yourself in your brother and your uncle and fucking weird fucking. All that stuff gone on with him. I. Don't judge me or I'll judge you. It's very sad and all and I wish it wasn't happening but fuck me you're not the center of the world. And I'm not helping you get fucked up more. Shut up. Shut up. Shut up.

I could rove through the flat for days not look see her if I could. I would. Do that. Get up. Get out. Out of her way of her hair. Fuck her everyone. Fuck them all for I'm being buried right here on my own. I say to him. That's it. Don't come, I think, anymore. Just come to my hotel once? No. I think. I think I'll not. But. I shouldn't do this it makes me. Something. Bye.

And I go down again always going back down. To home to you. Is well.

Ringing and ringing. Go on and on get that phone. Get that you says Mammy. Don't want to talk she says. I'm going I'm going. Hello. Who? I see. No my mother no. She doesn't want. No. You better talk to me. It's fine. Close the door. I'm. Yes. Sitting down.

You know we took the scan again last week the doctor says. Yes? I've the results here. Think I don't want to do this. There's a long way. Down this phone. This line. And I see him. Clicking. Looking at his does he see it through the light like x-rays? Scans. Like scans. Hiss myself concentrate. Now be calm.

Your brother. Yes? It's four months since chemo began. And yes. That's right. Will you get on. I can't. Fathom. As you know now we know what. What? We're dealing with. And to come. And that's? Ahem. What I'm saying. Listen. What I'm sorry to tell you. No. No. It's continued to grow. No. I'm sorry. But you said you would. Cut it back hedges weeds like grass? It's not working and what I'm saying is, it's a matter of time. He'll. He's going to die? My brother? I don't think that's right. We did what we could. We were trying for time. Time and that's all we have managed. No. I'm so sorry to have to tell you this. So. Can you say how long? Two months three if the. What? Going's good. Jesus not that. You said. He might.

With the all the things they can do. Remember? Sorry I'm so sorry. No you. God. That's not enough. Not. For him. Please calm yourself. I'm. Gasp at. Stop it. Is there anything you want to ask? Voices is all I have over a phone. I'm sorry I say will you tell me more? He shouldn't have any pain. He'll just fall asleep. Sleeping. Oh. My brother. This doesn't make. Doesn't isn't t t t sense sense sense to me. No. He'll be confused. Some of the time. Afraid? I don't know. If you. Oh God it's up to me to tell. My brother. I'm so sorry. Shall I go on? But. Ye. Yes. My my my brother but I think I see understand. He's slipping right, just out of the world. In a. Yes. In a way. Yes that's true. So I'll hold him as if. He's falling. Yes. He's going. Yes. He's already nearly gone. He is. I under. Understand.

Perhaps contact your hospice? No. We'll keep him. Me my mother. We. Will. Take care of him. Here. He won't. Let him be somewhere on his own. In the dark. He's a little boy. He's. Well then keep him home long as you can. I. Will. Thank you. Doctor for. Say. That's a. I know. Bye then.

My head. My head in hands in my feet in my jaws roaring blood I can't. Fine. Cold and fine. With our. With our. It'll be fine well. Knocking tat the door she is. Comes in and listens to what I say. Impart the. He's dying. The tumor. That living thing. It's kept growing on the chemo over it. Bastard it. In his head and. Shhh he's sleeping she says.

Mammy. No. Let's sit down. Bow our our. Intercede. No. Implored thy intercession was left unaided. Fly unto thee oh virgin of virgins my mother. To thee do we come. Before thee we stand sinful and sorrowful. No. Mother of the word incarnate despise not my pet. My pet. Ition. You listen to me. It's me. You. Listen to me. Mammy. For once.

One time. But graciously hear and answer us. Scream at. Do you hear me? Me. Me. Something awful's going to.

You can't believe it away. She is fever nibbling saying Do not be afraid I will save you I have called you by. What. Called you by what? I. Aye. Hi. Hello in there. Name. Jesus. Listen to what I've. Got. To. Say. I bless and cross in ainm an Athar agus an Mhic agus Spioraid Naoimh. Amen. Amen. He's going to die. Don't say that. Don't tell him. He'll give up. He'll lose his. Faith and then we're really done. Done. Really. Really. Is that that? What faith does he have? And are you thinking that? That?

Yes. You. Are. A. Fool. A fool in Christ. Shut up. Faith won't save him. The Lord. Shut the fuck with that. Langu. Stop it. He's a right to know. I'm his mother I forbid. He has a right to know he's going to die. Then let it be on your head. Let it be on you. If you he dies let it be on you. Mammy. Don't tell. Mammy. You heard what I said.

I'm soon. I don't look at you. I'm going home. Here. Up there. For a while. Need a. Think of. O. Kay. Okay. Have to rub it out off me. And I'll. Yes. I'll let you know. What? What's the thing. Mammy. The anything I can do about this.

I walk the street. City. Running through my mouth. Running in my teeth the. My eyes are. All the things. The said the done what there what's all this? That stuff. I could do. My. I walk the street. Who's him? That man. Who's him there having a looking at me he. Look at my. Tits. Ssss. Fuck word. No don't. Fuck that. No. Will. Not that. Not. That. But. If I want to then I can do. And it would fill me up fine. And I. I do. Do it. Take him back with me. Give him. The word. I want that. Hurt me. Until I am outside pain.

But I am ready soon after to take the. Walk back across the waves. Plunge. Say to her, friend, lookit well. I can't stay.

They need me you see need me. Home. So I have to go and put all those things down. The toys you see. Learning. Reading. Ranting the town. Fuck. You and me. Do you know all that's done now. All that doing going mad and like and it was. It was. Well whatever you want she says. Pay your rent up I'll get someone else in. Yep. I did. So. That's that then. Hope your brother gets well. Yes. Sure I'll probably see you around in the spring or what. I'll see you. Bye bye then. Oh I forgot to say. Your uncle called. Call.

He says. Thank God. Be quiet I say close your eyes. Open your fly. Just do it in your mind can't you. I want. To be able to now. So much. I can't. I want. My brother. Fucking where are you for me Fuck I. Sorry, he says Your aunt's just arrived but I. Good for. Good fuck for you I hope she dies. Don't hang up. I hope you die. Sssssss. Sorr. Fuck you. Fuck me too.
    I know. I'll lock the door and leave it behind. See that there. I'll leave it in the room in the bed and under those clothes. Hump. For I'm grown up and I don't need those childish. Those. I'll take them with me won't. No. That's the end of the end of that and I won't be seeing doing. Fucking. No more. No fucking much. My family. Need me. Shut your legs. I won't be. I won't anymore.

It's the train again. That train again and I am in. Safe. See that. Me. Me. Me. With my bags sitting pack on pack beneath. On my feet. Hem me. Pin me. Nail me in. And I left none behind. Looking out on it. See you city. I see you. My land love. City going. Out. On and on. That's the one I made. I went in. It was me my home. As. I don't know. I think. I did it. There. I liked. Thinking. That. I went in. All the way. Up to my hilt. My pelt. Leaving all it now. What's before what's before. Me. Spreading out like muck like shite. The future coming panic. And vibrating. Going somewhere in my brain. In my neck. Thump thump. The thing. Oh no. Oh not that. It is. And I know when those lights go turn on. You. Try to think of you. Think of your brother. Given fucking up for Lent. But I've done enough to know that. When it's coming. Itch will come. I can't. Squirming but panic this like I don't. I. Need. Someone. Catch out. Do I know not what I do. No and so. There now. There now. No good. Climb it. Comes for me. And I look up. Feel the wound going in. I did not. Not here. Expect.

I look about me see some man. Some sandwich quiet curly hair. Dip biscuit mild and not prepared for anything like that I cough. Cough to him. For I could choke. No I could choke and he might think look. The sweet the nasty. Thing. I am. Perfect. Ploy. Who can resist? He does not as I know. Knew. Rise his head. Oh God are you? Come beating on my back with the flat palm of his hand. Your arms up. He my aid. Try drink this that's it. Are you. Alright there now are you alright and fluster me fluster my hands. I put. On to his hands. Shall we begin at the beginning here. What I set myself to do. Don't. Too late miss too late for you. Oh thanks and thank you saved my life. The web and stick of it. I reel it reel him. Draw him over. For I can hardly breathe. You want. I want. Let him in. How do I know that, I do. I. It will conclude. This way. One way. Come.

Something in the toilets. He. My God I never. Sssss don't say anymore. Hold the basin sit rattle back. Spread as can. And he in his blood way up. Obliging and obliged. Fingers up me. Filthy round the quick. And I thought that when I cleaned between my legs. Press it in me. Pewled and scared. I'd be sick but what else. It's what I have to do. And watch him bobbing. For he must do my thing. Under my skin. Keep. So I can. That's it. Sit without. Something. Screeching. No not that. Other things. All the way home.

Jiggedy jig. Is that it? Let the pus run out.

At the end he want to kiss me. I've never done anything like that. You should wash your fingers. Can I give you a ring? Sometime. Maybe I'll see you again, I won't. That makes the sick of me. Check no skirt tucked in my knickers. All sedated. Bye-bye.

I limp from rail to home. Under some raining sky. Drag the bags all with me. Hold off. It does and I get in. Home and dry. It's what. It's dark. Hello? Where the lights are. Hello? And. Are you even here? Ah there. In the kitchen. In the kitchen in the dark. Doing something on the cooker. I catch you moving slow in the the lampless in the corner of my. I'm home I'm home now. Shall I turn on the light? Yes. You are. I hug you. I am really glad that you are here. What. There you say sit down. She. Gone praying for the something. I don't know what's it this time. I thought I'd make the tea, you say, so I don't know how long she'll be. I'll help. No I'll do it you say, you say for you to me. I. Sit. See pasta I can strain like this you say. I see your hand. Shake bad. You hold the sieve. See I'll pour it out just like this I watched a program. Mind you'll. Drop it you do. Try to catch. Ow. You. It falls. And scald your hand and food go flying all around. Sliding. All the way down. I jump up. Got you. You saying I can't. Can't I don't I don't see I don't understand what's why is this. Happening. To me. To me. My brother please please oh please. Don't say it. But. I run the cold water tap. Put your hand there let me. Do this. But dinner. It's fine. Don't you care I'll wipe. I'll fix it. But I wanted you say, I thought you'd like, I'd make you dinner for when you came. I knew see you were coming today I am right today? you say. Yes. Here I am. This is today I. And you start. To cry. Like my little boy I knew. I knew. When I was younger than you. So many years ago when. You sit. You say. I'm just so tired. I'm just so ill.

I thought about it and I could not stop. All walls mohow do I changiving around inside myself topple over. I can hold. I can hold them up if I I cannot if they'll fall in. Where I stood. Where I sat. What sat on my lips and in my mouth. Sour and rank. Like I could trip inside myself. There are so many things. I moved and caught. Who are you who are you now with this slip and nightdress on. With these jeans with this bright red hat. For in that I was swimming. I can do myself. Damage. That's it if I would. Do you hear me? Is it ever time for you to understand. I meant I meant that for I never thought you could think you were low. Were lost at the moment when they cut you off. Cut your head out heart brain. It is not I know was not that but to me it was to me. Like I could have seen you in the bright of day. Like the light could have come up from the sea and take you over. Me over. Is there. Forgive that. Forgive that me that I was fallen down. That I was under the weather under the same sky and did not. Not yet. If I took. If I had taken your good right hand I might have pulled you. Up. Pulled the black sea out of us. Saw you. Left you. Is there some truth in that? I went out to the cold. Thought I'd know what to do. Bring you with me. Bring you with. Sad and sad and sad fool me slipping down. Slope hill mountainside. Muck and stones on me. On my feet and rain in my hair. I thought about it but I could not stop. Pushed it further in. Needle and syringe. This will take me out of that. Like it could. As though it might do in

any way. Forgive. Forgive me that that I didn't see. Look out
my eyes. That I didn't know what I was doing though I did
though I did. Oh do you love me. Can you love me. Do you
love me still. My sins. My grievous. Woe my wrong. I went
out to him and said do what you will if you want. If you're
able will you save me from that. I put a pillow on my face
on your face and I said suffocate. It could have been. It could
have been that. If I chose if I didn't. If I knew what I do. I
don't so by the way I'm telling you. I'm warning now what a
monster I have become. Soap in my mouth my eyes my hair
turning bitter at the smallest drop. Of the rain give me the
rain and all that. Wash oh yes that's it wash away. My. Sin. Do
you see. I can do what I can and that is that's what I can do.
Yes I've done my worst now have I yes I've done my falling
down failed but will you. Let me. Pick you up. In some way.
Just a little? These are my bits. My pieces I have dropped and
thrown along the way. The pieces that were mine. Of me. Of
my leprous hands my skin my eyes that I do not. Have not
known too much. Held. Out to you. You need. I see that.
You have fallen down. My brother. My brother and my love.
For you're the first one that I ever had. And we'll be good
as good we ever were. Gold. Children with running noses
straggly hair and cheeks all chapped and braised by the wind
by the sea. When we fell off things and chopped and cut ourselves til we thought we'd die. Of blood. Of cuts. And all our
wounds we picked at. I yours you pick mine the scab of. Itch
it. Itch it scratch til we bleed. Till the guck pours out. See it's
better now dabbling a finger in. See it's running like water
down my leg. See that. You're my brother. See that. You are
he. The one you were and I was too. All our shit for brains.
Liked that. Swallow it down. We are. You are. No. That was
me. See that all that. How great I was. Sure I was then that I

might have been. Anyone. You too. Not. I'm so talented and you're so thick. Did I say that? I don't know. Do you love me? Can you love me even after that? Even now. I won't ask and I won't say that inside myself or ever out again. Forgive me brother. I know not what I do. Forgive me brother for I have sinned. We are all the things we'll ever be. Even when I go on after that. After what is coming. Though it's happening to you. Oh bless. Me. Find a way out of this. We were not meant. I know. Meant to go wrong. How we could not. How to avoid that I can't discover. When do you think I will see you again? Do you think that I will. I will. I will. For I won't let go. Even when you're gone. Time's going onward. See it in my clock head. Ticking until you are run down. And I am frightened and I am afraid of the cold. Of the dark. Of the sea. See. I will do my best. For all I am the thing I am for what I am. For you. You. Until the ships come in, is that the right way? I don't know now. I don't know much. At all. Almost a thing. Say you love I'll say I love you. Nothing better and nothing more? It needs an answer. Doesn't. Answer me this. Do you think you're going home? For a walk or for the night? Will it be good there? Any chance you'll let me know? No. How would that be just a bad idea. Just a thing wrong. You. Us. For the meantime. In the meantime. I'll say. Hold my hand. I'll do. My. For you. My best for you. For what we should be. If you can show me all the parts that are working. And the not. Hurting or sleeping. Show me this in secret code. To fix. I'll purge it. Kill it out. I'd kill anything for you. Rabbits and rats. Wring their necks to test on. Crushing flesh. Race round the world for only once born flower buds. Once thousand years I'd press their sap on you. Stick their thorns in you. Stick moss and weeds. Dance naked in the field horse through the town. Whisper that. You are sleeping. I know. I know. That dying way. Fully with your eyes saying last time for this. Last time for that. Open them up for me. Let me see in. To pluck out. To see it. A bit more. A just a bit more before. They are blue. So. Blue as up and up beyond. But they're not bothered with a living thing. Food or children fecking loudly over football on the street. Cats meowing or my good perfume I think smells so well. Open your eyes show me what's in. I'll pull it out. I'll bite it off like all wrong stitching. All wrong thread. Do I think I am who do I think I am. What did I ever do for you. I'll do something that you want once. What. You're off. Escaping all these things. Go away a little bit now. Now and more but still and still. I'd like to say. I'd like to say. Don't. Stay here. Please. If you will. I won't. I swear. Leave you alone.

PART V

The Stolen Child

Oh God light running through the room. I know. It's supposed to be. And burn. No. Shine. This is not for me. Turn. Quiet in the morning. Through the house. I'm caught where the light comes. Where the sun comes in. Twist. Wind blankets bandage done. I hurt. And ache. For I have done. What? Nothing. Nothing at all. Turn the. Light out sound out. If I could. Wake up. I've plenty things to do. Through the nets puff breeze from a sky of blue. Hot. I don't like. For aaApril this. Or May? I don't. What? Day going. Days go. And I've been here a long long time. Weeks or years or. There's a. Something. What? Surprise. Like I've never been gone.

I did not keep my curtains closed. They're wide as anything. What for. To see. I'm in.

The house. Is here. Where you. Are you. Sleeping. Through this wall. Sleeping hard. Tight with it. Days longer sleeping all the time. I am. Working on the. I am here.

Minding.

All these motes drizzle in the sun. I should set the day. For the. I am the first up.

Know that I will be watching. Listen for every hic and cough. See you and what's that? The corner of my eye. Are you slipping are you forgetting? No that's not right because. You. Not doing anything such as die. It's a while yet. That's for a time to come. In the weeks since I am back here. I think. Praying. She's right. That's the thing. My. Brother. Same as always. Doing all the same. You don't want gravy. You don't want jam on your bread. You want the TV and play kicking

kicking games. That's good that's right I am wrong. I heard every single thing wrong. Just that I'm here is the. What? Change. They don't know everything. They can make mistakes. I know I know that's true I know I. Don't do that I. Do it. But only when I can think this way. Now I'm here and seeing you doing right all the things you've ever done. And last night. Though. You. When I heard you singing some song. Wrong. Just. Something in it. Wrong. That line that. Went up.

Went down. Don't. Not that easy when that comes. That tumor. Floating sometimes in. In dribs in. Little niggles in. Like a something. Is it? Gone in your ear. That marauder. Is yes. Is really going on.

Turn the radio on. Up. You're alright sure you're alright. I'm. Yes there's a house sat under my feet. Creaking. Wooden floor. Creaking bed I. Stretch. Remember this. My room. What? Home. And I must wake up get up look around for things to do. It's a quiet world this morning. I'll make the. Get go. Get up out of bed.

While she sleeps, while you are, while I go crack and creak upon the stairs. On the carpet that's worn out. Swirly pattern there. Shoe scrubbed. Design. Me and you on it. Sliding on it. Good for us. I make breakfast. Sit there. Coffee quiet new beginning is the boiling kettle bowl of. Bran. Flakes. Good for. Good for me. Not the cold and a pint of milk. So quiet here after the night. Birds. When you are sound a sound asleep. I won't wake you up. Just yet. Let him I think be. Sit. Think for me of the rain when I went march off to school. A long and something time ago. Sweat bus sweat piny sweat me sweat me. When we you and I were. Oh no. Young. Is the right word is it for that smell of underarms and my own hair? All grown up now all grown fuck now ssshhh or they'll hear. And pick at pasta still there stuck on the on the bit there. Draining board. When we were we were we were young. See the cloud in where it's coming. I should I'll wash and dress for. The.

That water. Smells like onions. Growing in the hot tap. Flake of scale there. Mine. Rough skin. Scalp. Hard water soap doesn't lather and shampoo going down the drain. Gully lets the cold in like an open door. Get the. Let it in. I. Quiet down. Everyone's still and don't start singing you.

I comb up my hair. I'd snap it fray strands off. What's the? Coming. I. Don't know.

What's the. Another morning and doctor. Stopped car. He's here. That's. That's him coming. Up the. Stroking rain into his pants from the bumper of her car. Right. Galvan. Answer that. Quiet or they'll hear. They'll. I'll. Don't get that but I must. Hello. You're. How are. I'm calm and kind is who I. That's. Come in he's I. And shout are you awake? The doctor's here for.

Wake up sleeping thing. The doctor's here to. What? Your head. It's fine don't worry. Put your dressing gown on. That's it. There there. Now do you know who this is? Doctor. That's right. To see you. He's. Tired. Aren't you? That's. Fine. You can. Stand up. Walk around. His foot. I see. Is. Is trailing bored behind. A little. No doctor. He had that all the time. Before. Didn't you before you were sick at all? I don't remember, you say. Droop just a bit since he was young. Isn't that right? I want to say. See he's fine nothing's new. Miss. Shall I leave you? I'll leave. No. Examine. Him. I'll be down there. In the kitchen. Take your time. Take your time.

I pace chew. Jesus. Does he know a thing? You did always. Yes you. Always had. Your hand your foot a bit. No problems please here and nothing new. Hear Ahhh. Hear open wide.

Hear squeeze my hand. No. Harder than that. Now the hard-est you can. Both at once. Now right then left. Don't wig I say to myself. You'll soon know full well. Wipe the kitchen over. This j-cloth. This scouring pad.

Above I hear her turning. Hit her headboard with her prayers. Why don't you shut up? No now. You're here to care I say. I say so don't complain. You're clean here. You're calm and kind. I hear. Her shuffle. Her move. Across the floor. Are you down there? she shouts Did you get the door? Yes. Did the doctor come in he? Yes he's with now. Put that kettle on. I'm coming down now to see him. He's. I'll talk to him when he's done. Yes Mammy. Don't. He'll not I'd say be in there long.

She comes. All neat. All tidy down. All in state with her slippers. Make up the tea that's a good girl. And he'll want a biscuit. Yes. Sure I'd be lost without you she says and with-out the power of. Please don't. Prayer. Amen Mammy. I'll do that. Swallow my tongue. Amen again.

Sit down now til I talk to you he said. Eating biscuits. You might know what I'm going to say. A fine cup that. What? His room can't be upstairs. Up. What? It's a hazard. Crumbs everywhere. It's really time. I. If he stumbled if he fell. In the night he could.

That'd be very. Bad so you'd want to move him down. But there's. The power's much weaker in that side now. Spraying bits of chocolate chip. Like if he knocked his head. I. Please. Think what I'll do. I'll do everything I can I say. You understand. Yes I see I see. She turns. Do you Madam? What? Remember I'm the mother here. Sor. What I. I see doctor I see very well. I'll do all I can to make my son feel. Well. Comfortable. Safe. Down here. You're a credit he says slurp it up. No better one. Thanks be to Jesus. He gives me his strength. Only he helps me endure all this. Oh. And your daughter there of course. Ah I trained her well. So I see, so that's it then. He says. Settled. Call if. Thanks. Get the door you. Bye then doctor. I do.

I've a froth the mouth. In my head. What's all that? With her sniping? Now. Suddenly. She's all here mother. She. With scalding prayers. Forgotten her old lash phone calls. Am I not here? I. Give me a good punch on my face. Stop. It's fine now. It's fine now isn't that why you're came? To pick up. Bits and pieces. Let her do her thing. Name of the father but shhh. Lead us not into temptation. That's right. All very well. I. So I won't utter a single. No. I will. Do this. I will do this for you because. I can.

Well I'll leave that to you she says. Isn't that why you're here. I am. Spitting. What was that but? Don't you forget I'm the mother here. I. Didn't. You're not the only one. With this. You don't know what it's like for me to see my son and cannot do a single thing. Yes Mammy. It's hard I know.

So. I go. Getting some paint. Curtains. Curtain rails. Carrying in the wind and rain up the road. I am making. No. Say you don't want to. Don't worry I'll make it all as lovely as your room. Won't it be more easy and without those stairs? Think of that. See. No you say. You have to. Sorry. No. I'll make it. Nice. No. Sorry but. You do.

I do. That day and that night. Sticking paper. Stewing paste. Paint yellow and white for the. For you. Good for sleep I. She. You missed a bit you missed a bit. Just there look. Over there. I go on. With all my might. Paint. She's not around. Like she is not here.

Where's the lights? Turn the lights on. Now how's that for a room? She is non. She is unimpressed by me by my. Room I've made. But there's an air bubble shouldn't have

let that in there's crumple up the paper. I. Took me all night
Mammy. All night. Alright. I'm not saying. You are. Don't
be uptight. Your brother doesn't need that in the air. I. You.

Look. Leave me alone. She says don't think you can come
here with your tantrums. And it's not like you've done a lot.
What? For us. In the past. When I? Oh I see what you're at
Madam. I see you well, think you'll make up with him. On
the deathbed. I know you she says very well you selfish stupid lazy girl. Never bothered here and now. Don't. I'm not
impressed. You conniving jealous. Shut your mouth you.
Fucking. I'm just trying. My.

Best. Well aren't you lucky we'll have you. You. Just keep
to yourself. He needs his mother now not you.

Get out there burn my tonsils burn my eyes. Spit the
fuck the. Doorbell rings. Her jangle praying swaying crowd's
arrived. Answer that get that you she says. Holy Jesus. I
swing. Shout get in there and see your friend and say your
Jesus fucking prayers. Go on. I'm. Getting out of here. She.
You Miss listen don't you. Listen to me. No. I'm. I'm.

Have your lunatics. Anoint their Jesus crying eyes. Their
mouths slapping tongues. Their sing praise alleluias. So
levitate on the tiles. They sweep all Christlike in. Fat coven
descended to your bed. Your nervous face. Disguise. I can't
disguise. Some ancient thing that catch me make me panic
gag. Them. Doing it before my eyes. No. Announce yourself
and hear oh Lord. Between us chattels us vessels of shame
and you, blue conscious with outstretched hands will be
loaded up with all their sins. And to the wilds they'll send
you filled with that. I'm bad to my mother and I'll never
have luck. Fuck. Fuck that, this, all everything. It creeps and
crawls and. What? They'll grasp their hands and pray. Forgiveness. Absolution for you. I don't. I think. She bow her

head. Murmur holy spirit. She pray and whatsit she thinks she sees? Her son has failed her. Have put upon her these things. For she for her life shouldn't be this. I see her. I see. See. I'd like. I'll. Sit down, for God wants all our prayers. Hear that Madam? What you need. No I'm. Make a run for it. This time. Up up and away. There's a foul there's a wind where's the air. Catch me. Face. I'm going down the footpath and running from the door. Slamming. Fuck you. Where the rain is.

Narrow. I'm running. Between the trees. And the woodlands here and something primrose on the hill. It's the spring what's wrong here is me me me. Me the thing but I. Think I know. Is that the reason for what's happened? Me? The thing. Wrong. Strangling it is. Me. I have a juicy puke down like tsunami from my head. In the blackthorn in the hazel over there over there. Came out up all over. Carrots and peas. I paint what. Did I do? What a thing in my insides. Just sit still I say.

So afterward pick out of my hair glue strands phlegm bit insides no better than. I shake. Feel that dizzy. Sit but alone. With my vomit. Behind eyes blunt. What I'd be. Demure. If I could. With handkerchief blot ducts not glands race pump tears out and snot and fear like garlic through the skin. Out my mouth like a mad thing raving clawing out my eyes. This wrong doubtful body should not have been mine. Mine was. Not this. Was perfect. Once. Drag the. I will and sit and drown and drown if the. Come water. Over land. Swallow up. Swallow me down. Drag me in the gullies. In the pipes please and the drains.

I called your aunt. Your uncle and aunt. Asked them to come. No. I want. Somebody here. You. Do. Of my own. I'm.

And they said? He said. He? They'd come. Next week. How long? What? How. Long. I. He didn't say I just want my family with me. I am. You are my. Daughter much good that's showing to be now. Well thank you. Your aunt. My uncle will. Just keep clear she says. You I say, of me. Stick that in your pipe and smoke it. You and your holy joes. What they must think she says I don't know. I don't care. The future in future. Keep yourself to yourself when they're here. Nobody wants to hear your cheek. Nobody cares. For that thanks for that I say. Peel the skin off why don't you, rip it from my bone.

How are you? You not much open your eyes. Tired I'm sleepy. I know. Have to I get up. Have to go to work but my eyes. You know it's grand, they won't expect you in yet.

    You're here, play star wars here I'll get the tub you say. The men. I'm Chewy I am Luke. You're. Maybe later, I don't think, not now. But I want. I. Wanted to. Do that. I. Want to get up. I. Alright. Lean on my. On my arm. Pull the bedsheets. Bedsheets back. Swing. There's the ground. Fine you're. Lean on me. But I have to. There. Come on. Come on. You weigh. The weight you weigh on me bricks and stone. But. If I let you down. If I let go. You'd fall. You'll fall. No I won't. You will but sure, I'm here.

    You and me sit. Swing our feet. Watching TV. Watching films I bought. Here. Some sweets. Some penny sweets and toffee chews you like them I like them too. Don't slobber. Don't drop them on the floor. What's that? Feet up. Hold your feet up. Your feet cold. Touch. Look you've an ingrown toenail there. Where? I'll cut your toenails. You what, you say. You're an eejit, cut it badly when you did it yourself last.

I get my clippers. Get a piece of kitchen roll and snip snip. You hurt me. You say. Hurt me there. Point down to the foot I see. Little blood swell on the top. Jut. Blob the very edge. I. Sorry.

Kiss it better. There now there. Amends. I push toilet tissue under the nail. What. Raise it. Just up enough. Thhh stings a load. I know I know but that'll make it better soon. I'm better soon. Be better soon. I know I know you will. Shh now. Everything. Now that's enough. But hungry I'm so hungry. What'll I make you? Beans on toast you say. Hey fruit of the musical ha ha musical fruit good for your heart the more you eat the more you. Ahh 'sgusting 'sgusting boy. The musical fart the musical fart. You never used to. Don't tell on me. Won't. Don't don't. Don't be sssscared. Fooled you. Made you look made you stare made the barber cut your hair. I look you look. I look at you. Good to see the smile of you. He cut it long he cut it short he cut it with a knife and fork. Didn't know you liked hair so much I do. Beans on toast. I'll. Ha now that's enough. That's enough now. Just sit there I'll bring them in.

Now the window now I look out there. Smells of Fairy and damp matches stink in here. Hot swamp with condensation. Roll. What I'm. Help. I'm doing here. Light the gas just and put the pot on full.

What's the day? It's the day that they come. I know. Waiting. What. If I see? I'll. I'm in the window. Nets. No. Like a stomach I'm sick. I. Is that them? Pull up. Red car. They. It. Is. Yes them. How's his hair wet? It is. Curls. Curls a bit. With her handbag on her chest. Jesus. Cut her in half. I'd slice it at the neck. And he looks up. Don't see me. Pats her.

Cat. Close the door love. Go on in. I'll lock up. See me standing. Look down. Looking at me. This is not. I see him well enough. Bastard that he is.

Get the door. I can't. She goes instead and I'm just standing. Twist the usual. Twisting my hair. Where are you? Sleeping. Don't do that but. No. I hear her come in. I don't know what to say says our aunt. Put their arms round each. I'm so glad you're here. I'm just worn out. There there. She is comforted. I am standing on the stairs. Mammy catch me with her eye. That one there. Too much for me. Now says the aunt, we'll sort out all these things. I'm sure she's a great help, isn't that right? Don't you want to be a help to your Mam in her time of? I. Come on in and sit down you must be exhausted from the flight. Put on the kettle you. Aunt touch my back says your mother's overwrought. Try not to take what she says to heart. Yes I say. I put the kettle on.

Where'll I stick these bags? he asks. Oh I forgot about you, just so pleased to see your wife. Come in come in. He is also hers to hug and kiss. You show your uncle their room. Come on, it's upstairs.

Your room's there. Aren't you pleased to see me? Touch tips of my hair. Are you not going to speak to me? You can't ignore me the whole while I'm here. I. What did you come for? Bring down that tin of biscuits from the wardrobe she shouts I've been saving them since Christmas. Mammy which? Those Danish butter ones.

That's a quiet dinner. But least I made. Mashed potatoes and beans with a few rashers I grilled. Lovely plain dinner. Could do with a few fried onions mind. Ah one of these days she'll make someone a lovely little wife he smiles and I don't at all.

He is sitting on my bed. What are you doing here? They've both gone out. And what are you doing here? Your mother said she wanted us. You have to go, here's not the same, she is, me, I'm not that. I want you. Not here all that's done. I want he says. No. You to leave with me. No. I came here for. No. You need me. I don't. Touch. He does. Don't touch me. All that's done. I'm much cleaner better here. You're not. I'm something else and I can't. Not here. That's enough he says. And he wants. Loves to get me by the arms. Get away get away. Leave the fucking. Spitting out his mouth. Say. Leave me fucking lone. You're the one I. No fuck you. Don't you think I. Fuck you. To me you're not some. Fuck you. Fuck me please undoes his fly. No. I. Shut up. Hurt my arm I'll. Just be quiet. I won't be long he says. I shut the light out. Shut the air. Hurt wrists to breaking. Fall all his weight. Is fine. I can Fine. Hear him say, you know I know you now and to hurt you very well. Push it up. Me. I am dry and blind. While he goes on. Crushing all my bones. I refuse to breathe. Ha! And only when he's done let the light come through. I'm. Kiss my mouth. Get away from me you. That is the last time. The very last. You filthy bastard fucker cunt. Or cunt. Is me. For all time forward. For search he through my body rub. In the steeple. In the head. I'm. Now I'm. The wrong again. I shall. I'll. Calm and kind. Not dirty bitch. Feel. Jesus. That's it he says. No off get off. Just let yourself. Stop. You done in me what you done. Too late for frigged off making come get off. Please leave with me. No. I said I'd stay. I say to me my. I. I said. I said I'd never leave. Now peel his body off to kneel and while he will stay off I pray. Pray this will all be gone.

At the side of your bed I touch your hands. I know they are going wrong. They're not. Not doing all what they should ever should. Your eyes. Turned back. Sleeping in your head. That's it happening and I'm. No. I'm right. I'm staying here. I hear. Across the house. Like howl. Like wind. Fucking devil. My head. Come and get me. Jesus save. Jesus pray. Uncle that. Let him die. Let him be dead. He should he fuck. He fucks fucks me in me every day. I want to. Yes I'll. Here and now. I'm going to. I will. I will yes here with you. Must. And want to. Going to going to going to. Stay. Her. Here. Her. Not her here. Me.

I see they're not going. He pets her in the kitchen and she cooks the tea. Our mother wants them always. They are staying here. We're staying for the time being. Til the bitter. Fuck them. Bitter. They just want to see it to the end.

Mammy sitting one afternoon. We've something about which we should talk. Your brother. What? Can't seem to get up out of his bed. Anymore. I see you staggering. I see that. It means the end of things is coming. I know. Faster.

Around that dinner table. Stuffing all our mouths shut. She aunt going nack nack nack for she always has thoughts and always wants to say I. Spoon the peas the carrots in and dry spud choke me make sick I like. The best that way. Clinking he does drinking wine he bought petrol tasting and it get me in the throat. I warm though. Under. None the others won't have and you are sleep. You'll have a tray of neat and little cut-up things shush for later there. They thank you god for being so good thank you lord for all my friends thank you god for everything thank you god. Amen. Sing. Like I was at school. I sang each day. There eat up there it will make you strong. I strong I think I'm on the mend. I clean my everything. Feel the carrots dissolve and the spud go down. There's a whole clean world in here is mine. But he looks up at my face and I'm. Cough the dinner. Lights. Are dim but. Those eyes uncle eyes eat all things off my skin. He looks through the table smile at me. Burn and I'll look. No. Not at. Through the window at the rain coming in. Are you going are you staying? When's safe for me? He. Twist me. He see me in. This fucking house spring my neck trap he got me in. But. I. Yes. Can too. Do too. If I choose. I'm.

There's my plate on the worktop Mammy. I'm going out. Where you? See you I. I'm off. Put my coat on. Safe me. Out of here. In the black that gray that. Wet black sky. If I want to. There's something. Because I am able to say no. Because I am. I. Want to. It keeps me clean near you.

I know where the tarmac go. Where the lights fall gravel comes place for me. It hush in the dark in the night in the sky I hear I see. Ever up there something. I. Car coming down the road. Come for me. No. Pull up. Hear that. My uncle. Get in he says. You shouldn't walk here at night. He. At the steering wheel. I sit. Rocking with the engine with the petrol tank. Think. There's a there's a world's not this. Where you going? I. Your mother's very hassled. She could do without your antics traipsing off. Your brother. Don't you say. Just start driving. He pulls out. I'm going to take you where? What? Where you going? Going to the lake. Why? Things to do. I. I'll come with you you won't. Yes. No. I think I know. So? Gull the engine. Gull the traffic going by. You and me he say, we have things to. No. Just there. It's there. Pull in and. Here? Little road pull up. It's dark. Yes. What you do here? Not your business. But I but. Sssssh. I come here on my own. But I. Sit. You can wait. Here. Or go. I'll come. No. This is not for you.

I go into the black of trees. I wander over a silver of lake see the moon in. See the night and no one round. No one here. I sit on moss wet ground I sit and feel the. No. Don't feel here. In this moment in the place like this. I want the. Earth. My legs spread wide. The tremble moment men invade. Boys come in. I was small. I. Wounds were good for deep and. Quiet. Listen. Something. What's here? What's here? The crackling ground. Moving. Come the fucking soldiers for me. Come the heavenly host. That smell of stink cigs smell of stink of shit and cloy. Stink I want. Dirt clothes and mats and hair that.

Hands are. Greasy with oil or. They come. Here are two. Two with them with cans or them six-pack. Settle by the water. Settle by the edge. Toothing open bottles. I hear them laughs.

When it's black and still again. Light their fags. And I say. Hello. Sit with them. Be the smelt. I. Fucking. Game think I know you. From before. Hello you there they say. You know it's not safe to be hanging around here in the dark. I know you I say. Yes?

From before. Do you? he says Where? Have a gulp of. Fizzy under skin. Thanks for. He's older is he than I thought? From here. Maybe two months past. Really? Yes I know him fish shit man. Hmm he says. Oh yes, you called me a cunt. You were being disgusting. So I was but weren't you? No. Nice young girleen come down here doing. You do. I do. Well I won't hold it against you he says. Why don't you come here and sit on my lap? No.

Knotty fingers out. Black with something. Touch my leg. Say how you'd like come in the dark dirt with me? I. What else are you doing here? He stand up. Come on. Get me by the wrist. Lead me over the stones. I remember the rank. Go on. Teeth. See that hawthorn flower? Lie you down there that fallen tree. A lovely blossom teeth. He. No hang on I. Just shut up and pull your knickers down. Spread. I. His fingers. That. Ready now girl. There's a big. Now. Ready there. Fall on me. Fuck. Thhh. Hurts. Ow. I'm. Push my face on the. Pull my hair. Hold me down. I like the. I'm not. Work on the it's. In me. I. Fuck you I. Fuck you. He. Waddle happy there in me. I'm a cunt am I? Dabble. Give pain where. I. It. Extra. Hard work. Him. The. Ssssss the sting but. No. Go on. Mind that. Go on. Ha ha do you come here often? There's the. I know. This go. Well. Proper as it. Is. Feel that. Should I. Press into my ribcage. Push he. Push air out. Pin me there. I. Ow all all and there the. He so happy. Cracking ground. Sounds. Someone's come. Me? No. Shut up. Struggle up my head. I. In the. See. Rush in the mouth. I know that's the right thing. When I. Pus. Or spit the. Cough. I. Blood. Frail lady I would be. He. Who's that in the branches? What's that? Look at me. He in the pine trees leaning. Look at me. At the mount at the. Yee haa girleen. Jesus jesus. He. Come on. Spout up he up. What's the shower up the. Finsih in me. Fincsh. Good girl the. End of it.

Come out. Tidy there's a tissue. Now see I'm a gentleman. I take I. Fall in. Let the. What's the air. Oxygen. Get into me. And pull his pants up. Tucking the thing thought in. Nad byt ehn. What's that in my ear? Thanks good-bye. He says do you want to come sit with us. Have a few of our beers? No. A fine nice night. I pull up and down my clothes. No. Are you too good for us? Sit with. Down there. Come on girleen. Have my wrist I. Is there? Jesus though. He is. There Uncle. Turn.

What you doing? To that girl? You fucking. Pervert. Fucking. Scum you. Get you here he says. What's it to you? says my fucker. Uncle reach lands a thump on his ear so he stumbles. Get off me she wanted it. Blow again too hard on his face. He falls down. Don't I. Stop it. Pervert you. My niece. My. Stop. Kick him stomach. He holds out his scum hands Okay sorry I'm sorry just leave me alone. Stop it I. Shut up you. Kicks into him harder again. Harder. Stop stop it Jesus leave him alone. Fuck you he reach down and get him by the hair. He hit and hit him to curled up there. You bastard stinking fucking. Stop Jesus stop it I wanted him to. And that man on the ground. Pass out. Just stop. Come on. Spit on him. You fucking pervert you fucking dare. She's my. Leave him be.

And you, he have me. By the hair. Slut always you can't you keep your knickers to yourself. Let go. Slap me. More than ever before I. God my face. The. God my eye is coming out it seems. Falling over in the. See whore, what you done? Dragging through the nettles brambles. Onto the path I. Falling in. Like I can't see. He. Fuck you shake my head I. Don't. Please. He slap again my. Seeing. Falling through the trees I'm. Falling.

Catch. My love. He says. My love for. Shut the. Love for you. Is nothing I say and stretch my hands up til they tear the air behind. Til they burn on nettles and thorns barbwire. Do to me what you always ever wanted please. My head is singing. He kiss me. Please my don't make me do that again. I'm. I'll sing a song for you I say hobble with my sight. I'll sing. I'll sing. I am I I'm nobody's fool. I'm nobody's. Nobody's fooled. I am I am I am I am. Stop that. Never stopping sing again. Where's my. I can't notice anything stumble.

Til he stops til he touch me til he. What you doing? Stop leave me. Jesus. Bit me. Below the neckline of the dress. The.

Bite. Hurt that. My breast. Through the stupid white my bothered skin. See blood come. Rings I think of teeth flower. You. Don't. You don't.

Again. My lovely girl my love my. He says. Look at me. I'll always have you in the end. Because I love you. Shut up. Best. So so so so? Well fuck you then. He says. Wipe up that. Put your bra. Fucking state you're in. Don't know a man loves you. Don't know.

Fucking mental that you. Dirty cunt like him. Well I liked it and I fucked it and I wanted it some more. You fucking. Shut your. Caught my, the roots, in my scalp like they'll rip me. Coming. Uncle loving coming. Coming. We to. Home.

In the car driving. I won't take you in like that. Look in the mirror. Your mother brother aunt and. Jesus. I open car door. I can leap. Out. Swerve. Sit the fuck back in. I need the. Hold it now. Just wipe your face. Sit back I said. Sit back and put you seat belt on. Hahahahahahaha. Fucking stupid face. I'm. Shush. I'm off the world I need a think I think I need a drink. I still feel your disgusting run about in me, I say. Stop that talk you're not so. I'll tell your wife I'll show her what you done. The smell she'll know it's you. Disgusting you are you know you always led me on you won't say a thing. I. Won't. Say. If you hit me. If you tell me to. I do.

And we get to the house. And he got me by the arm. And he threw me in the door. And he said. I got her home. And he said. Go you to bed. And he said. Stop playing up. And he said. You've one last chance. And he said. You mother doesn't need antics. And he said. Now no more fun. And he said. Your brother's ill. And he said. You selfish madam. And he said. Now act your age. She's up to all sorts, that one. And they clapped they loved they worshipped him. I picked up sticks out of my hair. Dirt up off my tongue. I felt the loving smears go in. The loving blood. I felt water rushing in my brain. I dead the heart. I am for you alone.

I went in. I knelt next to by your bed. I put my face in the hook of your arm. I said please please you help me. I thought. I knew. You're dying soon. I wished for you. All the very good. Your life was better than it been I said I love you. Please tell me you love me. You sleep. You sleeping. When I know. I think your face the very best. When we were we were we were young. When you were little and I was girl. Once upon a time. I'll mind you mind you. Now. Not then. And I genuflect your quiet bed. I kiss your face. Leave the room. I'm going. Sleeping. Just like you.

I the morning. I the day. When the air was. The air is. Today. Today. When the bones hurt no I'm young. When the everything's sitting like. Right. What's happened? For the radio's somewhere play. In the house. I'm in the house. Today what's that? Today. Say.

Play. May. There's coming up out of my heads. A. Ssssss- someone's coming. Wwwwwho's a dddddoctor. Who'ssss going to. Llllllook at mmmmmy love. That is. Yyyyyyyou. I'll wash my. Clean my. Hide. Honor or the privilege of. Fuck- up. By my side. Your side. I know. Go down.

There's the kitchen air stink like fat. Mounging their breakfasts. Globle it up eat that eat that. They aren't look don't look at me. Like the look of me. I have my breakfast and I go in to see you with a scrambled egg. With a scab of bite marks on my chest underneath it all.

Your eyes shut on the pillow and your soft head. Hey morning you there. How are you? Not. Grog your eyes. Sleepy. Wake up wake up now. It's me here your. So quiet you do. Hello there that's my sister. Yes. I am. Are you alright? Hungry? I brought you something. What? A little scrambled egg. My favorite I love it. It comes from a hen. It does. It surely. Now have a little bite. Spoon you. My sweetness. I spoon in and wipe and lift. I tilt your head. There forward bit. I have my tender love for your sore head. For your dreams in there for all the things that are good to sleep for. Forget this house and world and stuff. We now. You and me.

The hours come. They come. Over all the clock. Around with time. I am sleeping my face on your quilt. Hear the doorbell ringing. Know the cock has crew. Oh come in. Make yourself. Sit down. Our mother opening the door. In. My daughter. Dr. blah and blah. If you want to sit there. Shall we leave you? No you can stay. Doctor is she? Hello. Stand up. Don't mind yourself what happened to your eye? I fell and hit my head. It looks sore did you put some frozen peas. Don't mind her doctor. She's grand. Well take it easy the next few days, sit down. I do again next to you.

This is a lovely peaceful room. Yes it is. My daughter made it before she. How nice. Round the bend. Well it's a hard old time for everyone. Hmmm she but she. Yes. In the end. And now your name? What's your name? she said all soft to you. I'm doctor from the hospice. This is my first time to you and I'm very pleased to meet you. Meet you you said. You're tired out. I am I am. There's a pulse in my mouth going round and round.

She took her things out things she need to do to you. And took your pulse and hit your knee and asked the day and date of week and you didn't know those things at all. It's alright she said sure when you're not out much it's easy to get confused isn't it? Yes you say. And I was glad she said that.

You smiling. Have not. In some time. Checked for bedsores. For stretch marks. I see. The weight you've put on makes flesh like rips under your arms and on your stomach I see. Like claws gone in lacerations and pulled off your skin. There she says some cream and says that's the steroids. Smooth your blankets out.

Tell me how you feeling? You say. I'm so tired now. All the time I. Wish I'd watch television I'd play some games with the other boys if ever they came round. I. Shush there, let him tell me. And how does it feel? Your head? Nothing I don't think anything's up in there. Nosebleeds? Headaches? Vision getting blurred? No. When I get better.

Sssssss that fills me so I get worse. How do you think you are yourself? she asks. I, you say. Haven't I? Haven't you what? Cancer somehow in there. I clamp. You do, I'm very sorry to say she says. Will I give it to my children when I grow up? You won't. That's good. And then silence here. Waiting. Swallow ocean. Waiting for. This is a moment when I want most to be dead. Face into the water or lying on the bank. Not around for this. Coming here. This sunny afternoon. This. When you say it.

When am I going to get well? She says.

You're not. I'm sorry to.

Am I

this silent moment you say, Am I going to die?

You are. She.

Clearer in this moment than you have ever been. Sooner or later doctor?

Sooner. I'm sorry. I'm so sorry to have to say.

And you. Filled up your bluest eye that fill and fill. Begin to cry. I'm going to die then. Now. I'm going to die.

Yes. Is there anything you want anyone to do? No.

Is there anything that you'd like to? Say sorry.

What?

You. Filling all our hands with tears.

I am sorry to my mother and I'm sorry to my sister.

And you held my hand. Though you could hardly could. I wish Don't say it but you do.

I'm sorry to you for this dying and all the things I've done.

Oh no oh no oh don't do that or say those things that are no matter anymore. Don't be sorry to me.

I want to. Don't.

I say

Shush silent night.

I put my head down beside. Fill my mouth up with bedspread. Fill the air out. Stop the. The coming in. And your hand on it. Down on my hair. You're crying and I am.

There there

You are saying to me. There there there.

Death falling through the room, sucking all words from air for us. And for quiet of five minutes we are just. The blasted moment. Crushing our every bone. Please God don't make me ever raise my face up. And you said

Why you crying? Why's everyone crying here? I was. I was asleep and now everyone's crying. She mother says

There's no reason in the wide wide world.

Comes pats you on the back and says to me go blow your nose and wash your face Madam. I do. I do obey and first kiss you and. Fine I say don't you mind about me. I'm grand. Then leave them to whatever they want.

In the toilet eyeballs bleeding it almost feels. Shussssh. Breathe. Wipe the burn out. Wipe my flesh. Deteriorating. No. Everyday. I know the end the end. We. And I'm the fucking one and please help. Da our father art in help. My prayer mine. Please. Don't. Do. This.

I come out. There there, white hall with tiles and doors, with pictures hanging up.

Work to do to make across it. Them standing open at the door. Her whisper saying tell me when? She doctor saying slow. No more months. Maybe weeks. One or two. Not any more. He's sleeping. Getting incoherent now. He could have stroke or just go. My son my son. My child my baby my boy my boy. I. There. And I am. She puts her hands on me.

She puts her arms around me. Oh my little. My boy my boy. My mother. Feel the. Strange and I am comfort there. I am the. Right. I am the right thing. In this time. Mammy. I will mind. This time. No shush. Take care of that eye the doctor hush and call me anytime.

Thanks doctor for saying all that. For him. Good-bye.

It is soup for dinner. My aunt made. This is her best thing. Chicken and bread. I dunk the fat slice. My mother hands crawling to eat. And uncle head say, so we'll do night about. He'll need someone always there. Yes I. Tonight I'll stay up he offers. All you go to bed and sleep. I'll call if. He does not look at me. Filthy. I wish we prayed. This quiet house. My brother. Good-night. I kiss you. I will. End this drum of day.

I dream of creeping under. I dream of underground where the warm earth is where the fire goes. Where we're sleep creep you and me in holes. In burrows rabbits safe from rain.

Roots growing caverns round our heads. And blind as mice popped out and new and cling and soft our bright pink skin. Who's there? There's no one. You and only me. We sing.

We lilt our chamber. No one coming. And we lie. A thousand years of sleep. And get beards wrinkle old and small and we. Troubleless in our deep. Eat the earthworms fat slugs things within. But I dream. Roots come growing. Slowly and tangle in. And roots come more. And fat and thick. And roots come fast. Roots fast in. Roots seek us. Catch us. Roots that want our head. Our eyes. We move about. The trees will have us. Have our brains for. No one in. That the trees will have us. Roots growing in the bursting through our skulls. Through in through our brains. Seeking out our noses. Seeking out our eyes for. Strangle. Choking out the air. Mangle organs. Tangle pain with us. The worming earth. Grown through. Pin us into soil. Grow life around and choke the air. Claw us.

Snare us. Grow through our hearts. Working through our lungs and brains and we and fight and we howl. To silent. No more. Make us dead. Make us into mud. Rotting in the down. Rot in the deep. Turning into stone. Dust we we were. Dust return.

I night watch you this night. I sit. Hands under your head say drink this. Just drink this. He. You won't. Not that. Don't like here. And I say. I wipe your face. Dribble I see it. Just there. And swim your eyes around your head. Thanks for. That I. It's alright my love go to sleep. I sit. These tick tock hours moving night across the ocean. Moving night across the sky. You moving once in a while. Say I want out of bed and I. There. You're fine. You know you can't. But I. Shush now. Read some flitter book while you are asleep and sleep and. I go under that. Until seven until eight. Until someone our aunt comes and says I'm up. You go on to bed. I do.

But the afternoon I am by your side saying wake you wake up. Don't sleep now and you are you are nearly done say just a little moment. Just one more. And I peel around the kitchen and I peel around her home. Yours. I know that. Lifting heavy fingers doing what. I don't. Still don't. I don't know.

When doctors come to visit saying. How's his back? How's his sores? Is he sleeping? Can you wake him up please? I can't I know. He won't. You won't. They shake. He's deepest deepest. Only when he wants to. Wake up. Anymore.

I can't wash myself clean. I cannot wash my hair my. I tie the long bit back. I lie on beds I stare and watch islands by in clouds of up. Where I would. You. When we were small would make our homes. Happy palace. Where you are going. Soon. And when you're gone.

We are happy cross each other. Everyone in the house. Eyes that wander off. Don't see. Don't see in the hallway on the stairs. Smelling dinner coming all the time and I say to you. Will you have a little something? You there. Can't hold your fork. Hold your knife. I cut. I say. For you. Open wide now let me put it in. And you won't smile and you won't chew. Please eat it. And it will do you good. She sit and says I will. Let me. She. Go on please. No. You won't though. No more eating for you.

She sits with you. That night I hear. Hail holy queen hail our life our sweetness and our hope to thee do we fly poor banished children. Of Eve. And in the morning. She is there. Cross her legs with her book down. Rosary wound like rope. Pulling in her skin going white til blue.

. . .

I walk and I buy you ice cream. That I can. No. For you, lick a little bit. You've done well done what she says to me. In the kitchen. Lean on the back of my chair. Get what we can down him. That's it.

So our uncle take this evening and will sit the night. Says he I will read the Irish Times he's fine with me. And I'll call if there's trouble. All of ye can go to bed. I put my face down in a pillow. Think if I were dead if I were dead I'd be the best best thing. All good and right and well. I hear nothing. I. The all the night because the sky falls down where my bones should break. Nail me right inside the blackness. That's a good night's sleep for me.

The morning's not so wild. He says that you ranted the all night. You up and down and up and down. What? How's that I say. Sure he can't move at all. He says you want the toilet. Twenty times last night. I could not lift him he says. The steroids filled him all up. You.
    Like a balloon. Too heavy for carrying. You know what. What's now. No. No. He wouldn't want. No. Yes. It's past time for it.

Nappies now. For you. Sorry. The nurse teach me and she. We'll do it. No one else will. For we're the secret flesh and blood. You won't mind us. You will. Roll him there. Roll him there she says. Like a baby. Stick on sticky tapes. Not so tight. There. Yes. I. There. It stick on there.

Tonight I sit with you. It's. It's fine. I. Secret in the whole house sleeping I am. Awake. And you are mine in the breathing. That breathing in and out remembers lost or quiet things you always wanted. Yes I remember those things too. Don't you like me best here doing things for you? When you breathe I know what you reply. Yes the. That's the.

Come up to the lamplight. To. What you say you will. Anything at all I. I would slavey on my knees or tightrope cross Niagara Falls. Would you like spaghetti on toast from me on my head at dawn? I would and you say. Oh afternoon have I slept all day? I. No sure it's middle of the night are you okay how do okay? I've just to go to the toilet. Shame you cheeks to say this word. I. You don't have to get up. I've to. You can do what you have to there. Shut what a thing to say. Give me a hand. Up. I. Listen you're alright there. You say. What? Your face red. What's that? There there I say. I have to go to the toilet. You can go there. I. No I can't are you gone crazy? No believe me you can, sorry. I'm. You have to. No. I can't lift you anymore. If you won't help me I'll. You can't. What's the.

Something. Words words. I'll go on my own. Your temper that's the devil up. Normal almost sight again. Pull the bed but melt like water. Gone to hell. All your muscles. You'd give me a hit but can't. I. There. Lie back. Lie back. You have to. Don't do this you say.

Don't. You have to. And I turn away. I say. Just go don't worry it's. Normal now. It's fine. You. Strapped up in your body. You don't live there. I. Don't look. I hear you. Crying.

Going in the nappy. Rage. Not fair. Not fair. You wait til I'm well. You can definitely kill me then I say.

Quiet.

Turn and you are back asleep. I. Know I lift the cover. Clean up. And now you're gone fast far. Breathing. Don't see me. Don't know I do. New one. Clean you. Put it in the bin. See. My one act. I might be a person. Beneath the. Where horrible can be a good act of contrition. Shush there. You there sleeping. My boy. My brother. Wish my eye for yours tooth for your tooth. You're a better. No. It's all fuck gone. Gone to the gone to the wrong wrong wrong. Be shush for you. I can.

Three days three days going. From here. Where's the time and everybody. All around here like. Tapping all the time out one two three. You there sleep go down to that. So we are going into the end. I am. Pool. We are where the blind go, I think. Cool cool days. Not a breeze even here. I'll be there. See. I am. I am. Already. It's a thing. It's a thing. Sing a song of sixpence a pocket full of. Fine. Fine fine. We're. That's your breath. Yours is. Watch it. Catch it. Catch it all the time. I'm. Watch that. We are. You see. Be here now. I see the curtains flap in it. Puffing dresses. Ghosts. Like big and pregnant. Takes the breath flip flap away. When I was little girl. Open up the door. Let the sunshine on.

What's that? Do you see that no you don't. I see you. And you're so quiet. Like a still. Like a Oh. Creeping on the floor. Spiders and flies.

Where's it going where's it going lights turning on they're not. I'm safe of, cured of now of that. When I love you that's all gone off where it should do. Out. He. Knows me. Not to choose. Though we smell each other all day long me she aunt he. There's no room for him in me. Or thing we did. Million million years ago fell off the planet. Good. Safe within my healed-up eye.

But.

She said you should go to mass. Pray for. Me. Think I might do. This is the time.

Sunday go. Sit rove praying. Not like when I was little long ago though, when I was some other thing. I bow my head. But the words of prayers are come coming into me as I have never been gone. Gone from praying or the house of God. You take away the sins of the world. Have mercy on us. Lamb of God you take away the sins of the world. Have mercy on us. Lamb of God you take away the sins of the world. Grant. Us. Peace. Fill my shallow breathing. What I could be. Be granted peace. After all this. After all I am Mary Magdalenish. I would wash with my hair, wash away sins. Lord I am not worthy to receive you but only say the word and I shall be healed.

After communion, after go in peace to love and serve the Lord, thanks be to God I step out of the church. Immaculate blue sky. If I carry my state of grace Hello girleen I thought it was you. Who? There is a man, sitting on the wall smoke out stub of fag his face black and blue, wrist in plaster arm in a sling. Not. Yes. I don't know if I see. Girleen girleen. What? Nice uncle you have there. Desiccation of faith, where's it going. Where's it going? Gone. Fuck you I say. Mouth going pound. We'll see about that he says but I'm already down the path glazed and shame before my eyes. I want you. I want to be home and when I am inside I do not think of him again.

New days. Sometime. I'm. Forgotten what's the past. And the doorbell rings and I answer the phone and the world's filled with people always doing something wrong like saying where you'll bury him, you know when he's gone? What? Well will it be a car trip or up the road? I know he hasn't long and I need to book the time off work. I. Don't know. But I laugh like I'm shot. Bang. Spray me about. I like that. For fun if you can or not for fun.

. . .

Next days. Fuck the future up. The undertaker's come for a good cat chat. Fat. I'll make the tea for him. I'll say I'll close the door, so you won't hear. Him our mother gentle bawling aunt gumped in a heap. Uncle arms on my back saying I'll pay. Do anything. Do anything you want at all. I want? I. Shut up. He says you know what I mean. Something simple. My boy. Mammy. Have I slept at all? I remember once. What. What? Wood. Brown. With a crucifix. With a plain white lining. With a plaque with the date and his name on top. My boy. Mammy stop. Leave your mother alone. It's hard. Shut up. Will you be wanting music? I asked the church choir if they. Did you? I did, she says. When was that? Don't grill me. Your mother's tired. Alright shut up. Play what you play. Nearer my God to thee. Be not afraid. Flowers lilies roses white for him always him my. Brother. My son. And the funeral parlor? We'll be keeping him at home. Yes. On the evening of the second day you can come. We'll lay him out in bed til then. My brother. My Son. And people can pay their respects. I'll make tea and scones aunt. Thanks for that. Not the time. I. Bite my. So we'll process him from the house here. He'll be carried on the shoulders of the men. I want, I say. Of. The. Men. Amen. To the end of the road and then driven in the hearse, who's talking? I think our uncle might but I'm. To the church. Yes, very good I'll see to that. And up out of me is all I suddenly want to know. Is he be buried here Mammy? Where? I'm taking my son home. Home? He'll be buried with his grandfather. No. Yes. He's my son. But I. Too bad for you. When he's gone sure you'll be gone. Back up the city doing your own thing, God knows, so I'll bury my child where it's good for me. I'll join him one day. I. But I. See your mother's point of. Fuck off you, uncle. He doesn't belong to her, he doesn't. All that you care Madam. Not that. I'll want to. Don't you bother telling me about you Miss.

I feel the lights but I'm going lie down by your bed. I won't be stuck up. Anything I. Want to hold your hand and let them what they do I. Understand the end's the end. I can. Have you now. There is so little time.

Hey, do you know me? I pinch I pinch. I say. Do you know me? Wake up. Please.

Please. Do you know me? I know you. Good. You know all those things I did? No. Your eyes rolling. You do, I'm sorry for it. They were the wrong thing sorry I sorry I did that to you. That's alright you say in your going to. Wait. Don't go to not just yet. What's the.

Falling your eyes falling in. I love you. Do you know I love you? I saying I. Yes. Do you love me? Hold on wake back. Come back one minute. Do you love me? I. Do you love? I do. There now. They open the door. They stick their undertaker heads in. He say I like to see them while they're. Shut up. He's a fine-looking fella God love him he's a fine-looking man.

Did he eat today he didn't. Will he. Please get something in you now. She sits by your bed saying you, say you're sorry for all the things you done. Aren't you? When you were. My little boy. When you were bold to me. To me. Leave him. Mammy, does it matter? He must die without sin. I. He couldn't sin if he wanted. What does it matter anyway? Wake up son. Mammy. Leave him. He's going to die. My son. I won't let him in a state of sin.

I walk a long way off. Get out of here. From you. Feel I could clean my head with a. View of mountains. With a view.

Where God is looking in he isn't if he was. He wouldn't do. He wouldn't do. Where's the air out here?

Shush. Aunt saying. The priest is in. Why? To give your brother the sacrament of the sick. She lay the white cloth down. She put candlesticks and candles in. Twig of palm in holy water. Napkin stuck there under your chin. Wake up there son. Wake him. Put his chasuble on. Kiss this bit. Kiss the end. He wash his fingers. Do you renounce Satan and all his ways? Oil on his thumbs. Draw the cross on you. Your eyes and ears. Your lids clappered shut. Don't wake I pray into my fingertips. Oil on your nose and lips. Sign of the cross and. Spread his hands there. That's the way and draw the cross again. Again. On your palms where you have sinned. And feet. There. All the oil stops the devil getting in. Out. Places where the sins come in. He says this is to comfort you in your mortal pain. To fortify your soul I. Remitting all your venial sins. Cleanse your, what's it here, your soul. And restore your health if God sees fit. I pray I pray I pray I pray. For. Him to go. For you. You will not know what this priest's done. What cross mean. What oil. What stink where you have been sanctified.

You're doing, ah you're all doing great he says. Come in Father for a cuppa. For a bun a slice of fruitcake. They. Well alright so. I'll sit with you instead. And when the kettle's boiled I toilet roll your face. Pressured blood pressure going. Yours then mine. I clean the oil from your skin sore red and tired. For what need? You're more perfect than you were before. I'll wash your face of sacrament. Let sin to sinner return. Like me—for I know it very well.

. . .

Pedaling days are pedaling. Jesus coming in. Off from heaven off the gutter off the street for. I know. Jesus is coming. Jesus be here soon. I'll rip his arms. I. Won't have God's son here I. Won't. Jesus will lose you. This time I say I'll win. I. Will. Make you safe this time.

At night I dream. Always. God is. Give me unquiet dreams. When the world. That. I dream. I see the plains of the sea, turning over. Tar. Black as. Black as. Through the. My nose press. Open. Close. Like a seal on the ice. Against the smell of rot. Come from black come from. Where the. Where the world is. Turn like that. On the face of it. Diving. Feel I that. Where we ought to. I am of the. Off the. Who are you wake. Up. And the window is filled with light. Off the street. And the it rises. Sun. Come up. I see through the water. I am right back where I. All that. Where all that. Me. Running. Went from the start of time to here in the next room or down-stairs. And radios and dog bark and cat meow. I'm the. Start now. The beginning. Of. You. End. The end. Begun. Where the lights are. Turn on. Panic. Who do you look like who you are. And I. Running. Think I pull my cool jeans on. Full of. Skin. Something. Bits of me. Fell off that. For he comes the comes the human child to the waters and the wild. Me hand in hand. The world's more full of all those things than we can understand I'm singing. Running. Sing out loud. Oh God the look the state of that see him now. Come Jesus. See he's falling fall fast asleep like an old man tired man sick and. My brother for me. Sick and. Save the. Fine above the rushes. In the hills above Glen stop. Don't. Stop it now. Wake up. I wake. My eyes shut. Run. From a world more full of weep-ing than you can understand.

. . .

But I know now this morning. I know it will be today. And I am white as any creature ripped down to the self. In my quiet in my bedroom in my on my own. Where there's a mirror that is empty. Where there's a worn-out pair of pants. Where my shoes lie turned over. Where hairs are knot and fall behind the radiator. Where the smell of empty spreads out across the air. The thing the thing is. Kingdom come.

I know I must wash and clean my hair my teeth. My putting on my clean my jumper my skirt. People will be here I. Put my lipstick on my mouth. Perfume on my neck my hands my knees where's right. My face don't have its night eyes on. Only day eyes are here. For you. I go down. And I turn room to room. I close I closing all doors. Keep it out while I can. The more. A minute more will win me minute more you.

In the kitchen and in their beds the others move and move the place. Teacups bedsprings flushing toilets. I hear floorboards open. I am coming. Coming today. For you. I come into your room and close the door. I am here. I'm here remember. I love. I. Sit. In your room. In moment caught. Shot. I sit with face smiling black. Please pour the amber in we. Ever ever ever would sit in this moment here.

Hello morning my love. And kiss your face. That's warm. And hard with sleep to the touch. Closed. I know what today is even if you're unaware. I know you'd tell me if you could say. Today. Is the day you'll die. You're going off to leave me and I. I wish you would. I wish you'd learn your lesson and still come back. Wish you. Fuck you. Open your eyes. Please. And you. For the moment show me all that blue there is. World that's falling off the cliff into a farer crashing blue. Do you see me this time this day? I see you.

I. See you today. Don't you close them. Closed and gone

away. Your mouth rattles. I know this. I know what it means. Death rattle like a. Something. I'm.

Close the door and doorbell rings. She bustles to it. Come the holy holy holy things. What? Mammy. Not. Come in come in. No no not today not not them. The district nurse came and said. Today. So I have gathered my friends in. Help him on his. My boy my little boy. It's not right he won't like. All these strangers it's not for gawking Mammy it's not a show please please. I'm asking. Please send them away. No.

They troop. Them large them heap of things and come in smile and go cluster in your room. There bring more chairs down. Don't move. I stand. Get them. I won't. Or you can stay in your room. And leave my brother? Too late for sucking-up miss. I won't do that. Go. No. Go and get or get out and get to hell.

I bring one five six seven in.

I eat my butter bread across the table from him uncle. Look at me he say. Sorry. For this. For your mother doing. For. Today. There isn't. Anything. Feel blood in my neck my head. Fighting in veins in eyes and on my hands. All wrong hands. That I wash them now. Again. Again. Kiss the side of my face. Give me your dishes. Go on in to your brother.

I'll do them up for you.

In the hallway. By the door. Catch the handle I hear. The long complaining prayering sound. Acts contrition reciting it as one. For you. For your sins. Frightened for the dying soon. Their hands laid upon. Bless everywhere on you. Upon your forehead. Upon your feet. Upon your chest. Chant it shout it almost down. You. Please. You sleep please don't you hear what's going on.

Oh my God I'm heartily sorry for having offended thee and I detest all my sins because I dread the loss of heaven and the pains of hell but most of all because they offend thee my God who are all good and deserving of all my love I firmly resolve with the help of thy grace to confess my sins to do penance and to amend my life.

Life. Death. Amend your death. Amen. I go in. Is there any chair for me? No one.

Holy sitting next to thee. And I. Excuse me. Move out of my way I'm. My brother. I get there. That one. Give me his chair. Thanks she says to him. I say nothing. Don't dare look at me.

I hold your hand that was hot and sweat when it was smaller and would fight with me. Stump of nails and stupid. Short they are. I notice this. I see. I see you. I'm there I here. Now. And even here it goes. Your palm. Cooler. Calm when I have it in mine close. What your feet doing. Still growing your hair. Still growing your. Stop that. How's the ingrown nail I'd like to see. See. Stop it doesn't matter. Here. Shush. Cough a bit. You. Don't wake up. I rest my face down on your shoulder she. Stop that. Sit up. Sit up he doesn't like it. I won't. Leave you and me alone.

If thou oh lord will open my lips.

My tongue shall announce thy praise. Incline to my aid oh God.

May the lord make haste to help us.

They sing. Rosary like a lullaby like a song. I know well.

Keep off my breath my head and your rising falling shoulder whisper to you I'm here as well as fecking eejits. Don't forget that I am here.

The door aunt uncle come. Sit watch too. Asking hushly how you do and does anyone want? Then they are terrible and subdued in the corner where they hold hands. I do not see. I am holding yours. I am holding your hand close. My love. That's the best in the. Sssssh to me. In the land. Couldn't help ssshhh. I'm here. Think I think all about, all I can, about you now.

In an hour. There's still time. There's still. Some time. Your hand is getting colder mine. I see. You are going white. Wait wait. I'll tell you. It's all wrong. It's not.

I whisper in your ear over psalming going round. The world around the room around. Tell you every perfect all I can. There's a story now you know. I done it all. I did all for. There's a story. Have it for your own your. Entertaining God when you are gone. Do that. And remember me when you come into your kingdom. Remember me when you've already gone. Today. Is still here. I'll be. At your. Right. Hand. And will you tell me when everything is done? Everything is done. You are. Ready happy go to. Bed. You are my.

Bite.

And all your. Sudden body. Where's the. It. Comes for you. Come blistered breath.

You. Strain. I see. Your heart I see your chest is move is moving is time to. You are. Struggle. Where the air in. Let the air come in it won't it soughing out. Gushing like water. Where's the. Your face that eyes are open wide. See the land and all above mine. Your eyes are where are. They look. When and a tinge purple on your cheeks choke the purple blue. Across your mouth. Across your lips. I see your suffo-

cated eye. Please don't go no. Not. Go. I. Please don't leave.
There's the. Air flying out. Your eyes on me. They. You are.

Silent.

Breath.

Lungs go out. See the world out.

You finish that breath. Song breath.

You are gone out tide. And you close. Drift. Silent eyes.
Good-bye.

My. llllllllllllllllll. Love my. Brother no.

Silent.

He's gone. He's gone. Good-bye.

No. Oh please. My.

Done. And. Quiet.

And.

Gone.

Where the sky burst. They started to cry weep the cry out
Oh why oh lord oh why.

Shut. Your will be done not mine no let mine let mine.

My tears coming blind my eyes my. Face of me. You're
white as. All this sudden.

Moment back. Where have you gone. Breathing. White
your face is not like that. New the awful of the. Awful you.
Stop the. What's that? Nn. My heart. Comes broken now.

Broken off in me. Some flake falling off the sky. Off the.
My. You. Where the day is light the sun come in. Give me.
Not your face. You're. Marble in the mountain. See you. I
touch your. Awful face. Cooling like. I don't even think
can't even think. Do that. You're making my hands cold.
My hands for warm you. Not only. No not this time. The
only. I put my face. Inside your arm. Hold the wave of the
the. Ocean of that. Torn me. In two. Save. Clinging on the.
No. No one. Drag me down.

Who am I talking to? Who am I talking to now?

In the afternoon the undertaker came his hands are ready. Wrap you in your sheet and he and uncle put you in a coffin. Put the lid on tight. Put you in the hearse back. He take you away. We can't clean. We won't do those things. And fill you with formaldehyde.

Cleaning you all you away. Later. When they'll bring you back here. Again.

Goes goes the holy joes. Going to spread the good clean word. Going to say what a good death you have made. What a saintly. What a sad. Young one. Gathered to himself the very best. Left. The shit and trash behind I sit on the kitchen chair and someone give me shepherd's pie. I sit on the kitchen chair. I sit on the kitchen chair. I drink my water. I've gone to the blank. I've gone to the. Gone to the. Eat some more. You'll need your. My eyes are burning up the inside of my head I'm. Something gut the insides something. Pulling out the entrails something. There. Something there. He slurp the chew the. Mince. Like dog sucking marrow in a bone. That mother of us took to her bed. Hear her there.

Screaming there of. My son. My son.

I lie on the carpet floor. I. Hear the bedsprings go. Where she thumps them where she batters. Where the walls are banging. Where the ceiling's banging. And aunt upping down the stairs there there. There there. It's a trag it's a. Nothing.

I am sitting in the toilet talking to talking to the. Smells like molded is like. Fungus creeping up the shower curtain. Fat like vomit. Growing there. Knocking on the door. He. Are you? Come out of there. Come out of there. I'm. Washing my face with my hands I'm. Coming out. I'm. Come.

I am crouching by your bed they've stripped the sheets the bare. I see that. Mattress. You were just there. I rub it with my hands I. Smooth it. Your. It. Bed. That you sleep on.
Every day. That you're sleeping. Smell that. Every. Day. Come back. Not. That's the. Shush. Is it him? Touch my head. Touch my face. Your poor eyes what have you done? Nothing. Shush shush darling. Leave me alone. Scratched them. Left. I. I am. Left alone.

I kneel in my room. Where I pray that. Where I pray that. I pray that. I. Who's though who pulled out my tongue? Don't let the air in. Don't. Hours and hours going on and on. Til I close my eyes I keep them shut. I know where the darkness goes.

The doorbell ring again again now. This is the day when the heavens and the deluge came. For they're coming to say sorry they're. I heard about. I brought a wreath. But it's only a few hours since. I hear the hum. Of buzz of them. The everyone who ever knew are coming in are coming in. And someone's making sandwiches and someone's pouring tea. Not. I'm not. Kneel on the carpet rub my skin to burn. Someone else can let them in. I'm.

Hours and hours passing. Bursting house with all the sorry ever heard. All the flowers they fit in. All the Virgins Child of Prague the Sacred Heart St. Anne I. Can't. I hear. I. I hear the coming like it's miles away. He pulling in the drive. Hearse. That uncle going out and rustle all them. They're here again.

The body poor boy's home again. That's that how it should be. Would you let them in. I hear them stagger. And cross the threshold with a coffin scratching on the doorframe. All the. Way. In.

I think I'm sleeping now. Come down to pray. Get down and pray for your brother. If you cared at all. The house of silent people here. Me. Gone to the dogs she is my mother say.

I. Go into the landing.

I can go down the stairs I. I stare into the candlelight and cigarette smoke was here. In the kitchen. Not in here.

You there. Sleeping like you never gone. Not. I've not seen this face of yours so pale before. Where's the kicking and the little man. Where's that bad auld temper and the and the. You're not here. Not like that empty face. Not. Unshakeable not un. Fightable. Come in say the rosary. No. That's not. That's not even a bit. Come in say the rosary. Like you. I. Can walk in that room. Where they part for me. Looking in the. She the creature thing who. I put my hand down. I put my hand on. No it isn't. Put my hand. Down. Put my hand. On you. Like a. Something. Cold and. Wrong. You. No I get up. I have to leave here. Come back she shouts. Back in here.

I run. No. To get out quick I. Out of my way. Run the run the. To the door. Down the street and on til the house rips out of my head. Where the what's the. Something fix this. I know to fix this. I want. And I fix this place where I can run. This gouge will drive me mad. Where's comfort where's safe. From here. I run from where you are not.

The pant of it. In the dank of. White shooting streets cars by. Lungs heave up blood they would if I. Hedges. Don't stop running. From my. Stone walls and schools and hospitals.

Eyes burn with thud through arteries and eyeball veins. Street lamps curling light. Restaurants and pubs I twisted that. I hear. My tongue. I hold. My scream mouth shut. Turn the little road. This little road. Go in here. Now you. Go in the. Black.

Across the lake the lights of cars and bikes and roaring off somewhere I'm here. In the dark. Where the lights. Where the water. Calm and kind. Benevolent with thorns and stones I. Know. I smell the same. As something. Once is me. Where I walk. Don't think. Where I'm not frightened. Face of the water. I know. Face of the grass I lie in. Lay broke upon. All these times. Where I come to see the. What's. It's the devil. I do here. Said you would not yes I will. Shsssh. Before I'm well. Before it's time. Swallow glass the whole way down.

Where's everybody now? Where the. This I must this. I. Don't. I do. In my own. This the blister. Doesn't matter. Nothing wrong with. Don't be I'm not. Frightened. Hear the. There must be someone in the. Do to you here. What you. Shush. I hear no one no one here for me and so I make. The gravel. I hear make. Some. Picking stones don't look make. My. Someone coming I make. It look. Down from mountains and hills. Angel save me. Fill my mouth. Comes. And so I make. He comes and comes til I see. Through the broken trees. Through kicked-down weeds and nettle all the same. Through eyelids I have. Close. I make. He says out from the twilight. From my brain. You've come here. I know. Quick and should be done. Give myself to the. My will be done.

He says. I've been waiting for you. Days and days. I knew you wouldn't be long. Where's the. Not. Looking close til I see him in the dark. Behind my eye. That man whose face is broken up. That man whose face is scratches and cuts. That man who say girleen girleen like a song. I know something. Your family love you very much. I. Wrong. But you're here again. Don't think it not you. Say it. I'm here again I say. Hear him.

What I'll do to you. No. He says Thanks for all my pain. I. I'll fuck. So you'll know what I mean. Don't know. But. Get off me. By the wrist and the hair on my head. I'm. No this isn't. No I. Slap. My brother. No. Shut up. Shut up. My brother died. He's died he's. I don't care a single fuck about. Where's your uncle is he here? Is he here? Scream until I. He. That means no. Enough of that and strike. So hard. Home. On my face. Spew I think of blood or words I bit down on my tongue. Turn the eye off it won't. Perhaps. He punch the bag me stagger. From. Now for you. You aren't leaving here. I. Don't that. Slap me harder. Never speak again or you're die and gone. I. Comes the black is fallen down. He got. Thrash. Can't see his faces hands fingers in my eyes. My nose. You're hurt me. This is my. Make. Dragging by the gruaig. He is I know. Across the stone my legs to flitters when you pulled me up the stairs. Breath. My eyes I can't. Full of my own hair. Screaming. Shut up. Is that me I am I. I think. There's a my body he push back. I'm. Fling rubbish thrown I am am I I. Falt. Where until I crack. Break my. Face. Head. Something. Smash. On a stump. Where on the back of my head on the back of my back my back crack that's my eyes fucking up with tears. Scare me. Punch me there fright. Stop stop it you are who are I do I don't want. I want to. Not this I don't not for me what he will. You. Jesus. Got. Jesus on his knees pull me up pull me. Fuck. Not. Fuck not.

Help. Grab me. Fingers of my skin. With his filth hands I hear. All the sounds tonight. Raddle fuck in my head. Tonight I hands up my. Knickers up my. Hurt. Not me Jesus. His nails too sharp are you. Did that. Did I make. Stop. Don't don't. I changed my. Jesus he. Not. No. Jesus me. Rips the I think dig them through my leg he. Spread fucking open up you sick fucking stupid bitch want the fuck you just like this I. Kick the kick. My heels dragging blood through the muck. Want to catch to prise to lift me. Save. Off off him fuck off me off me. He'll. Pulls me up away. Kill. Me. Rake my hands I fingers in the dirt in the stones up my fingernails. Stones powder clawing them to. No. Get off. They're off fuck knickers off. Fuck. Whore. You. He pulls like mad I I. Hear the sound. That fly. Zipping. Fuck out. Spring it out. Thighs in claws I vice. Rip m open. I make this. I make this. Undone he push my face hye pusk my head. My eyes flat of his hand. In the skull my. In the muck my crown of stones. Don't break me open face open. Crushing I hear boines on done he up me fuck me. Smeeling he I don't not do this I a don't know he's fuck me. Stucks the fck the thing in. Me. In. Jesus. I nme. Go. Away. Breeting. Skitch. Hear the way he. Sloows. Hurts m. Jesus skreamtheway he. Doos the fuck the fuckink slatch in me. Scream. Kracks. Done fuk me open he dine done on me. Done done Til he hye happy fucky shoves upo comes ui. Kom shitting ut h mith fking kmg I'm fking cmin up you. Retch I. Retch I. Dinneradntea I choke mny. Up my. Thrtoat I. He come hecomehe. More. Slash the fuck the rank the sick up me sick up he and sticks his fingers in my mouth. Piull my mth he pull m mouth with him fingers pull the side of my mouth til I no. Stop that fuck and rip. Scin. Stop heeel. Tear my mouth. Garble lotof. Don't I come all mouth of blood of choking of he there bitch there bithc there there stranlge me strangle how you like it how you think it is fun grouged breth sacld my lungs til I. Puk blodd over me frum. In the next but. Let me air. Soon I'n dead I'm sre. Loose. Ver the aIrWays. Here. mY nose my mOuth I. VOMit. Clear. CleaR. He stopS up gETs. Stands uP. Look. And I breath. And I breath my. I make. You like those feelings do you now. Thanks to your uncle for that like the best fuck I ever had. HoCk SPIT me. Kicks. uPshes me over. With his brown boot foot. WitK the soLe of it on my stomik. Ver. Coughing my. Y hard. He. Into the ditch roll in gully to the side. Roll. I roll. For it. He. Turn on the. I. Hear his zip. Thanks for fuck you thanks for that I hear his walking crunching. Foot foot. Go. Him Away.

I lie thisright place for me with my fingers ripped onthebody Mine is Lie in the ground faceWhere I Right for meyes. Think about your face. Something. Shush now. Right now. FullofslimeThere better now. And I am. Done with this done. Fill the air up. Smear the blood up is there any no no t reeeeelly. My work is. I've done my I should do. I've done the this time really well. And best of. It was the best of. How. Ready now. I'm screaming in the blackness. Scream until I'm done my body. Full of nothing. Full of dirt the. I am. My I can. There there breath that. Where is your face off some-where. Where am I lay down this tool. I fall I felled. I banged my face head I think. Time for somewhere. Isgoinghome.

I get there I get. I get to the door. I am. Bleed blood on my mouth. Gone. My I know it's there. Was. Salt and iron. Gone. I lick tank taste water taste brack there I. In my gob.

Vomit on me. Gone. My hair. But in my eye. Just all is there is in my eye gone. Gone it back to. Bed. But the silent. House in there I know. Bleed my knuckles find if I. Some-thing. Key. Hear the swarm hear the queen in the hive I.

Turn the handle round about I push the glass door goes I go. Go in.

Under your door I know they're. Swaying sing on you doing. And you are scared by if you're awake that. Not you no that there's I. Forget. You are. Gone. You would be though afraid of that. Aunt are here. Is here. They in there no not. No nright mright rong wrong they won't be there. But I will I. Me me. Will I get in this room or go orgo or goon wash myself blood I know that my cheek no there isn't. My mouth. Plunged and red and purple swoll like a lemon melon swoll like riped ripped like shreds my tongue my salt my. Who kissed me? Burn of it god that torn. Open the door. They you who are there?

Oh Lord God. Oh Lord God of might where were you? What happened you? What happened your face? It looks it looks like. Oh sweet Jesus someone say sit and let me look. At. That. They come like locust clusters of bees on me land on me don't shh I know don't don't move or the you what makes them angry let no you don't sit. Don't move.

And she my mother look at that what. My torn-out mouth my ripped-out hair my puke vile blood clothes holes with mud grass on she does not see they do not see. Maybe. I. Eyes burst with rage she. Seeming. She will. I've no. I look at you there, spread light their candles by your bed and you asleep and you. So white and clean my. Speak if it were not for my tongue I wish I was. Sssss. She has me. Come you out here. Close the door on them. What have you done?

What I've done. Nothing ever ever Mammy. Don't you cheek me, clip on the ear. Ow Mammy. How can you do this to your brother to me? No. Where were you? I fell I hit my head I fell I got my mouth I caught my pulled it on a bramble pulled it on. What are you on about? Your lies and lies are. Have you no shame? Mammy. All my shame I give to you. I'm turning off the lights I'm shutting down my doors. What do you mean by that? Don't you turn your back on me. What do you mean? Nothing Mammy. I've had enough do you hear me? Enough of you. Your face. You're a state. Making a show of yourself on today of all days. Go she says and have a bath. Lie down and later someone'll take you to get a stitch in that. I open the door look at. You're awake saying what's gone on you're not. I wish. You were. See do you see what I did to my face for you for you lying there? Oh I. No I don't. They look at me. I fell and wish I fell don't. I just fell. You should. Can hardly talk your voice comes up but far away from me. I know you know the. Sound of. Sssh you can't talk to me. I know I don't I do. Peel off from you what face once was. I'm going no. Go out of the room. Get out of my sight she says.

I climb the up the. Hurt. Stairs. I go. Behind I hear them close your door and pray.

Do not be afraid—I will save you.

I have called you by name—you are mine.

When you pass through deep water, I will be with you; your troubles will not overwhelm you.

When you pass through fire, you will not be burned; the hard trials that come will not hurt you.

For I am the Lord your God.

Near me I turn the bath light on I see I think that fuck punge of my face. It tore it shred of. I see think I must she creature fuck that me that what have you? Sssh wash it off. I see floorboards in the bathroom coming up for me. Wave. Do I see. In the trees in the hunted. Fox and goat. No. Where's the. On my hand. My face the blood on. My lips. Teeth. Rust on my dirt or me. Where's the. Nothing. Water. Turn what at the taps to do. Burning. My the. Oh what's the words for the. Where are you? Where are you? I. Door handle turn.

Don't come in it's. For him the who's there uncle looking in at you. No. At me.

Jesus Christ you're green. Look my face. What have you done? See there see it? See it? Oh my God, they said but. Me. See. Me me me not her. What? He. I don't know.

What's that inside you now? Hwta the knewit. Gone s. Lost but something. What I.

He stretch his hand out on my soft head. He puts his hands on. Touch my hair. The. Dirt in it. Picks. You done, you done this to yourself this? This? Know me you know he know me. I. Yes I. So I did. I was good and I was strong. Oh his f. He is crying. I. Something. He. Put. He put me in his arms he catch the. Stroke my. Don't do that again. Don't do that I. Whatever it. You have done. He I. No get off I. He. I squirm he. Got. He. On my back his soft kiss and hands and hands and. I fall in there. On what I know. H. He turn. He lock the bathroom door. In there. There there there. In the dark there's no light on. My eyes. For a long time Shush love shush you now. No one's here and others praying can't hear can't. Why I'm here. Let me do for you. He say. He this. Comfort. To stroke me down. Yes hands on me I let. In my long hair. In my jumper. He feels. In my knickers. Don't. In my bra. No. He find the trail leading. All the way back. I love you. I love you it's he says I love you. That is love evermore for me. He say open let me. In. I'll mind you. No. Shush there. Lift my skirt up I think knicker hands. Runs hands on score thighs dirt. There open my love I won't he says open and undoes. The trouser the spring the needle stick the knife. Let me. I won't. Don't scuffle. I'll take care of you. No don't. Take it all out of the inside. No. Push back in. Knock me on the door. Ssssh. Don't let everybody hear. I lo I lo. I'll take care of you. Let me. Oh no no no no no. I don't want. Want. Quiet pet. There he does it. Says come on now it's what's good you and us. Stick it ionthe don'tinside wwherhtewaterisswimming htroughmynoseandmouth throughmysense myorgands sthroughmythrough. That. A. My brain. He. Like. Now. Ithink i smell of woodwherethe river hits the lakebrownwashfoamy up the bank side Isee allcreaturesthere fish ducklings inthespring spring water going throughmyveins sinktheocean seeoutfar my salt my. Sea firsttime. Ahhhh pisses. Up me. Is the love that. No the other. Finisch lovely. He is done. Drop to earth. Tender. Can't smell this room.

He done and shake the. Let me. Fall down there. No the usual it is but i lost the. See I love the. Clean my little girl I'll wash your face. I'll kiss your face. I'll see you sore. I'll touch your mouth. My eyes. He. Pat my girl. My soon I'll take you far far away. Kiss my girl my poor poor girl. We'll. Had such a hard time little girl. Take care of you. I'll mind you now and tuck his thing. And there and now and calm. Love now I'm going down. See if I can help your mother. Keep everything normal isn't that right? You should go to sleep. You should go to bed. It's a long and terrible day for you. He. Sit me on the bath. i hold on there. Now love. Tight until he's gone.

Stag i can't stan i cn.an't stan i fall down on the splish of the water run it. See my invisible face. i'm drowned i'm awake i'm drowned. No your brother is and not you. Clickedy click the lights are off. Are on. Water take all. Boil up. i slip in the deep. My face go under there. Purple waves and taste of foam. You. No. Not here. i'm burn.

Think get up now go in your room and later when they've all gone i'll know the thing. Alright. Later then.

i go i off to the room where i lie and lie down on my face. Think of this. Did i give him all he asked for then? Mouth tasting of sick. Eye back in my head. A burning stomach. A body wet from the rain. It did tonight I remember. I recall. Wet and freezing. No it. Did it? I. Give it to him if he wanted it. I don't. I think he did. Fuck the. I'm the girl. Did that is that love to me. I'm. Spite and spit and sick. That's me that was. Is now. What me? In the layers of makeup? In the smear on his shirt? In the cold pocket between my legs? Where do I live? Where am. Someone he can see and cut into. Good to be. Butter and knife. No. What he takes. What he takes is the what there is of me. Now you've. I thought was nothing left. Now you've. How he knows it. He knows it is there for the beating the stealing the. I. Some place around that. No. I am there. Now you've. I. What's it like in the silence when. You. I. Where. I. Hello. Hello. Is he are you there? Ssssss. There? I'm only here in my bones and flesh. Now you've gone away.

The night is quiet. There are no dreams.

But this morning no one came for no one comes for me. How can I. Wake. My face is brick. My everything sting and swollen. Up. I am. Something. I am sore. Do you. I go I. Down the stairs. Cold. My mouth hurts against the light where it shiddent and it shouldn't lick it smart. My back. Thinks it feels too riddled with holes. Dead. This. I. In the kitchen no move no one. Everyone quiet is sip their tea. Aunt there in the cornflakes eating.

Uncle mother not you but me I. Go and will not look

up. Have a cup of over there. I. In this house of. I am left be-hind. Is your face sore? Not too. Teach you what. Teach you go walking all times of day and night. House I am left behind. Yes Mammy. You're a disgrace. I am. I am. If your father was. House I am left behind in. If your. I am sit. Curl table body and face. Sit up while I'm talking. I'n mammy I. Feel my ebb to the grass and tea with leaves I'n. Going. Sit up I said. Sit up. Where's my skin is black with. Ants and. Where's my brother? She says I've had enough nough to last a lifetime. Ma. Your brother's dead my girl. Lying stretched out in there as you know well. Left behind in. Your brother's dead and all you can think about is. Before everyone. Before everyone you came here and displayed yourself looking for sympathy. From me? From me? You dirty. Don't now our uncle says. Says she you keep your nose out if nothing else. I've only so much patience and I've bitten my tongue too long. You have shamed yourself and me and your brother most of all. I can't even look at you. I haven't wanted you in my home. But I allowed you because I thought you were making amends. But not you. Of course not. Selfish to the last. You couldn't even let your brother's wake pass without making a show of yourself, showing everyone your contempt. Well my girl, you may look down your nose at my beliefs and friends but I wasn't out throwing myself on every man passing while my brother was dying. You are disgusting. You are. Sick in the head. How you've lived. This filth you've made of yourself. So now your good kind brother is gone and God forgive me but it's true. I almost wish it was you lying there in that box. You. And not. My. Son.

I am. Get up from that table. Slide the. Cold hard tiles. My the. Oh my brother where have you gone? Where've you. What I've done. Where you going? she says. There are so many doors here. So many so many that. Open. Open it I am. I'm. Where you going? I'm so many doors I can knock knock knock. Where's my coat. My hat. Where you going?

For a walk. Down. You be back here in an hour and you be washed and dressed and clean there're people coming. The priest is coming and you be here for the prayers. I. Don't want to hear it she says and cover that bruise, it's the very least you can do. You're a disgrace. Yes Mammy. And true but. I am gone gone gone.

I go into your room. You are breathing no not. Like stone. I kiss the all. Wrong head poor head. Was yours. Where. White. Touch all wrong hands folded over like. Now and at the hour. Of prayer and say now your eyes are shut on me. There's a white patch drift.

See it? Where I have. Rotten. Been. Where we have. Brother and. Brother and. Go round my head. Simple as it was. Gone. Wrong. Where my hands are. Hold out for me. Hold. I never asked I never did I. Moving. Don't see through you. Is silent and blank. Don't.

Don't forget me because I won't be long. I'm going walking. Over the stones. Close out the cold door. On me. My love. Close out those old stones.

I go walk blacks of road go cars there white as. Rubbish passing on my feet are hurt and. Blind my lips. All that's. No speaking. No speaking here where the sunlight and cold wind blow me quiet. Burning motors. Crows go round the sky. I'm. Walking where that's home. And wind blows thistles on me. Nettles to burn but. Turn the little road. I see there. The little road down.

Pass the lampposts. Out of sight where the trees are. Cover me. Turn the corner spread before. What I want to. I go down. Walk gravel off the path where grass is trodden, rabbits been and maybe cows have. Suck of hoof marks. Filthy ditch strangle grass, sticks bottles petrol scum of. Rushes. Twisted wind. To the end there. Look. And stand.

There's water I see. Light of. Sunlight catch my eyes where the small drops trickle in the small wet streams. I see the water. Look upon the lake I've been in. I've been known of. Come to know. Well. Touched and loved and ripped here all the same by hands teeth and claws and waded in. Swim. See my scrawl there. Under my feet. Mud and weeds where I was, my blood split on. Running in running in among the reeds where the ripple fish go. And vomit and some half-drunk can, some things, some paper bags some cigarette rolled and stuffed and smoked. Ground to the heel. This home I know.

I see water. That under eyes is pool as deep as the far sun. Wider than sky is wide with herons fly up and swans all swan tongues clacking. Clack for me. And wings beat in air. For me. This morning. When the mist is gone. And rubbish drift is left behind.

I step in water on my cold feet. Touch the white flesh. Damp the. Walking where the mud slips into my shoes. Rushes pricking winding ankles trip the. Not a new girl here.

Go out. Go out further where the water is fine.

On my bare legs. On my thighs. Knowing what I am. Come the. Still. My. Slipping over hips and stomach. On my mind. Through fingers combing there. Soak in my white shirt colder. Up the spine. Duck it duck now or I'll never go in. The browny foam.

Baptize. Creep up my throat. Above my head. Wash away all blood. I'll under. Start to swim and water rolling through my hair. Scrape me free of. Clean now. All the purity I can. There is for me here. Far out. Far out.

Water blaze across with sun. No one to touch. Far out. Far gone the ground. I do not need I do not. Carry me over. And silent morning. No one to hear the lap lap on me.

Island. Moving stealth and through the clear the brown but all the same. It lick off hurt my face and hands. Strip pain all the parts off me. Wash away. Wash into the deep with it. Go down there.

I see. That face mine in the water. I'm. Crying laughing always happy where water is.

I am. Kicking my kicking legs. Extinguish all the lights I can. That's gone. And now that's gone.

More slowly on this water. More slowly. Where the center is the darkest. Cannot see is black down in. That. A far far I am far from ground.

The black I swim in filled with light and things and clouds that were the sky. The coldest water. Deepest mirror of the past and in it I am. Drowned no fine. Fine look because I see you under. Because we are very young. And we are very clean here like when we wash our hands. When we're in the rain. I was. His fingers in my mouth my eyes my hair. Stop. You break the surface up. Gasp. Air is. That's what air is again.

We are in the water. Hands as white as numb and you splash brack and twigs at me above the black. With your good hand. Float. There is every missing bit. All bits of me

I. And kicking my legs like I'm out to sea they are cold going cold on me. And plastic bags and bottles go by. When I was. When we were. Do you see? My feet are silver kicking through the frozen clouds beneath us. I know below me this water goes all the way down. I see the murk where fishes live. Those churned-up leaves silt where I look down. Those houses for the dead where cold is coldest. Cannot see. This lake. This water going to the center of the earth.

And I know what you say. Come on you say. Come with. Come down. Come down where the water turns to hot and rivers flowing rocks go by. Dive the. Dive with me. You say. You tell. You tell me your name and tell me the truth this time. Ssssh. We'll live there for a thousand Lir years. There now. There now. Take my hand.

Let water take the thing away. Take body. Tired as I am as you are. Full and watered down and sure that oceans underground will take us. Everywhere we desire. Say yours I say I'm scared now. No you tell me. I never understand. And you say. Say it once. Hail holy queen. Poor banished children of Eve and you say oh sacred heart of Jesus I place all my trust in thee. There is no other one. No person more inside for fuck for work for. For I'm twenty now whenyou were gone. When were you gone?

Rise up the lake above me. Take me where the waters go. I'll take your hand. You'll show. You'll show me all my lands and evil heart as you know it. Brother me. Clean here. Show me all the places of a soul. Where I will calm. And calm now. Give up dry land.

I'm. Tired. Let it.

Go there.

Struggle down.

We are down. We are down down down.

And under water lungs grow. Flowing in. Like fire torch. Like air is. That choke of. Eyes and nose and throat. Where uncle did. No. Gone away. Where mother speak. Is deaf my ears. Hold tight to me. I. Will I say? For you to hear? Alone. My name is. Water. All alone. My name. The plunge is faster. The deeper cold is coming in. What's left? What's left behind? What's it? It is. My name for me. My I.

Turn. Look up. Bubble from my mouth drift high. Blue tinge lips. Floating hair. Air-famished eyes. Brown water turning into light. There now. There now. That just was life. And now.

What?

My name is gone.

Acknowledgments

Thank you to Edward Carey and Elizabeth McCracken for their unstinting support and encouragement. To my mother, Gerardine McBride, for the same. To Jarlath Killeen for being a friend indeed. And most of all, to my husband, William Galinsky, without whom this book could not have been written.